Murder Revisited

A Jack Mallory Mystery

William Coleman

MURDER REVISITED

Dedicated to my lovely wife, Vicki, who has supported me every step of the way through each of my novels by allowing me the time to write, being my first beta reader as well as my main editor. By being my biggest fan and my sharpest critic, she has helped me produce final manuscripts for you to enjoy.

1

A single light source illuminated the alley, a bare bulb over the receiving door to a mom-and-pop hardware store. Long shadows stretched in both directions intensifying the darkness of the crevices where light did not reach. It was the kind of alley parents tell their children never to enter, the kind kids dared one another to go.

The girl's broken body lay on the damp pavement in the darkest area of the alley. In a shallow alcove, she could not be seen from the street even in daylight. Whoever found her had no good reason for being in the alley at night. The call had come from a payphone two miles away, one of the few remaining in this part of the city. The caller could be poor, homeless, with no cell phone. Or they may have preferred the anonymity the payphone provided.

Each end of the alley was blocked by squad cars, emergency lights disturbing the darkness. The intermittent flashes washed the walls in alternating colors yet never reached the girl. A man next to her squat in such a way that he was balancing on the balls of his feet and sitting on his heels. A penlight held between his teeth lit the area next to the girl's face. In one gloved hand, he held a small evidence bag, in the other a pair of tweezers. It was protocol to wait for the lab boys, but Detective Jack Mallory always worried they would miss something.

He pointed the thin beam at the young woman's hands. They were misshapen as if someone had stomped on them repeatedly. Her forearms were bruised and bloody. But most of the damage was concentrated around her head and neck. She fought for her life but her assailant had been determined.

A crime of passion or anger Jack summarized. The killer was emotionally involved with the victim. Whether fueled by anger at this girl in particular or just a hatred toward women in general was impossible to say.

Jack's light fell across a single eye staring blankly toward the moonless sky. He was struck by a sense of recognition although he did not know her. Had he seen her somewhere before? It was possible. In his work, he crossed paths with hundreds of people, maybe thousands. He couldn't possibly remember them all.

What was left of the girl's face, bruised and swollen, could not possibly represent her former appearance. How could he recognize anyone from just one eye? He stared at the iris for a moment. Her dead stare was gazing up at him pleading for help, or at least answers. It was something Jack could always see in the faces of victims.

He moved the light away from her face and followed the line of her body down one side and then the other. A reflection when the beam struck her left hand caught his attention. Jack leaned in close and saw the young woman was clutching a piece of jewelry in that hand. Was this the motive? Unlikely. A necklace or bracelet was hardly enough to evoke the rage for this brutal beating. And if the killer was after the jewelry, why leave it behind? He would have to wait for the lab boys to take their pictures before he could study the piece more closely so he moved on.

One of the girl's knees was shattered and Jack had an image of her down on the ground with her arms and legs pulled up to protect her body, begging her assailant not to hurt her only to have him strike the knee with a bat or lead pipe. With the knee crushed, she would have no chance to run. Jack considered the attacker may have crushed the knee to keep her from running a second time. Had she run once before? He flashed his light down the alley in each direction considering which way she might have come. The bulb was not powerful enough to penetrate the dark.

One of the squad cars on the east end of the alley moved. A van backed in and rolled to a stop just far enough for the squad car to block the alley again. Two men stepped out and began gathering their gear from the side door. The lab boys were here. It was time for Jack to hand the crime scene over. He walked toward them, meeting them halfway.

"What've we got, Detective?" the taller man asked when the space between them was almost closed.

"Caucasian female just past those trash bins," Jack pointed. "Beaten badly. She has a piece of jewelry in one hand. I'm thinking this is a secondary scene though."

"You think she was dumped?" the tall man asked. Jack had worked with him before. He was good at his job, but Jack could never remember his name.

"No. She was killed here," Jack shook his hand. "But I think the attack started somewhere else, maybe further up the alley. She may have gotten away, ran and he caught her here."

"We'll work the whole alley then," the tall man said.

"Thanks," Jack said. "What time is it?"

"Almost six," the man checked his watch.

"I'm going to go get some sleep while you guys do your thing," Jack let his shoulders droop. He turned away and walked to the end of the alley. He would be going to bed just as the sun broke a new day.

2

The phone rang and Jack moaned, rolling to one side covering his head with his pillow. It was no use. The ringing was persistent and the pillow did little to block the offending noise. He sat up and rubbed at his eyes before reaching for his cell. Jack fumbled and the phone fell from the nightstand to the floor where it bounced under the bed. With a heavy sigh, he rolled off the bed and dropped to floor level feeling for the phone in the dim light coming through the window blinds and clutched it in his fist. He pressed the talk button with his thumb and held the phone to his ear.

"Mallory here", he said in a hushed voice.

"Jack," the woman on the phone was tentative. "Is that you?"

"That's what I said," he growled. "What do you want?"

"Jack," she said again, "this is Kelly Walden."

"Oh," Jack sounded disappointed. "What is it, Kelly?"

"He wants to see you," she answered.

"I'll stop in when I get there," Jack yawned.

"He wants to see you now," Kelly said. "Like ten minutes ago."

Jack pulled the phone away from his ear and looked at the screen. The time in the upper corner read eight-fifteen. He rubbed at his eyes again. "I just got in bed an hour ago. He's going to have to wait."

"He's not going to be happy," she lowered her voice.

"He's never happy," Jack had no intention of missing his sleep.

"This is different," she said. "He's yelling."

"He always yells."

"Not at me."

Jack stopped at that. It was true. Terrance Singleton did a lot of things Jack didn't agree with. On the whole, Jack could honestly say he didn't know anyone he liked less than Singleton. But the man was always political when it counted. And he never raised his voice to his secretary. He claimed it was because he was a gentleman. Jack suspected the man was afraid of women, going back to his mother. No proof but the thought made Jack smile.

"What's this about?"

"I don't know," she was almost whispering. "The governor called first thing this morning and he's been really upset ever since."

"Governor, huh?" Jack nodded even though Kelly could not see him.

"Yes," she said. "As soon as they hung up, he told me to get you into his office. When I tried to explain you wouldn't be in yet, he yelled at me."

"Harsh," Jack said more to himself than to her.

"I know," she agreed. "He never does that."

"Tell him I'm on my way." He disconnected the call and started for the bathroom.

The hot stream of water stung his skin as he leaned against the wall under the showerhead. Jack watched the water swirling down the drain without thought. Out of the shower, Jack leaned into the mirror trying to force his dark brown eyes to stay open. Shaving, he noted that the brown waves of his hair were getting too long. If he let them go too long, they became tight curls which he hated with a passion. He stretched to his full six feet and inhaled deeply to expand his chest, releasing his breath slowly through his nose. He was finally awake.

Fifteen minutes later he was dressed and driving through heavy traffic toward the station. He listened to a talk radio station as he went. The radio personality was discussing the upcoming elections and offering his advice about each of the candidates for state government. From what Jack could gather the man was not fond of any of them.

Jack braked hard and turned into the station parking lot. He parked in a space reserved for one of the captains that worked second shift and jumped out of his car. Just under an hour from the time he answered the phone he walked into the chief's office where the secretary sat with a nervous expression on her face. The expression softened when she saw Jack, but not completely.

"Thank God you're here," she smiled faintly.

"I told you I was on my way," Jack said, sitting on the front of her desk and grinning down at her. "I wouldn't let you down."

"I know," she said. "But he doesn't." She indicated the door behind her that led to the chief's inner office.

"Being a bear, eh?"

The phone beeped and the chief's disembodied voice crackled through the speaker. "Where is Mallory?"

"See?" she shrugged at Jack. She reached over and pushed the intercom button. "He just arrived, sir."

"Send him in then," the chief barked.

Kelly waved an arm toward the door. Jack slid off her desk, winked, and crossed to the dark wood door. Shiny brass letters spelled out: Chief Terrance Singleton. Jack considered briefly pulling out his pocketknife and popping a couple letters out. It was not the first time the thought had come to him and it wouldn't be the last. Jack's mother would have said it was because he did not like authority figures. Jack, of course, knew better. He simply didn't like the chief.

When Jack joined the force as a beat cop more than ten years ago, Terrance was a detective. The first time Jack found a body while making his rounds Terrance was called in to investigate. The future chief took one look and reamed Jack a new one for disturbing the scene. Jack countered, insisting he hadn't disturbed anything any further than determining the woman was dead. He never even touched the corpse. One quick look at the woman's face was all he needed. The two men were at odds from that day forward. Unfortunately for Jack, Terrance had friends in high places. By the time Jack was promoted to homicide, Terrance was a senior detective.

He turned the knob and pushed the door open. The inner office was a corner space on the second floor of the station. The two outer walls were lined with large windows. The shades were pulled all the way down and closed. Terrance was the only person Jack knew who would shut out natural light in favor of fluorescent. Terrance sat in a high-back leather chair, his elbows on its padded arms and his chin resting on the tips of his fingers.

In the dim room Jack made out several stacks on the chief's desk; envelopes, manila folders, loose sheets of papers, stapled sets of papers. Jack scanned them and wondered what amount of time they represented.

"Where have you been, Mallory?"

"What do you want, Terrance?" He never referred to him as chief. It didn't settle well in his stomach.

The chief hesitated before saying anything. "I have a case for you."

"I'm already on a case," Jack informed him.

"No you aren't," the chief said. He had a matter-of-fact tone meaning he had the final say.

"Listen, Terrance," Jack yawned. "I just spent most of the night in a dark alley that smelled like human waste. I was examining a crime scene where a young girl was beaten to death. Beaten so badly we may never get a positive I.D. I already have a case."

"There's nothing I would like more than having you spend your days in dark alleys," Terrance said. "But, you're off of it."

"You can't do that," Jack argued.

"Already done," Terrance sat back in his chair with his head resting on his fingertips again.

Heat spread through Jack's body. He wanted to reach across the desk and grab the chief by his necktie and pull him out of the chair. He clenched his hands into tight fists and stared at the man he had grown to hate. Doing so he asked, "What is this all-important case you want me on?"

Terrance took one of the manila folders off the top of a stack of what looked like a hundred of them and dropped it onto a shorter stack of papers right in front of the detective. Jack took the folder and read the identification tab.

"Elizabeth Mitchell?" He opened the folder and started scanning the first page, a homicide report. "This case is twenty years old."

"Twenty-two years," Terrance confirmed. "The girl would have been forty next month."

"I don't have time for this," Jack closed the file and set it back on the desk. "I have real cases to work on. Give this to the cold case nuts."

"It's yours," Terrance stated, pushing the folder back toward the detective.

"Why?"

"Elizabeth Mitchell was the daughter of the, then, mayor of our city," Terrance explained. "Now, Governor Steven Mitchell."

"Oh," Jack let the word linger. "Now I understand. Your old friend says jump and you jump. He wants a real detective on his daughter's old case and you throw him me."

"Something like that," Terrance said.

"So, why the sudden interest?" Jack asked. "It's been twenty years. Why wait 'til now?"

"Twenty years ago the case was solved," Terrance explained. "We found blood samples under her fingernails and the blood type matched with her recent ex-boyfriend. We made the arrest, convicted him, and sent him upstate."

"But...," Jack prompted.

"But, the guy filed an appeal," Terrance sighed. "Third time actually. But this time his lawyer was able to get an audience with a judge. The judge ruled the evidence used at trial was insufficient and overturned his conviction. He let him walk. That was yesterday. Obviously, the governor is furious. He wants the guy back behind bars. I told him I would put someone on it. He insisted it be one of our senior detectives."

"And you picked me?" Jack said.

"I know the boyfriend did it," Terrance said. "We had the proof we needed. We got a fair conviction. I want him back behind bars. But like you said, we have real crimes to solve. I want you to hound this guy and get the proof to put him away again."

"You can't retry him, Terrance," Jack said.

"Find me the proof, Jack," the chief said. "We'll charge him with something."

"Why don't you put Peterson on it?" Jack suggested.

"I put you on it," Terrance snapped. "I want you to take care of it."

Jack rolled his eyes and picked up the folder again. He rose to his feet and turned away from the chief. He was across the room with his hand on the doorknob when Terrance called out to him.

"One more thing Mallory," Terrance said. "I don't want you bothering the governor. Everything you need from him is in that file. I don't want him reliving the whole thing again. And, Jack, I want you to keep me up to date. Every day. I want reports so I can keep him informed. Understood?"

"Yea, Terrance," Jack said. "I understand. You want me to waste my time on an old case that probably won't be solved and you want me to let you know how much time I'm wasting on a daily basis."

"I want your all on this, Jack," Terrance sneered.

"And I want nothing to do with it," Jack said. "Doesn't look like either one of us will get what we want."

He pulled the door open, stepped through, and closed it hard behind him even as Terrance was responding to what he had said. It wasn't the smartest thing Jack ever said. Wasn't the wisest for his career. But he couldn't remember anything ever feeling quite so good. He winked at Kelly and walked out of the office.

3

Jack left the chief's office, drove home, threw the folder on his dresser along with his keys, and crawled into bed. He was asleep almost as soon as his head hit the pillow. When he opened his eyes, more than five hours later, he was disoriented until the events of that morning came rushing back at him.

He sat up, yawned, and headed for the kitchen. He hadn't eaten since before he got the call about the murder in the downtown alley the night before. Within minutes, eggs and bacon were sizzling on the stove and coffee was brewing. The morning paper was still on the ground in front of his apartment door and he scanned the news briefly while eating. He found the Elizabeth Mitchell story on page four. Deciding it would be better to read the case file before getting the journalist's point of view, he folded the paper and set it aside.

He opened the file he had only scanned that morning and started reading. Elizabeth Mitchell, age seventeen, was found in the back bedroom of an empty house that was listed for just under five hundred grand. The owner of the house had been transferred by his company to the West Coast nearly a month earlier. No one besides the realtors showing the house had access to the keys. A broken window next to the back door indicated no key was used to gain entry. Jack jotted a reminder on the pad he had laid out for taking notes, to try to locate the listing realtor.

The realtor had brought prospective buyers to the house for a showing when they discovered the girl. Jack could imagine a young couple in search of a new home where they could raise their family only to find a dead teenager in the master suite. That would put a damper on things in a hurry. She was found lying in a fetal position with a blanket drawn up to her shoulders. The realtor claimed he thought she was sleeping when he first saw her. Only after he saw her face, eyes wide open, did he know any different. They left the house and called the police from the safety of his car.

The crime scene reports filed by Officer Joe Baxter were written like any other reports he had read or written before. At 10:15 a.m. on Saturday, November 30th, 1997, a real-estate agent who discovered a body while showing a house placed a call to 911. Officer Baxter was the first officer on the scene. He arrived shortly before 10:30. Finding the girl as the real-estate agent had described, Officer Baxter checked for a pulse and determined she was dead. Baxter called for the coroner and a homicide detective, then he secured the scene.

While waiting for the others to arrive, Baxter took statements from the agent, a Mr. Wayne Fenton, and the couple he brought to see the house, Mr. and Mrs. Edward Vine. The three of them all gave the same story of discovering the body while on a tour of the house. It was noted that Mrs. Vine was hysterical and an ambulance was called. The case was handed over to the homicide detective on duty when he arrived at the scene.

A crime scene investigator who gathered evidence from the scene filed the next report. There was a precise description of where things were in relation to the body. Several pages detailed the girl's appearance and the state of the room where she was found.

At first glance, the girl appeared to have been strangled, as made apparent by the bruising around the neck and face. There were signs of a struggle, but they were not severe. Jack examined the accompanying photos to orient himself. Indeed, the items disturbed at the scene did not amount to much, but he also noted that there was little in the house to disturb.

Jack paused. The girl could not have been strangled while she lay in the fetal position. Not consistent with the bruising pattern Jack saw in the close-ups. The murderer would have had to be facing her to get the dark purple thumb marks under her chin. The killer arranged the body to give the appearance she was sleeping. He had to know this wouldn't fool anyone. In most cases where the body was arranged peacefully, the killer turned out to be a close friend, lover, or family member. He wrote the word 'governor' on his pad.

Jack put the report aside and picked up another. It was a copy of the autopsy findings. The pages were wrinkled and the edges torn, as though it had been read again and again. Cause of death was asphyxiation caused by pressure being applied to the throat. The bruising was consistent with the shape of a pair of hands.

There were signs of semen on her inner thigh. The girl had intercourse recently. Force was not evident but was not ruled out either. The sweater was torn at the shoulder. The skirt was disheveled. No panties were found at the scene. The killer apparently took a trophy. Blood under the girl's nails suggested she put up a fight. More bruising on the wrists was a sign of being held down or tied, possibly while being raped.

The food in the girl's stomach was not digested. She had eaten within a couple of hours of her death. Had she eaten with her killer? The contents were fast food, burger, and fries. The major organs were healthy, as they should have been in a teenaged girl. There was nothing more. The report was incomplete.

His cell phone rang and Jack looked at it as a stranger in his home. The screen announced that the caller was Chief Singleton. He let it ring three more times before answering and announcing his name. The sound of his boss's voice made Jack's skin crawl.

"Jack," the chief said. "How's it coming?"

"Coming?" Jack was incredulous. "Are you seriously asking me how it's coming? It's not coming, Terrance. I haven't been on the case long enough to do anything. You want to tell me how it's supposed to be coming?"

"Calm down Jack," the chief said. "I just wanted to make sure you got everything you need."

"I don't know, Terrance," Jack said. "I don't know what I have. I don't know what I don't have. Do you know anything? Why don't you tell me what I'm missing?"

"What is the matter with you?" Terrance snapped. "What are you trying to say?"

"I'll tell you what's wrong with me," Jack's voice rose. "I'm taken off a fresh case with the chance of catching a killer before he tries it again so I can work on a twenty-year-old case with no good leads so the chief of police can tell his friend the governor it's being handled."

"Damn it, Jack," Terrance yelled. "I didn't want you on this case. I wanted someone I could work with. Not your sorry ass."

"If you didn't want me on it," Jack asked, "Why did you dump it on me?"

"The governor requested you," Terrance's voice lowered considerably. "He read some damn article about you in the paper last week. The reporter claimed you always got results. That's what the governor wants on this."

"Did you explain to him I don't always get results?" Jack asked. "Did you explain there was little chance of finding anything new in this case?"

"I told him all of that," Terrance said. "I also told him what a pain you are to work with. Nothing helped. He wanted you on this case. So, here you are."

"Here I am," Jack said. "Meanwhile, there's a killer running around downtown and I'm not even trying to catch him."

"Peterson will get him," Terrance said.

"Peterson couldn't find his own badge," Jack said.

"You told me to put him on the Mitchell case," Terrance said.

"Because there's nothing to find. It doesn't matter if you don't find what isn't there. Peterson would have been perfect for this." Jack never understood how Bret Peterson made detective, he couldn't even figure out why the man was never relieved of his badge and gun. Of course, Peterson had been around long enough now there was probably no getting rid of him.

"Just do it," Terrance said. "And Jack?"

"What?"

"Do it well."

4

It was early in the morning when Jack finished reading all the coroner's reports, initial police reports, and the crime scene investigator's findings. Combined they provided a snapshot of the events leading up to the murder. Coupled together with the photos of the victim and the room where she was found, Jack had a very good idea of what might have happened to the girl all those years ago.

He poured a cup of coffee into a tall dark blue mug with a chip on one side of the rim. It was the mug his wife had given him while they were still dating in college. He used it every day, even though she had left him more than three years ago. There was no great explosion, no final straw. Their marriage had simply become a victim of his career. A victim he couldn't help. All the late nights and the not knowing if he was going to make it home took their toll on her and she had to get out. He had helped her move. They called each other on special occasions, even her birthday which, ironically, he usually forgot when they were still married.

He set the mug on his desk and sat back in his fake leather chair. The springs underneath moaned with the shift of his weight. The next batch of papers had a note paper-clipped on top. It read 'Case Notes' in clear block letters. Jack had only seen one person in all his career use this method of storing his notes from a case. He pulled off the clip and removed the cover page. His eyes quickly scanned the page until he saw what he was looking for. The name of the lead detective on the case was written halfway down the page. It was Terrance Singleton. Jack sat up. The chief had not mentioned this detail. Being the arresting officer meant he had more interest in this case than just knowing the governor.

Jack sorted through the remaining papers, pulling the transcripts of Singleton's interviews with witnesses. There were only four: someone noted as the girl's best friend, the real estate agent, the agent's clients who found the body, and the boyfriend, Timothy Waters. None of the interviews were very long. Most had the feel of being an afterthought. He read each one of them carefully and learned very little from the content. The only interview that went into any depth was the one with Waters. It was obvious to Jack that Waters was the prime suspect from the very beginning. In fact, he was the only suspect.

He examined the short list. It would be difficult to find them after all this time. He wrote down their names and the addresses where they could be reached twenty years ago. He added the names of the men and women he wanted to speak to who were not on the list: the coroner, friends of both Timothy Waters and the victim, and the victim's parents. The last would be the easiest to find and the most difficult to meet with. Singleton already told him to stay away from the governor and his wife. But Jack wasn't one to follow rules or listen to his boss. He would speak to them. Terrance wouldn't like it, but Jack would deal with that when the time came. He would have to interview Terrance as well, to get the full picture.

He spent the next hour examining the photos of the scene again. This time he concentrated on each photo individually, one section at a time. He memorized how the body was lying, where the items in the room were compared to her. An overturned candle, a paper cup, a plate of grape stems. There was something not right about it all, more than a dead teen-aged girl. There was something missing and if he was going to be stuck working on this case he was going to find out what it was.

One photo showed a close-up of a bruise on the girl's thigh. It was older than the other bruises she had. Jack wrote a note next to the coroner's name on his pad. It was a name he didn't recognize and he wondered if the man still worked for the county. The main challenges of investigating this case would be finding new clues if they existed and finding the possible witnesses who may have moved from the area or even passed away.

Another photo was a school portrait. The young girl in the photo was pretty. She was smiling broadly and had the look of happiness in her eyes. She had flowing blond hair and smooth tanned skin. She wore a silk blouse, a pair of gold earrings, and a diamond necklace. Some would call her a rich brat, or privileged and she may have been. But Jack got the sense Elizabeth Mitchell was the kind of girl everyone liked. The good girl type who never had a bad thing to say about anyone. Not the kind of girl a boyfriend would want to kill. As Jack studied the photo he sensed that something was wrong. Not with the girl so much as the photograph. He studied it a little harder, leaning in close but nothing presented itself to him. With a heavy sigh, he set it aside and picked up another photo. This one was of the cheerleading squad from her high school. Elizabeth was sitting front and center on the grass of the football field. She was sitting with her legs extended in front of her pointed at the camera. Another girl sat next to her mirroring Elizabeth's pose.

Jack's eyes moved from face to face in the group shot of girls. He didn't know what he was looking for but he searched for it anyway. When he came to Elizabeth he lingered, staring at the girl's features for a clue of unhappiness or worry. He didn't see anything. This time the earrings were silver, but she wore the same diamond necklace. Jack flipped through the family snapshots and school pictures. In each of them, she wore the same diamond necklace. Then he looked through the crime scene photos one at a time. There was no necklace visible. A quick run through the cataloged items of evidence revealed no necklace.

Jack wrote a note on his pad. A souvenir for the killer? A motive for the killing? It was something he didn't have before. An angle not followed before. A place to begin.

Jack checked his watch and saw that it was going on three o'clock. He stood, stretched, and headed for his room. He would get some sleep and start with those on his list he knew he could find. Chief Singleton topped the list. He wanted answers he couldn't get from the paperwork. A lot of years had passed since this case was closed, but Jack had an idea Terrance would remember it well enough.

He lay down and stared up at the ceiling for a long time before drifting off to sleep. In the back of his mind, he imagined Elizabeth leading a cheer with her friends, laughing. And just over her shoulder, a shadow lurking in the darkness. Someone took this girl's life in the prime of her youth. And if Jack was right, Timothy's was taken from him at the same time, locked away for a murder he did not commit. Jack did not want this case, but now that it was his he was going to see it through to the end. He was going to find a killer. It was what he did best.

5

Eight o'clock came far too fast. Jack turned off the alarm then forced himself into a sitting position, his legs dangling over the edge of the mattress. He stayed there for a few minutes, letting the fog lift from his mind. Rising to his feet he quickly readied himself for the day. He was out the door before nine and in the office by nine-thirty, where he drew stares from his day shift colleagues who were not used to seeing him in the morning hours unless he was on his way home. The night shift had been his domain for most of his career and he was comfortable with that. He knew the night and the night knew him. There was a respect between man and nature he did not have during the daylight hours. This case would require a change in his routine for its duration. All the more reason to finish this investigation quickly.

Kelly Walden was sitting at her desk in front of the chief's office door. She was so intent on the work she was doing on her computer she did not notice Jack's arrival and jumped in surprise when he made his presence known.

"You could warn a girl," she said.

"Is he in?" Jack asked.

"Yes," she answered. "But he's with someone."

"Anyone important?"

"You know I can't tell you that," she smiled.

"I'm going to know when they come out," Jack said, nodding at the door.

"I guess so," she leaned forward conspiratorially. "He's with Judge Watson."

"A judge came to see him?" Jack asked. Usually, if you need to see a judge, you went to him. "What on earth for?"

"Something about an old case," Kelly shrugged. "You know he doesn't tell me anything."

"An old case?" Jack said more to himself than her.

"I think that's what he said," she answered.

Jack tried to remember the name of the presiding judge in Timothy's trial. He was sure he had read it but couldn't recall the name. Kelly must have been confused by his expression.

"You okay?" she asked.

"I'm fine," he nodded. "Look, it would probably be best if they didn't know I knew they were meeting. I'm going to go wait over in the corner and come back when the judge is gone."

"I knew I shouldn't have told you," she pouted.

"Kelly, it's okay," he assured her. "If you hadn't told me I would have waited here and found out when the judge came out. The only difference is now they don't have to get all uncomfortable with me knowing they were meeting."

"Why would they be uncomfortable?" Kelly asked. "If they were trying to hide something, they would have met somewhere else."

She made a good point and Jack had to consider what she said. If they did not want people to know they were meeting, they would have chosen a meeting place where they were unlikely to be seen together. They would not meet in the chief's office.

"I'll just play it safe," he said. "Back in a few."

She watched him walk across to his chosen waiting spot. When he reached it, he turned and waved to her. She waved back at him and smiled shyly before turning back to her typing and was soon punching the keys the way she had been before his arrival.

Jack waited in the corner for twenty minutes before the door to Terrance's office finally opened. A tall light-skinned black man in a tailored suit stepped into the outer office where Kelly was working. He was still talking to the chief as he made his way down the hall. Jack tried unsuccessfully to hear what was being said. Their hushed voices did not carry. Reaching the corner, Terrance stopped and the two men continued their conversation for another five minutes before the chief retreated to his office. Jack emerged from hiding and returned to Kelly's desk.

"He in?" Jack asked with a friendly smile.

"No," she answered, sitting back to wait for his reaction.

"Cute," he said. "Let him know I'm here."

She picked up her phone and pushed a button. A second later she told Terrance that Jack was waiting for him. She listened for a few minutes before agreeing and hanging up. She looked up at the detective and pointed to the door behind her. "He'll see you now."

Jack smiled at her and moved to the door. He reached out, took the knob, and turned. Before pushing the door open he turned back to Kelly. "I'll be right back."

"I'll hold my breath," she said, feigning infatuation.

"Don't pass out," he smiled then pushed his way into the chief's office.

Terrance was sitting in his big leather chair leaning over the desk as though Jack had interrupted his work. He raised his eyes to the detective without visible emotion. It was common practice for the two men. They had given up fake pleasantries years ago. He waited for Jack to sit in the chair opposite him before shifting his body in that direction.

"What do you want, Jack?" he asked. "And don't tell me you want off the case because it isn't going to happen."

"No," Jack said. "I'm here to ask questions of the detective in charge of the original investigation."

"Questions?" Terrance became defensive. "Did you read the files? All of my reports are there."

Jack sat for a moment before responding. "First of all, why weren't any other suspects considered?"

"There were other suspects, but I didn't look into them much because we had the guy," Terrance said. "There was no doubt Timothy Waters--was guilty. There is still no doubt he is guilty. You are supposed to be finding proof."

"Why didn't you interview the girl's parents?" Jack asked.

"You listen, Jack," Terrance raised his voice and a finger to the detective. "You stay away from the governor and his wife. I already warned you about that."

"Did you interview them or not?" Jack asked.

"They weren't suspects," Terrance said.

"Did you talk to them?"

"Of course I talked to them," Terrance snapped. "We were friends. I talked to them all the time. I'm the one who had to sit them down and tell them their daughter was murdered. I'm the one who told them I found her killer. And two days ago I had to sit them down and tell them the courts were letting him go."

"Where are the notes?" Jack said, ignoring the man's speech.

"What notes?"

"The notes from the interview," Jack clarified.

"Are you listening to anything I say?" Terrance asked. "That's the problem with you, Jack. You don't listen. You don't pay attention to the important details. That's why you're still on the streets. You won't get anywhere if you don't listen."

"No notes then?" Jack said jotting in his own notepad.

"Don't push me," Terrance said.

"You put me on this case," Jack argued. "You don't like the way I'm doing it, take me off it. From the information I have on the investigation I'm surprised you got a conviction twenty years ago. Or did Judge Watson have something to do with it?"

"What did you say?"

"I was wondering why Judge Watson was visiting you in your office," Jack said. "Not very common."

"If you must know," Terrance narrowed his eyes on Jack. "Judge Paul Watson is my brother-in-law."

"He's black," Jack pointed out. "Your wife isn't and you don't have a sister."

"He's Heather's half-brother. Same mother, different father," Ter-rance explained. "He came to talk about the game this weekend. He's coming over to watch at our place. Wanted to know if he should bring some beer. You want to know what we're serving at half-time?"

"Is the governor going to be there?" Jack asked.

"Get the hell out of my office," Terrance growled.

Jack rose and started for the exit. As he reached the door he stopped and turned back to the chief, saying, "One more thing."

"What is it?" the chief huffed. "And it better be good."

"Did you ever find the necklace?"

"What necklace?"

"The girl had a necklace she always wore," Jack said. It may or may not have been true. But then, he was fishing and you don't always use real bait to fish. "It wasn't on her body. Did it ever turn up?"

"No," Terrance answered. "Now, if that's all, get out."

Jack left the office with a quick wink and smile at Kelly. He was surprised the chief did not claim he didn't know about the necklace or that it wasn't important. He only said it hadn't turned up, so he must have actually tried to find it. Maybe, and Jack admitted it was a stretch, maybe the chief wasn't a complete idiot after all.

6

Timothy Waters sat at the kitchen table in the house where he had grown up. He constantly tapped his finger on the tabletop, not so loud as to be annoying. He simply never stopped. His mother, a short gray-haired, thick-boned woman, stood at the sink washing dishes. A pan slipped from her hand and clattered on the counter. Timothy jumped.

Jack sat across from him trying to find the nineteen-year-old boy in the face of the forty-year-old man. Timothy was adorned with a tattoo on each arm. On the left, a cracked heart with a teardrop. On the right, a lightning bolt. Both were prison tattoos, unprofessional and faded. A pack of cigarettes and a lighter rested on the table next to his tapping fingers. He snatched them up with unexpected speed.

"Mind if I smoke?" he asked taking one from the pack. His mother glanced his way. Jack had learned from Timothy's file his father died of lung cancer two years ago. The woman resumed her dishwashing without a sound. Timothy put the pack back on the table holding the cigarette between his fingers.

"Go ahead," Jack said, knowing it made no difference what he said.

Timothy put the cigarette in his mouth but did not light it. He pointed at his mother's back and gestured to Jack, "Come on."

Jack followed the man out the back door into a small yard overgrown with weeds. Flowerbeds ran the length of the house and along the fence but showed no sign of life. The screen door slammed shut behind them, but unlike the dropped pan, extracted no response from Timothy. He had been an athlete before his conviction and it was obvious he remained active in prison. His shoulders were massive, his arms and legs thick with muscle. He flicked the lighter and raised the flame to the cigarette. Once lit, he took a long drag, the tip glowing as the fire ate away the tobacco.

He held the smoke in his lungs for a moment before blowing it skyward.

"She hates smoking," Timothy gestured toward the house to indicate his mother. "Even twenty years ago when dad was smoking three or four packs a day she made him come out here to light up. Now, she doesn't want to say anything to upset me."

He flicked the end of the cigarette and ashes fell to the ground. He focused on them, "She was a vibrant woman, you know. Back before all this crap. You couldn't tell it now. We used to talk and laugh. Used to enjoy each other's company. The last twenty years she's had to see me through a pane of glass. We talked about appeals and lawyers and money. She told me dad died through a goddamn piece of glass. It eats at your soul. Now, we don't know what to talk about. No more lawyers. No more appeals. What is there now?"

He took another drag then pinched the butt between his fingers before flicking it into the yard. He turned to Jack. "You didn't come to listen to my problems. Mom thinks you're here to tell me there was a mistake and I have to go back."

"What do you think?" Jack asked.

"I think you would have brought more men if you were going to try to take me back," Timothy leveled his eyes on Jack. "Cause I'd rather kill you than go back. Or die trying."

"I'm not here to take you back," Jack assured him.

"Then why are you here? Checking up on me?"

"No," Jack shook his head and looked away from the man into the yard. "Fact is, with your release the Elizabeth Mitchell case has been reopened. I'm here to get your side of the story."

"My side of the story?" Timothy said. "Mister, I've been trying to tell my side of the story for twenty years. No one ever listened. Now you want to know what happened?"

"Anything you can remember," Jack agreed.

"I remember everything like it was yesterday," Timothy said. "In a sense, it was yesterday seeing as how I lost all the time in between."

"You met with Elizabeth at the house where she was found that night didn't you?" Jack asked, already knowing the answer from the case file.

"She called me that afternoon and asked me to meet her there," Timothy recalled. "Had something important to tell me. You know how women are. Everything's a drama. So, she set this place up for us. Stole some wine from her father's liquor. Had candles and everything. Wanted to tell me something important. I thought she was going to break up with me."

"Why did you think that?" Jack asked.

"Well, I had been away at college all year," Timothy said. "You know how it goes with long-distance relationships. I figured she was lonely and found someone else. The end of us and all."

"What about you?"

"What about me?"

"Did you find someone new while you were away?"

"Can't say I wasn't tempted," Timothy said. "But I was planning to marry Beth. Didn't want to screw it up."

"Did she know you wanted to marry her?"

"Sure," he said. "We talked about it a couple times. We were going to wait 'til she was out of high school so she could move up to the university."

"Yet, you still thought she was going to break up with you?"

"She was acting strange when I came back for spring break," Timothy said. "Kind of distant. Wasn't her bubbly self. I figured her feelings weren't as strong as mine."

"So, you met her at the house," Jack said. "What happened? Did she call it off?"

"No," Timothy took another cigarette out and lit up, talking even while he was puffing, "She asked if she could go with me when I went back to college. Wanted to leave high school and come live with me."

"Did she say why she wanted to leave school early?"

"You mean like someone wanting to kill her?" The sarcasm in Timothy's voice could not be mistaken. "No, she didn't say why."

"Did you make plans to take her with you?"

"No," Timothy said. "I told her it wasn't a good idea with her parents and all. They would never forgive her for dropping out. Would never accept me into the family if I took her away."

"What did she say to that?" Jack asked.

"She agreed," Timothy said. "Reluctantly. She knew it was a bad idea when she asked."

"Then what happened?"

"Then we had sex," Timothy said. "Not the first time, but it was really nice. I think it was the candles and being in a house rather than a car. It was almost like we were already married, you know?"

"What I don't understand is why you left her there alone in the house," Jack said. "Why didn't you take her home?"

"Couldn't." The man took a long drag from his cigarette. "She told her parents she was spending the night at her friend's house. So she was going to spend the night in the empty house and go home in the morning. My parents were expecting me home so I couldn't stay with her. Besides, she said she had a friend coming to visit her that night."

Jack turned sharply. "She said she was expecting someone else at the house?"

"Yes."

"Why didn't you ever mention that before?"

"I did," Timothy said. "Like a thousand times. No one listened."

"Do you know who this other friend was?"

"She didn't tell me," he said. "Just said she needed to tie up some loose ends. Needed to talk to this friend so she could move forward. Some kind of crap like that."

"And you told this to the police?"

"I told everybody," Timothy said. "Like I said, no one would listen. They were convinced I did it and wanted nothing to do with any other possibility."

"Could she have been meeting another guy?"

"She wasn't some slut if that's what you mean," Timothy said sharply. "I don't know who she was meeting. I can't tell you anything else about it."

"Okay," Jack said. "You said goodnight and then what?"

"I went home."

"Did you stop on the way?"

"I told you," Timothy sighed. "My parents were expecting me. I went straight home. I was already late. I didn't want to get in trouble. Kind of ironic, huh?"

"I need to ask you something a bit sensitive," Jack said.

"Mister, I've spent the last twenty years in prison," Timothy said. "You can't shock me."

"When Elizabeth was found," Jack started, "she wasn't wearing panties. They weren't found at the scene. Do you know anything about that?"

"She had them when I left," Timothy said. His head dipped a little, his eyes drifting into a far-off stare. "Bastard. They told me she was raped. Of course, they told me I did it."

"You sure she had them?"

"I took them off her," he said. "Gave them back to her after. She had them."

"What about the necklace?"

"Necklace?"

"She had a diamond necklace," Jack said. "Was she wearing it that night?"

"Oh, yeah," Timothy said. "I remember that necklace. She was wearing it when I came back from school. Told me her father gave it to her. Yeah, she was wearing it that night. Played with it when we talked."

"And she had it when you left?" Jack asked.

"Why wouldn't she?"

"She didn't when she was found," Jack said. "Just wanted to know if she gave it to you."

"What would I do with it?" Timothy asked. "It was too girlie for me to wear. No, she had it when I left. Her killer must have taken it?"

"It's a possibility," Jack commented. "Anything else you can tell me about that night?"

"I've been thinking about it for twenty years," Timothy said. "The love of my life was murdered and before I could even start to mourn I was arrested for doing it. I didn't even get to go to the funeral to say goodbye to her. If you're serious about this, I hope to hell you catch the bastard. Probably not likely after twenty years."

"Not likely," Jack agreed. "But since I'm on the case, I'm going to try my hardest to find the real killer. You can count on that."

7

Jack stopped by the last known address for Angela Grimes and learned that Elizabeth Mitchell's best friend from high school was married and living on the opposite side of town. By the time Jack arrived at her house, it was well past noon. He pulled up to the curb and saw a middle-aged woman down on her knees pulling at weeds in her yard, a stark contrast from Timothy Waters' home.

He walked up the driveway and cut across the grass to where she worked. When his shadow crossed her she looked up at him suspiciously. He stopped several feet away and pulled out his badge, identifying himself before getting any closer. Even after twenty years, Jack could recognize the young girl from the cheerleader picture he had seen the night before.

"Are you Angela Grimes?" he asked anyway.

"I was," she said rising to her feet and brushing blades of grass from her knees. "Haven't been Grimes for sixteen years. It's Hastings now."

"I apologize," Jack said. "My files are rather dated."

"Your files?"

"You may have heard Timothy Waters was released a few days ago," Jack said. "His conviction overturned."

"I heard," she said, flatly. "I never believed he killed Beth. He was crazy about her."

"I have been assigned to Elizabeth's case," Jack explained. "It's been reopened."

"Figures," she said. "Her father is the governor."

"All cases are reopened when a conviction is overturned," Jack said, adding, "But I'm sure her father got the investigation rolling a little faster than it might have otherwise."

"What can I do for you Detective?" she asked.

"I want to ask you some questions about Elizabeth," Jack said. "And about the night she was killed."

"That was a long time ago." The woman looked off into the distance as if she were trying to see back the twenty years. "I don't know what I could tell you."

"You'd be surprised what you'll remember once you get started," Jack smiled at her. "Do you mind?"

"Why not," she said. "Let's go inside. We'll be more comfortable. I'll fix you some tea if you'd like."

"That would be nice," Jack said. He watched her gather lawn tools then followed her into the house. The interior was well decorated and very clean. He sat at her kitchen table and waited while she moved about the room gathering what she would need to make the tea. She did not speak while preparing the drinks. When she was finished she set one glass in front of Jack, the other in front of the chair facing him. She pulled this chair out and sat uncomfortably on its edge.

"What do you want to know?" she asked.

"First, what can you tell me about Elizabeth?" he began. "What was she like as a person? As a friend?"

"Beth and I were best friends since we were in first grade," Angela said. She said it with little emotion, almost as if she were tired of saying it. "We were opposites that attracted. She was from a wealthy family and I lived in rent-controlled housing. She was flamboyant and I, well, I was shy."

"You were on the cheerleading squad," Jack said. "Not easy when you're shy."

"That was Beth's idea," she gave a half-smile. "Her way of getting me in with the rest of her friends. It didn't work though. I never cheered at any of the games."

"So, the photo I saw . . . ?"

"Was taken at the beginning of the season," Angela finished. "After I quit the squad, Beth and I didn't see each other as much. She was busy with cheerleading and I was . . . I don't know. Ashamed, I guess. I didn't reach out to her because I thought she might be mad at me."

"She was dating Timothy Waters," Jack said.

"Yes," she confirmed.

"Then he went away to college," Jack said.

"He was a year older than us," she nodded.

"Did Beth date anyone else while he was gone?"

"The magic question," she said.

"Pardon?"

"That's the magic question," she repeated.

"I don't understand," Jack said. "Magic question?"

"I have been waiting twenty years for someone to ask me that question," she said glancing out the window to her manicured lawn.

"So she was dating someone?"

"I think so," Angela turned back to him.

"You waited twenty years to say you think she was dating someone else?"

"I know," she folded her hands in her lap. "It sounds stupid."

"No," Jack said. "What makes you think there was someone else in her life?"

"As I said before," Angela leaned forward conspiratorially. "After I dropped out of cheerleading I didn't see much of her anymore. And when I did, she acted strangely. At first, I thought she was mad at me for quitting but then I found out she was missing cheerleading practices sometimes."

"You think she was skipping practice to meet a boy?" Jack asked.

"Well, at first I thought it had to do with me quitting," she said. "Then around Thanksgiving Timothy called to tell her his parents were driving up to get him and they would be going to his grandparent's for Christmas. She didn't take it well."

"What did she do?"

"She started missing more and more practices, and games," Angela said. "And I saw her even less than before. I think she was going to get kicked off the squad before . . . you know."

Jack nodded knowingly. "Why do you think there was another boy?"

"I didn't until," she paused for a minute, "it must have been about three weeks before spring break. She started coming to school late. And she started calling me for her missed assignments. But after I gave them to her she stayed on the phone to talk, like old times. She talked a lot about missing Timothy. We talked about what it would be like if she married him. She told me once she was going to run away to be with him. But every night the conversation would end with her crying. I would ask her what was wrong but she wouldn't say. Eventually, we would hang up and the next day at school she acted like it never happened."

"I don't follow," Jack said. "If she missed Timothy so much, why do you think there was another guy?"

"The night she died," Angela said. "That night she called me. She knew Timothy was coming home that evening and wanted to surprise him. She was so excited when she called me. But she also asked me a very strange question."

"Which was...," Jack prompted.

"She asked me how to break up with a guy," Angela said. "I said, 'With Timothy?' And she said, 'No'."

"She wanted to break up with someone else?"

"That's what it sounded like to me."

"What did you tell her?"

"Boys weren't exactly knocking down my door, detective," Angela said. "I hardly ever had a date. I never had to break up with one. I couldn't tell her anything."

"You think she was going to break up with the other boy?"

"Had to be," she said. "Who else could she break up with if it wasn't Timothy?"

"You have any idea who it was?"

"Until that night I had no idea there was another guy," she said. "And she wouldn't tell me who it was."

"Did you tell the police about this?"

"Yes," she nodded. "But without knowing who it was they couldn't do anything. They just went after Timothy."

"On the night of her death, Elizabeth told her parents she was going to spend the night at your house," Jack said. "Did you know anything about that?"

"No," she said. "But it doesn't surprise me. She had done it before. Her parents never called to check on her."

"Where did she usually go when she did that?"

"Wherever," Angela said. "When she wanted to go somewhere her parents wouldn't want her to go, she told them she was at my house."

"Like where?"

"Parties, dance clubs, anywhere she could have a good time."

"Did you go with her?" Jack asked.

"My dad was too strict," Angela smiled. "He would call to check on me. I couldn't get away with anything. Beth would tell me about it later though."

"Beth had a necklace," Jack said. "A diamond necklace she was wearing in most of the pictures taken her senior year. Do you know anything about it?"

"I know she wore it," she said. "I think Timothy gave it to her."

"He says Elizabeth told him her father gave it to her," Jack said.

"Really?" Angela raised an eyebrow. "That doesn't sound right."

"Why not?"

"Beth's father was hardly ever around," Angela said. "He wasn't one to give her gifts either. And that necklace was gorgeous."

"Did you ever ask where she got it?" Jack asked.

"Yeah," Angela said. "Right after she got it, while I was still in cheerleading, I asked and all she did was grin. That's why I thought Timothy gave it to her."

"Did she have it before he left for college?"

"No," she shook her head. "A few weeks later. I thought he must have mailed it to her."

Jack remembered the house where he had interviewed Timothy. It was the same home Timothy had lived in twenty years ago. Even then the house would have been considered low-end. He asked, "How do you think he would have paid for it?"

"I don't know," she paused. "I never really thought about that."

8

Angela Hastings gave Jack the names of several women who had been on the cheerleading squad with Elizabeth. He spent the better part of the afternoon tracking them down. Of the three he found, only one provided information he could use. She didn't know whom Elizabeth might have been dating but she did remember seeing a car pick her up once. The only reason she remembered was because the car was a sporty model. She didn't know who was driving the car, but she was sure it wasn't Mr. or Mrs. Mitchell.

"How do you know?" Jack asked.

Tina Shelton juggled a toddler on her knee. She was a new grandmother at thirty-nine. Her eyelids were drooping, her hair unkempt. The room where they sat was filled with a playpen and dozens of toys. The child giggled for no apparent reason and a spark came to her tired eyes.

"How do I know it wasn't her parents?"

"Yes," Jack said. "How could you be sure?"

"Because her parents always came in big fancy cars," Tina said. She kissed her grandson on the forehead. "And they always came right up to the sidewalk. Probably would have driven onto the field if they could have. This car was parked a half a block away. Beth had to walk to it. Then it sped off in a big hurry."

"You didn't see the driver?"

"It had those dark windows," she said.

"And Elizabeth never told you who it was?" Jack asked.

"No," she said. "But not because we didn't ask. We all wanted to know. She told us it was a cousin of hers or something like that. None of us believed her but we could tell she wasn't going to tell us more. So, we stopped asking."

"Do you think she might have been dating the driver of that car?" Jack asked.

"It's possible," she grinned at the child. "But I suppose it could have been her cousin like she said."

"But you said you didn't believe her," Jack reminded.

"We didn't want to believe her," she said. "We were teenagers. We liked the idea of a mysterious man."

"Man?"

"A figure of speech."

"You don't remember what kind of car?" Jack shifted the conversation. "Anything you might be able to tell me could help."

"I didn't know it then," she shrugged. "I sure don't know it now."

"Would you know it if you saw a picture of it?" Jack asked.

"Sure," she nodded. "I see one from time to time. I could pick it out easy enough."

"I'll try to get some pictures to you in the next couple of days," Jack said. "Is there anything else you can remember about Elizabeth that might help? Was she acting strange or different in any way during the days leading up to her death?"

"That was a long time ago," she said, sounding a lot like Angela Hastings. "I really don't remember her that well. I do remember the squad was talking about kicking her out. She was missing too many practices I think. Of course, everyone liked her, so no one wanted to vote on it."

"She was popular, then?"

"Very."

"What about her friend, Angela?" Jack asked. "Was she popular?"

"I guess not," Tina said. "I don't remember an Angela."

"She was in your squad that year but dropped out before the first game," Jack said.

"Oh, Angie," Tina said with a smile. "God, I forgot about her. No, she wasn't one of the popular girls. She was okay. She just wasn't fun."

"Wasn't fun?"

"She was a good girl, detective," Tina explained, rubbing noses with the baby. "She followed the rules. To be in the popular crowd you had to break the rules, or at least bend them."

"And Elizabeth bent the rules?"

"Bent them?" Tina laughed. "She broke them into tiny pieces. She never did things by the book. I think it was her way of rebelling against her parents."

"You're saying Elizabeth was not a good girl?" Jack asked.

"Not even close," she confirmed.

"Yet she and Angela were close friends?" Jack said.

"They knew each other for years," Tina said. "I think if it weren't for Angie, Beth would have been worse than she was. Angie kept her in check. It was something Beth needed; to be kept in check. After Angie dropped out of cheerleading I think Beth stopped spending so much time with her. That's probably why she started missing practices. Angie wasn't there to keep her in line. God knows the rest of us couldn't do it."

"So, Angela was the voice of reason for her?"

"More like her conscience," Tina said. "Having Angie nearby toned Beth down."

"What was she like when Angela wasn't around?"

"Party girl," Tina said. "She would do anything to have a good time. She used to go to all-night parties. Some people said she never went home. But, come to think of it, she stopped coming to the parties, too. We thought she might have gotten in trouble with her parents or something. Never got a chance to ask her."

"Do you think she might have gotten mixed up with the wrong kind of people?" Jack asked. He waited while she thought it over.

"I know whoever was driving that car wasn't from East High," Tina said. "And the only kids from West who could afford a car like that weren't good kids."

"Could she have been involved with drugs?"

"I suppose it's possible."

"Anything else you can tell me?"

"I've already told you more than I thought I remembered," she said. "Sorry I'm not more help."

"You've done fine," Jack said. "I'll be back with those car photos."

"Okay," she said. "And if I remember anything . . ."

Jack handed her a card. "Call me at this number. If I don't answer, leave a message and I'll call you back."

"I will," she said placing the card on the table. She hefted the child so she could stand and walked Jack to the front door. She waved the little boy's hand at the detective as he made his way to his car. As he was about to get in, the woman opened the storm door and called to him.

"I just remembered something," she said walking toward him at a brisk rate, the small boy bouncing on her hip.

"What's that?" he asked, leaning on the roof of the car.

"Tim had a friend," she said. "A guy named . . . what was it? . . . Oh, I know, Lance Carpenter. When everything happened, he insisted Tim was innocent. Even said he could prove it. I don't know how. No one really listened to him. We figured if the police didn't listen he was probably full of it."

"Carpenter?"

"Yes."

"Any idea where I might find him?" Jack pulled out his notepad.

"He disappeared about the same time Tim was found guilty," she shrugged. "There were lots of rumors. No one really knew."

"What were the rumors?"

"Oh, you know, all the basic ones," she said. "He ran away and joined the circus. He ran away and joined the army. Some said he went to work for the CIA or the FBI or something. Another said he was killed by whoever killed Beth and was buried in a field."

"That covers a lot of territory," Jack grinned.

"Rumors usually do," she said.

"Thanks," he waved to the boy. "I'll look into it."

9

Next, Jack wanted to talk to the couple that found Elizabeth's body. Unfortunately, he could not find an Edward Vine on record. He checked with motor vehicles, the phone company, and the post office. There was no Edward, Ed, or E. Vine anywhere. No one by the name Edward Vine was paying utilities of any kind within the city. He was going to check under the woman's name but found it was missing from the reports. Either the officer questioning them did not ask for it or he did not write it down. Whichever it was, Jack was blocked by the officer's negligence.

Jack feared the couple, then young and just starting their lives, had moved away. He finally moved to police records and searched for the couple. There was no criminal record. He found Edward's name in reference to being interviewed after he discovered Elizabeth Mitchell's body. And then Jack found one more entry. It was in a highway patrol report. Mr. and Mrs. Edward Vine were killed in a head-on collision with a drunk driver ten years ago. There was no way to get a new statement. Frustrated, Jack moved on to the next witness on his list.

Wayne Fenton was still a real estate agent. In his early sixties, he was a gaunt man with stark angular features which made Jack question if he was ill. The man greeted Jack with a firm handshake and a broad smile common to persons of his profession. Jack flashed his badge and the smile faded. Jack couldn't help but wonder what the man might be hiding behind that artificial smile. Wayne showed the detective to an office and closed the door behind them.

"What can I do for you, officer?" the real estate agent asked.

"Detective," Jack corrected.

"Detective," Wayne repeated dutifully.

"I have some questions," Jack said. "If you have some time."

Wayne tilted his head at that. For a brief moment, Jack thought the man was going to claim he was too busy to answer questions. In the end, the man gestured at a chair for Jack to sit and circled the desk to settle in the more comfortable executive-style desk chair.

"I'm not sure what I could possibly know that would be of use to you," the man flashed his smile again. "But I will help any way I can."

Jack smiled as well and pulled his notepad from his jacket pocket. He deliberately took too long finding his pen. He watched the man shift uncomfortably in his seat. Beads of sweat formed on the man's forehead and he whipped them away with his hand. Jack squared his shoulders and leaned forward slightly, staring the man straight in his eyes, holding his gaze.

"I want to talk to you about Elizabeth Mitchell," Jack said. After twenty years, would Wayne remember her name?

"Who?" the agent asked, apparently not remembering.

"Elizabeth Mitchell," Jack said again.

"I think you have the wrong man," Wayne said. "I don't know anyone by that name."

"I'm sorry," Jack grinned and sat back a little. "Elizabeth Mitchell was the name of the girl you and two of your clients found dead in a house you were showing them about twenty years ago."

The man's face paled. It was not the reaction Jack was expecting. He actually thought the man would be relieved. Jack was convinced Wayne was hiding something about his current life he did not want the police to know about. He was sure when the realtor heard Jack ask a question about the twenty-year-old case he would be overjoyed. Yet, there the man sat without a drop of color in his face.

"You okay, Mr. Fenton?"

"Uh? Oh, yes," Wayne nodded. "I just . . . well, you know . . . that was an awful sight. I had put it out of my mind years ago. Had to if I wanted to sleep at night. When you mentioned it, all those images came flooding back. I'm okay now. You say you have some questions? That was twenty years ago. I thought it was solved. Some guy was sent to prison, wasn't he? I was sure they had caught someone."

The man spoke fast and gave no time for responses. A nervous habit from childhood, he had worked hard to control it. But in times of stress, there was no stopping it. He had lost more than one sale over the years by driving clients away. Jack had dealt with far worse over the years and he waited for the proper opportunity to interrupt.

"Mr. Fenton," he said when the man took a breath. It was enough. Wayne offered his full attention. "You are correct. The case was twenty years ago. A young man was arrested, tried, and sentenced for the murder. But recently his conviction was overturned because of a lack of evidence. Therefore, the case has been reopened and I am in charge of the new investigation. Because of this, I need to speak to as many of the witnesses as I can."

"Witness?" Wayne faltered. "No. No. I didn't see it happen. I only saw . . . I just . . . I . . . "

"Wayne!" Jack snapped.

The agent's mouth stopped wide and he closed it slowly. He looked at Jack with a tinge of fear in his eyes. "I'm sorry."

"Let's try it this way," Jack said. "I'll ask questions. You answer them. And if you'd like to tell me why you're so nervous about my being here, I'd be glad to listen."

The man said nothing. His shoulders sagged and he let out a long breath. Jack was not sure what Wayne was hiding, but he was convinced it was something he wanted to know. He glanced at his notepad to orient himself and to buy time to organize his thoughts before starting the questioning.

"When you arrived at the house that morning," Jack asked, "did you notice anything out of the ordinary? I mean before you found the body?"

"No," Wayne said. "It was just a simple showing. Normally we would have been in and out in less than fifteen minutes. I had almost a dozen houses lined up to show that couple. They were one of those needy clients. And picky. They didn't like anything. Except this house. They liked it. But finding a body in the master bedroom took the thrill out of it for them."

"I can imagine," Jack said. "Was there anything missing?"

"From the house?" Wayne said. "No. It was an empty house. The previous owners were transferred months earlier. Eager to sell. I was sure I had it sold that day. Then your guys came and threw crime-scene tape all over it. Couldn't give it away then."

"So, as far as you knew," Jack said, sternly. "Nothing was disturbed in the house? The only thing out of place was the girl's body?"

"Yeah," Wayne said, nodding his head vigorously, trying hard not to say more than he should. But then he added, "Well, that and the window."

"The window?" Jack asked. "The broken window at the back door? I know about it."

"I never understood why they broke the window," Wayne said, not at Jack specifically. "With her having the key and all."

"Pardon me?" Jack sat forward. "What did you say?"

Wayne's eyes went wide as what he said replayed in his mind. He glanced from side to side trying to avert Jack's gaze. There was nowhere for him to go, nowhere to hide. The man's body went slack and he sank deeper into his chair, looking very small, very vulnerable.

"She had the key?"

"Yes," Wayne said in a weak voice.

"How did she get the key?"

"I gave it to her," Wayne said.

"You knew her?" Jack demanded.

"Yes," Wayne said, quickly adding, "Well, not really. I met her that morning. Or rather the previous morning."

"Mr. Fenton," The authority in Jack's voice startled the agent. "You better start explaining what you're talking about right now, or I'm going to haul your ass downtown on suspicion of murder."

Wayne's wide eyes widened even more. "No. No. I didn't kill that girl. I . . . well, I couldn't have. I would never . . ."

"Then tell me what happened," Jack said. "I could already bring you in for obstruction for not telling this twenty years ago. Why would you give a teen-aged girl the key to an empty house?"

"Well, it all started with my son," Wayne said.

"What does your son have to do with this?"

"With the girl?" Wayne was taken aback. "Oh, nothing. He never met the girl. But my son convinced me one day to let him use an empty house for a poker party. His mother would never let him have one at the house. And I had been young once. So, with a promise from him to clean up afterward I gave him the key to a house where I knew no one would notice a few cars."

"You loaned out someone else's house?" Jack asked.

"It didn't hurt anything," Wayne explained. "Danny cleaned up the place like he said he would and no one ever knew."

"And how does this tie into the girl?"

"Well, after the poker party," Wayne continued. "Word got around the high school that Danny's father could get them into empty houses. Soon, Danny was bringing kids to me with requests for houses."

"And you handed them keys?"

"No," Wayne held his hands up in an effort to stop the direction the conversation was taking. "I made them swear they would not have parties, would clean up the place before they left, and return the key first thing the next day."

"And they did what you asked?"

"Well," Wayne looked away. "I required a deposit."

"A deposit?"

"Okay," Wayne nodded. "I charged them fifty dollars."

"You made money off of them?" Jack said.

"Yes."

"And Elizabeth was one of your customers?"

"She wanted a house for that night," Wayne agreed.

"Did you know why?" Jack asked.

"I never asked why," Wayne said. "I just insisted they follow the rules I had set."

"And you never mentioned this to the police twenty years ago?" Jack asked.

"No," Wayne shook his head. "And I never, ever gave out another key after that."

"A little late," Jack said. He stood and opened the door. He turned back to the man who seemed to shrink more every minute. "Keep yourself available. I may need to ask you more questions."

"Yes, sir," the man squeaked. "I'll be here."

10

Eight years ago, Officer Joe Baxter had been moonlighting as a bank guard on his days off, to supplement his income and provide a better life for his family. One morning just after the bank opened its doors for business, a man walked in waving a gun and demanding money. Joe pulled his weapon and a shootout ensued, leaving two dead, including the would-be robber. Joe took two bullets. The first was a through and through in his upper arm. The second shattered his kneecap, ending his career in law enforcement.

He answered the door leaning heavily on a hand-carved oak cane. He smiled broadly at the sight of Jack on his doorstep and used his cane to push the screen door open, beckoning the detective in. He limped into the living room collapsing into an overstuffed recliner. Using the cane, he pointed at another, smaller chair and told Jack to sit.

"Sally, bring us some tea, would you?" Joe shouted over his shoulder toward the kitchen. To Jack, he said, "Would offer you a beer but my doc won't let me touch the stuff, so she won't buy it for me."

"Tea is fine," Jack said. According to Joe Baxter's service record, he would be fifty-two years old. The man sitting next to Jack looked to be pushing seventy. His hair was thin and gray. The skin of his face was loose, his complexion patchy. The evidence of a hard life was limited to his appearance though as he maintained a jovial persona that was contagious.

"You said on the phone you wanted to discuss an old case," Joe said. "Which one was that?"

"Elizabeth Mitchell murder," Jack said. "Twenty years ago."

"Thought so," Joe grunted. "I saw in the news they released that boy. I never figured him for it anyhow."

"You didn't?" Jack's eyes widened.

"Hell no," Joe shifted his weight and stretched his injured leg out. "I knew the kid. He wasn't a bad egg. But Detective Righteous wouldn't look anywhere else. Said the boy was guilty without a doubt and he put enough evidence together to convince a jury."

"Detective Righteous?"

"You know," Joe grinned. "What's his name, Singleton. He's your chief now I heard."

"He is," Jack confirmed. "Why do you call him Detective Righteous?"

"It's Chief Righteous now, I suppose," Joe said. A middle-aged woman emerged from the kitchen with two glasses of iced tea. She handed one to each of the men and retreated to where she had come. Almost as an afterthought, Joe twisted in his seat saying, "Thanks, dear."

He turned back and took a long drink from the glass. When he stopped more than half the cool liquid was gone. He held the glass out and admired it before setting it aside. "She makes good tea. Now, where was I? Oh, that's right. The other boys and I called him Righteous because of the way he acted, always critical of everything and everyone. He was especially harsh on anyone breaking the rules."

"Sounds like Singleton," Jack nodded.

"Yeah well, one of the guys in my squad found out our Mr. Righteous had a not-so-righteous secret," Joe smiled. "Found out he had a couple of mistresses. He's telling us to follow the straight and narrow and he's cheating on his wife with at least two women. That's when we started calling him Detective Righteous."

"No kidding?" Jack said and he found himself wondering about Terrance's secretary, Kelly.

"Oh, sure," Joe said. "But he stopped that years back. Some of the boys thought he got caught with his pants down. His wife stopped showing up for the dinners and such for a while. Real pretty thing, too. Never understood why he would cheat on her."

"How do you know he stopped?" Jack asked. "Maybe he just became more discreet."

"No, he quit," Joe shook his head. "I worked around the man for several years. He changed. Went from a big pain in the ass to a huge pain in the ass. Spent a lot more time at home. Some of the boys verified that. He definitely quit. That was right around the time of this girl's murder too. The governor, he was mayor then, anyway he and Singleton were friends. He wanted someone to pay for killing his daughter. Singleton was stressed out so badly he snapped at anybody daring to walk by him. We think that's how he got caught cheating. Snapped at his wife, used the wrong name or something. Anyway, after the trial was over he seemed to be pissed at everybody."

"What kind of detective was he?" Jack asked, cautiously.

"He got results, I guess," Joe said matter-of-factly. "Of course, as I said, I never figured that boy killed the girl. He closed the case and sent an innocent kid to prison. I don't know if that makes you a good detective or a bad one."

"You said he was stressed," Jack said. "Could he have made mistakes? Other than arresting the wrong man. Could he have mishandled the investigation? Or the evidence?"

"I can't answer that for you," Joe said. "Only Singleton would know. Not sure how we got on the subject of him anyway. Don't you have some questions about the case you want answered?"

"Yes," Jack settled back in his chair. "Yes, I do. You were the first officer on the scene according to the records."

"I was the first to respond," Joe agreed. "It was such a strange call."

"How so?" Jack asked.

"I get there and there's this couple," Joe said. "She's crying hysterically and he's trying to console her. Then there's the real estate agent pacing back and forth chain-smoking like nothing else. I ask where the body is and the woman starts wailing and the husband has to try even harder to calm her down. Then the agent points to the house. Tells me there's a girl in the master bedroom. I'm thinking I'm going to find this bloody mess and discover new ways to torture and dismember a human being.

"I walk in with my weapon ready," Joe said. "Do a room-by-room search. The house is empty, and I mean completely empty except for this girl. And when I see her, the first impression I get is they made a mistake. She looks like she fell asleep on the floor and just needs someone to wake her up. I call out to her and move closer and closer until I'm close enough to see she isn't breathing. So, I go back to the car and call for the coroner and a homicide detective. All by the book."

"What's so strange about that?" Jack asked.

"Aside from the way the girl was positioned?" Joe asked. "Well, the way the whole thing was handled. First, Detective Righteous shows up in record time. Then he tells me to make sure no one goes into the house. Like he thought I was going to sell tickets or something. Then he goes in without asking where she is. A few minutes later, he comes out and tells me again not to let anyone in and to talk to the couple.

"A few minutes later he's in the trunk of his car. And I remember that because I had worked with the guy a few times and he was never fast about getting his equipment. A lot of the time he would have one of us uniforms get it for him. I think it made him feel important. But this time he got it himself. Then he goes to the radio and calls dispatch for support," Joe said. "He went back in and didn't come out until forensics arrived. They weren't too happy with him. But he insisted he wanted everything done right since he knew the girl's parents."

"Let's go back to when you first arrived at the scene," Jack said. "What do you remember about the room the girl was found in?"

"I was only in there long enough to determine the girl was dead," Joe said. "I didn't notice a lot."

"Come on," Jack said. "You're a cop. You're trained to see things just like the rest of us. What did you see?"

Joe nodded. "I guess I saw a young girl who was murdered then positioned to appear like she was sleeping. The killer even put a blanket over her as if to keep her warm while she slept. I assumed the killer knew the girl. I think that was what led Singleton to the boyfriend."

"Probably," Jack agreed. "What else?"

"You know what I really didn't get?"

"What?"

"My wife is a fashion nut," Joe said. "And teen-aged girls are crazy about fashion."

"Okay?" Jack wondered if the retired officer was drifting onto another topic.

"This girl," Joe continued. "She was wearing a pink sweater. She had on pink pumps. I found out later her skirt was white."

"What's wrong with that?" Jack asked.

"Nothing," he said. "Nothing at all. It was the purse I didn't get."

"The purse?"

"Yeah," Joe said. "I go in there to check on the girl. She's lying there in her pink schoolgirl clothes. And next to one wall there's this blue designer purse. I didn't get it."

"An expensive purse?" Jack asked.

"High dollar. But it didn't match her outfit."

"Maybe she was proud of owning the expensive one and carried it to show it off," Jack suggested.

"Maybe," Joe said. "It just bothered me. But I wasn't on the case after I filed my report so I never got to find out."

"Well," Jack said. "I'll look into it and let you know if there's anything mentioned in the file."

"Thanks," Joe said. "Not that it really matters now. But I am curious."

"No problem," Jack smiled. "I should get going. Thanks for talking to me."

"Any time," Joe said. "Sure you don't have any more questions?"

"I might," Jack said. "I'll be back if I think of something. Don't get up. I'll see myself out."

Back in his car, Jack pulled the file from the passenger seat and started thumbing through it until he came to what he wanted; a crime scene photo of the girl lying in the room. It was a wide shot taken from the doorway. It showed nearly the whole room.

Twenty years was a long time. A lot of cases to remember. Joe could have been confused. But Jack didn't think so. The old cop was pretty clear and Jack bet he could remember the details of most of the cases he was involved with during his years on the force. But staring at the crime scene photos, it was obvious there was no purse in the room.

11

Mrs. Alyssa Jackson was still teaching although she had not coached the cheerleading squad for more than five years. Jack found her in her classroom grading English papers with a red ballpoint pen. She glanced up when Jack entered the room but returned to reading the paper she was working on. Jack stood off to the side waiting patiently while she continued. She made marks with her pen from time to time and finished with a large letter 'C' at the top of the page.

"Thank you for waiting," she said, looking at Jack over the top of her reading glasses. "I didn't want to have to start over."

"No problem," Jack said moving forward. He pulled out his badge as he walked. "I'm Detective Jack Mallory. Are you Alyssa Jackson?"

She removed her glasses, laid them on her desk, and stood in one graceful motion. "Is there a problem?"

"No," Jack said. "I just need to ask some questions. Are you Mrs. Jackson?"

"Yes," she said. "What kind of questions?"

"I wanted to know what you could tell me about Elizabeth Mitchell," Jack said.

"Who?"

"Elizabeth Mitchell," Jack said. "She was a cheerleader on your squad a little over twenty years ago. She was murdered her senior year."

"Oh, Beth," Alyssa said with recognition. "I haven't heard her name in years. You say you have questions?"

"Yes," Jack confirmed. "You may have heard that Timothy Waters was released from prison because his conviction was overturned."

"Really?" Alyssa was surprised. "I hadn't heard. I was so shocked to hear it was him. He was always such a polite boy."

"You knew Timothy?"

"Yes," she said. "I had him in a couple of English classes while he attended school here."

"What kind of student was he?" Jack asked.

"A good one," she smiled, thinking back. "He wasn't like the other jocks at the school. He was sweet. Always did his homework, scored high marks on his exams. He spoke with respectful politeness. He was the type of boy who opened doors for the girls and teachers alike. I can't think of anyone who didn't like Timothy."

"What about the girls?"

"The girls?"

"How did they like Timothy?" Jack asked. "Was he popular?"

"Are you kidding?" she said. "He was a handsome young man, the captain of the football team and he was sweet. Every girl liked him."

"Were any of them jealous of Elizabeth?"

"I see where you're going," she said. "You think one of my girls might have killed her to get a shot at Tim?"

"I don't think anything yet," Jack said. "I have very little to go on. I have to follow every angle and some of them won't be pleasant, but I have to follow them just the same."

"I understand," Alyssa said. "But to answer your question I would have to say no. I don't think any of the girls were jealous of Beth and I'm sure none of them would have killed her."

"What about other boys?" Jack asked. "Timothy was away at college. Any chance Elizabeth was dating another boy who became jealous when Timothy returned for the holiday?"

"I suppose it's possible," Alyssa said. "But if she was seeing someone else I wasn't aware of it."

"What about the weeks leading up to her murder," Jack said. "Did you notice any change in her personality?"

"Now that you mention it, I do remember she started changing there at the end," the teacher said. "She was missing practices and games."

"Did you talk to her about it?" Jack asked. "Ask her why?"

"I talked to her," Alyssa nodded. "Had to. If I remember she said she was having problems at home. I asked if there was anything I could do and she said there wasn't. So, I warned her she needed to start showing up for practice or I was going to have to remove her from the squad."

"What did she say to that?"

"She told me to do what I had to do," she said. "Very unusual for her."

"Did you remove her from the squad?" Jack asked.

"No," Alyssa said. "I told her I would give her some time to decide what she wanted to do."

"Did she ever make a decision?"

"No," she said. "She was killed about a week later."

"When she told you she was having problems at home," Jack said. "Did she give you any indication of the type of problem? Was it with her parents or siblings?"

"She didn't say," Alyssa said. "Her parents were very supportive of her. But she was a teen. You know how it gets between teens and parents. I assumed it was normal adolescent problems."

"You teach English?"

"Yes, I do."

"Did you have Elizabeth in any of your classes?"

"Twice," Alyssa said. "First in her sophomore year. Then again when she was a senior."

"So she was your student as well as on your cheerleading squad?" Jack asked.

"Yes," Alyssa nodded.

"What kind of student was she?"

"Her sophomore year she was a delight," Alyssa said. "Her senior year started wonderfully but there toward the end she was faltering. Like with cheerleading, she was missing classes. And she wasn't turning in her homework. The work she did turn in was second-rate. She was a better student than that. When I talked to her about her grades, she blamed them on the same problems at home."

"Did you ever speak to her parents about the problem?"

"Her father was the mayor then," she said. "They never came to parent-teacher conferences and they never returned my calls. It wasn't easy to talk to them."

"You said they were supportive of her," Jack said. "How is that if they never talked to you about her?"

"Well," the woman stopped to consider. Then she spoke slowly. "I don't know. I assumed. I mean, she told me they were. I never thought otherwise."

"Yet you never spoke to them?"

"I talked to them," she corrected. "They came to . . . Or did I? I really don't remember."

"But you had no reason to believe they weren't supportive?"

"No," Alyssa shook her head.

"Other than when Elizabeth told you she was having problems at home?" Jack asked.

"Well, I guess," she said. "But like I said. I never thought it was anything more than normal teen problems."

"And now that she's dead?" Jack asked. "Do you still think her problems were normal?"

"I have no reason to believe the two things were connected," she said with wide eyes. "Were they?"

"I don't know," Jack said. "I'm investigating a murder. Until I can prove otherwise, anyone who had contact with the girl is a suspect."

"Even me?"

"Even you," Jack smiled giving Alyssa a sense of unease. "You're just not very high on the list."

Jack closed his notepad and stood, excusing himself from the interview. He walked out of the school with little more than he went in with. In his car, he steered north. It was time he paid a visit to the coroner.

12

Elizabeth Mitchell's autopsy was performed by then Medical Examiner Simon Penske. After more than two decades on the job he retired from the coroner's office. Finding the man was simply a matter of Jack dialing the phone number listed in his personnel file. He agreed to meet with Jack at a small mid-town diner to discuss the twenty-year-old murder as long as Jack agreed to bring the original case file for Simon to review and pick up the tab at lunch. Jack gathered the file and arrived at the diner at a quarter past eleven, fifteen minutes ahead of their scheduled meeting time. Simon Penske was already there.

Simon was a short stout man with thinning hair that he combed to one side. He wore his glasses low on his nose and scrutinized Jack with piercingly blue eyes. Having left the job five years ago, Jack expected a man approaching seventy. The man before him was barely sixty. He did not smile as he greeted Jack with a firm handshake. Jack noted the man's tired expression as the hostess guided them to a booth near the back of the restaurant. They sat opposite one another and Jack slid the file across the table.

"Thanks for agreeing to see me," the detective said.

The man waved him into silence with one hand while he began turning pages with the other. He scanned the report quickly, making grunting sounds from time to time while he read. Jack sat quietly for another five minutes only disrupting the silence long enough to order two cups of coffee from the waitress whose eyes remained transfixed on the photographs Simon was examining. When he finished, Simon returned all the pages to the file in their proper order and set the file to the side.

"I remember this one," the man said. As if to prove it he added, "Mayor's daughter. Governor now."

"That's right," Jack said. "What can you tell me about it?"

"You mean, what did I leave out of my report?"

"I didn't mean to imply...," Jack defended.

"I never said you implied anything," Simon waved his hand again. "I'm saying this case was a mess from the get-go. You had a dead girl whose father was a prominent politician and your lead investigator was a close friend of the family. It was a lousy deal. I didn't like having any part of it."

"What are you talking about?" Jack asked. "You didn't like being part of the autopsy?"

"I was only allowed to report what they wanted," Simon said. "I don't work that way. As soon as the dust settled I transferred to the north end. When I heard Singleton was going to be chief, I took early retirement."

"So, you left things out of the report?" Jack asked.

"Oh, yes," Simon said. "Son of a bitch told me what to leave out. I said I don't leave things out of reports. He told me I would this time or he and the mayor would ruin me and my family. I told him he couldn't get away with blackmailing me and he told me he could and would. I had a wife and three kids. I couldn't afford to take the chance. So, I left out what I was told to leave out."

"And what was that?" Jack asked.

The waitress came with their coffee and asked if they were ready to order. Her eyes kept floating back to the manila file folder on the table's edge. They ordered quickly and she retreated to the kitchen.

"What did you leave out?" Jack repeated.

"For one thing," Simon started. He took a drink of his coffee and stared into his cup as if he were reading tea leaves. Head still down, he continued, "The blood under the girl's fingernails and the semen I found on her thigh were not from the same person."

"And Terrance had you withhold that?"

"He said the proof was in the blood," Simon said. "The blood type matched the boyfriend and the semen just clouded things."

Jack shook his head. "Did you do a tox screen? There wasn't one in the file."

"I ran all the standard blood work," Simon said.

"Find anything?"

"Yes," he answered.

"Drugs?"

"No," Simon took another drink.

"What then?" Jack pressed.

"She was pregnant," he said in the same tone he used when he ordered his lunch.

"Pregnant?"

"Yes."

"How far along?"

"A few weeks."

"Far enough she might know?" Jack asked.

"She could have known," Simon nodded. "Probably did."

"That would fit," Jack said to himself.

"Fit?"

"I interviewed a couple of her friends and they said she had been acting strange the couple of weeks prior to her death," Jack explained. "I thought it might be drug related. I bet the pregnancy had something to do with it."

"And you think that might have something to do with the murder?" Simon asked.

"I don't know," Jack said in a sharp voice. "But we can't question the father since we never had the chance to identify him. How could you withhold something like that?"

"I told you . . . "

"He told you to bury that?"

"He told me it had nothing to do with the murder and that the mayor just lost his daughter and didn't want her memory tarnished with an unwed pregnancy," Simon said. "So I left it out."

Jack looked at Simon with a long stare. The retired coroner returned his gaze to the coffee cup. Jack said, "Nineteen."

"What?"

"That's how old Timothy Waters was when he was convicted without the benefit of all the facts for his defense," Jack said.

Simon did not speak.

"What about the bruise on her leg?"

"Old," the coroner said. "Not related to the attack that killed her. I assumed it was from cheerleading."

"Anything else you left out?" Jack asked.

"Isn't that enough?" Simon raised his eyes to Jack's.

"More than enough," Jack said. "Do you know what became of the evidence? Did you make it disappear for them?"

"All the evidence I had was cataloged and taken to long term storage after the trial," Simon's brow furrowed. "Why? What happened?"

"Timothy Waters was released because they couldn't produce the evidence," Jack said. "It wasn't in storage."

"None of it?"

"None of it," Jack confirmed.

"How can that be?" Simon said. "I checked it in myself. You can't just walk in and take it."

"Apparently someone did," Jack said.

The waitress brought their food order and set their check on the end of the table so either man could reach it. Jack read the total and pulled his wallet out. He dropped two twenties on top of the check and stood. He shook his head at the coroner again and turned to leave without touching his meal.

Simon contemplated the plate of food, then slid out of the booth and made his way out of the restaurant. In the parking lot, he searched for Jack but the detective was already gone. If Timothy Waters was really innocent, Singleton had misled him all those years ago. There was a chill in the air and Simon turned his collar up against it. He moved down the aisle to his car and drove away.

13

Jack drove home exhausted from chasing down and interviewing witnesses. He threw a frozen dinner in the microwave and stood in the kitchen reading over the case file again. He re-examined the coroner's report comparing what was there with what Simon told him. Without the knowledge that Elizabeth was pregnant, and had become so while her boyfriend was away at college, there was no evidence to suggest she was dating someone else. Without the existence of another possible suspect the only direction the case could take was to Timothy.

The microwave sounded and Jack took his meal to the table and continued to read while he ate. Many of the things he read had new meaning when tied to the fact that Elizabeth was pregnant. Missing her morning classes could easily have been caused by morning sickness. Missing cheerleading practices could easily be tied to the pregnancy either because of her emotional stress of dealing with her condition or the physical changes she was going through.

The cheerleading coach told Jack that Elizabeth was having problems at home. She was pregnant. She was missing classes and practices. She had talked to her best friend about breaking up with someone. There was a lot going on in the life of this seventeen-year-old girl. Jack was beginning to believe the timing of her death was not a coincidence. Someone had become angry enough with Elizabeth Mitchell to take her life. As many problems as the girl was juggling, Jack was sure she would not have been able to hide it from her family. He believed they might know something that would help him with the investigation. In spite of Singleton's warning to stay away, he was going to talk to them.

Besides her parents, Elizabeth had an older brother and a younger sister. Jack thought it would be best to start with them. If he could stay under Terrance's radar long enough, he might be able to talk to them all before getting shut down. The brother, Donald, was a bank manager downtown. The sister, Virginia, was a housewife in the suburbs. She would be the easiest to approach and the least likely to blow the whistle on him. And as Elizabeth's sister, she might have more knowledge of the murdered girl than anyone.

He finished his dinner and went to bed setting his alarm for an early start. When he woke the next morning it was past nine. His alarm clock was lying on the floor next to the nightstand. Reality hit him and he jumped up and headed for the shower.

It was a little after ten when Jack pulled up in front of the two-story brick colonial. Jack placed the original construction in the 1850s or '60s. He also guessed its value was over a million dollars. He parked in the street and made the long walk to the front door, a wonderfully manicured lawn stretching away in both directions. He climbed the red brick steps to a porch of polished wood slats. On one side a porch swing hung on thick chains, on the other a pair of high-back rocking chairs painted a glossy white stood on either side of a small table. None of the furniture appeared to have ever been used.

He stepped up to the door and pressed the bell. Listening to the chime inside the house reminded him of church bells. The ornate wood door was large, common to higher-priced homes. To either side were windows the height of the door and about eight inches wide. The glass was opaque. Jack stood looking through one of the windows at moving shadows beyond. A moment later the door opened and he moved back to where he could get a full view of whoever was greeting him.

Virginia Mitchell-Clifton was a petite woman. She wore a simple summer dress but Jack was sure it cost more than his suit. Her hair was pulled back with a pink scarf that matched the flower print of the dress. She tilted her head at the sight of Jack, glancing past him briefly like she was expecting someone else. "May I help you?" she asked tentatively.

"My name is Detective Jack Mallory," he held his badge where she could see it plainly. "I was hoping to ask you some questions."

"Is there something wrong?" she asked. "Is it Brandon?"

Brandon, her husband, was the son of Nathaniel Clifton of Clifton Construction Inc. There was a lot of money in their families, a lot of power. Jack did not like the woman as soon as he saw her. It wasn't fair really. It was stereotyping to think she was a spoiled rich girl.

"No," Jack said. "I'm sure Brandon is fine. I wanted to ask you some questions about the past. About your sister, Elizabeth, and the days leading up to her death."

Virginia stood in the open doorway of her home staring at Jack like he had struck her. Jack remained unmoving while he watched her gather herself and her thoughts. She was contemplating his request. Jack was surprised, expecting she would be eager to discuss her sister's case.

"I really don't know what I could tell you," she said. She made no move to invite him in or to close the door in his face. He stood still, waiting for her. They were silent for a long moment before she broke. She pulled the door open and waved her arm into the house. "I can give you a few minutes."

The two of them entered a room just off the foyer. A high ceiling with bookcases that stretched the length of the walls and nearly the full height dominated the room. Track lighting illuminated the volumes of books on the shelves as well as the leather reading chairs. The only breaks in the walls of books were the windows, the door and a fireplace. Jack was standing in a library for the wealthy. He had an urge to whisper. Virginia sat in one of the soft leather chairs and waited for him to do the same.

"What is it you want?" she asked, not a whisper.

"As you probably know," Jack said, "Timothy Waters was released from prison. It was determined by the court there was insufficient evidence to uphold the conviction."

"Yes. I heard," she said. "And I really don't know how I can help you."

"The case has been reopened and I have been tasked with the investigation," Jack explained. "All I want to do is ask you some questions about the last couple of weeks of your sister's life."

"Detective, Beth and I were not close," Virginia said, "and it has been over twenty years. I don't know what I can tell you."

"You weren't close?" Jack asked.

"No."

"May I ask why?"

"You may ask," she said, adding nothing.

"But you won't tell me?"

"We were teen-aged girls," Virginia said. "We fought. A lot. Over clothes. Over what to watch on TV. Over boys. You name it, we fought about it. Typical teen stuff."

"What about the two weeks before her death?" Jack asked.

"What about them?"

"Did you fight during the two weeks leading up to her death?" Jack said. "Was everything normal?"

"As normal as ever," Virginia huffed. "I'm sure we fought. As I said, we always did."

"Nothing out of the ordinary?"

"No," she said. She opened her mouth then closed it again. Her eyes changed from argumentative to quizzical.

"What is it?" Jack encouraged her.

"Well there was one thing," she said. "It's probably nothing though."

"Tell me," he said. "I have very little to work with right now."

"Well, at the time I thought it was strange," she said. "But I didn't question it because it worked in my favor."

"Yes?"

"Beth came home from school early one afternoon," Virginia said. "She was supposed to be at cheerleading practice so I was in her room trying on some of her clothes, a big taboo with her. Anyway, I was admiring myself in a mirror wearing one of her favorite sweaters and she walked in. Of course she starts yelling at me and I yell back and everything proceeds as it always did. She insisted I give her the sweater, so I finally took it off and threw it at her.

"Next thing I knew she started crying," Virginia said. "She sat on the side of her bed crying and hugging the sweater. I was so confused I just walked out of the room. A few minutes later, she came to my room, threw the sweater at me and told me to keep it. She said she didn't like it anymore anyway. But I knew it was her favorite sweater."

Virginia looked at Jack as if waiting for him to explain what this event in her life meant. Jack looked away and then back again.

"Do you know anything about the necklace she wore?" Jack asked. "The diamond necklace that disappeared after her death?"

She paused a moment and said, "I don't remember a necklace."

It was Jack's turn to pause. He did not believe her. The dislike he had toward her when she first opened the door returned.

"Virginia," Jack said, "besides Timothy Waters, do you know anyone your sister may have been dating?"

The woman checked her watch. "Goodness," she said. "I'm going to be late. Can we finish this later?"

"Was Elizabeth dating someone other than Timothy Waters?"

She looked at him. "Yes, Detective. She was."

"Can you tell me who it was?"

"No. I can't."

Jack stared at her for a second. "Why can't you tell me? Because you don't know? Or because you don't want to?"

"I'm really out of time," she said rising from her seat. "I would like you to leave."

14

Standing well over six feet tall with an athletic build and a summer tan, Donald Mitchell reminded Jack of his father, the governor. When Jack arrived just before noon, the banker was not surprised. Jack got the impression the man had spoken to his sister.

When he asked to see the bank's manager the receptionist asked Jack to take a seat. He settled in expecting to be there for a while. But Donald did not keep him waiting. Jack spotted him in his perfectly fitted suit from across the room. His gray-blue eyes were locked on the detective as he walked confidently toward the receptionist's desk.

"Suzy," he said to the girl behind the desk. "You can go to lunch now."

"Yes, sir, Mr. Mitchell," she said pushing her chair back and collecting her purse from one of the drawers.

The man turned to Jack in a smooth, practiced motion with hand extended, "I'm Donald Mitchell. And you must be Detective Mallory. Let's go back to my office. We can have some privacy."

The toothy smile never left Donald's face and Jack took an instant disliking to him just as he did the sister. He followed the banker through a maze of desks, each occupied by employees busy doing whatever it is bankers do. Jack paid little attention to them, keeping his eyes focused on the pinstriping of Donald's designer suit.

They came to a large wooden door with a bronze plaque featuring Donald's name and title mounted at eye level. Inside was a large office furnished with dark cherry wood and leather. A print of the original bank building dominated one wall, a second wall was a collage of plaques and degrees with Donald's name on them. A third wall was decorated with tasteful artwork with more bronze plates identifying the work and its artist. The fourth was floor to ceiling glass revealing the busy street outside.

"You were expecting me," Jack stated.

"Virginia called me," Donald acknowledged.

"Then you know why I'm here," Jack said.

"You have questions about Beth's murder," Donald confirmed. "Maybe about Tim as well."

"Did you know Timothy Waters?"

"He was a couple years younger than me," Donald said. "We weren't friends. I knew him through Beth."

"When you say you weren't friends...?"

"I mean we didn't know each other before he started dating my sister," Donald said. "Otherwise he seemed to be a decent enough kind of guy."

"Do you think he killed Elizabeth?" Jack asked.

"I don't know," Donald said. "He was convicted so I thought he did. Now, I don't know."

"From what you knew of him," Jack said, "was he who you thought of when you heard your sister had been murdered?"

"No," Donald said.

"Why?"

"Because he treated Beth better than she deserved," Donald said. "Better than she treated him."

"It sounds like you weren't fond of your sister," Jack said.

"Don't get me wrong, Detective," Donald said. "She was my sister and I cared about her. But I would never have introduced her to a friend of mine. She didn't treat people well."

"Can you give me an example?" Jack asked.

"An example?" Donald thought for a moment. "She was the type to make plans with someone then call to cancel at the last minute because she got a better offer. She broke up with one guy on his birthday so she wouldn't have to give him a gift. She decided to break it off with another guy but waited until the day after Christmas so she could get the gift he bought her. It was all about Beth."

"Not too popular with her ex-boyfriends?"

Donald chuckled.

"That's just it," he said. "Sure some guys were pissed. But the fact was she had them all dangling on a string. Sometimes she would pull them in. Sometimes she would throw them farther out. But they were always on the string."

"Was Timothy on the string?" Jack asked.

"I'm sure he was," Donald said. "He came back to see her. Sounds like she pulled him in."

"You don't think it could have been something more than a game?"

"I was away at college," Donald said. "I suppose it was possible. She dated him longer than anyone else. But I don't see her changing that fast."

"What about the other guy she was dating at that time?" Jack asked.

"Other guy?" Donald said. "Which guy?"

"There was more than one?"

"Couldn't tell you," he said. "I was away, like I said. No one told me she was seeing anyone else."

"Virginia seems to know something," Jack said. "But she didn't tell me."

"That's Virginia," Donald said. "She's very difficult to talk to. She never got over Elizabeth's death."

"She told me they didn't get along," Jack said.

"They didn't," Donald said. "But if you crossed one, you crossed them both. I only made that mistake a couple of times. They fought all the time. But if you picked a side, they were both on you just like that."

"What about you?"

"Me?"

"Did you get along with Elizabeth?"

"As well as a brother and sister could," Donald said. "I loved my sister. I didn't respect her sometimes, but I cared for her a great deal."

"Did she usually talk about her boyfriends?" Jack asked.

"I guess so," Donald said. "Not constantly. But she would usually mention them in one way or another."

"Yet she never mentioned she was seeing someone new?" Jack asked.

"No. She didn't," Donald said. "At least not to me. But as I've said, I was away at college."

"Do you have any cousins who might have driven a sports car twenty years ago?"

"My father was an only child," Donald answered. "My mother was from a large family back east but we seldom saw our cousins."

"None of them lived around here?"

"No."

"One more thing," Jack said. "Of all the jilted boyfriends, or even the friends she had upset, can you think of anyone who might have wanted to hurt your sister?"

"I think everyone wanted to hurt her," Donald said. "But I don't think anyone wanted to kill her."

"Well, Mr. Mitchell," Jack said rising to his feet, "at least one person did."

15

Time to make an appearance at the station, Jack pulled out of the bank and drove north. During the twenty-minute drive, he considered his conversations with Elizabeth's siblings. The way they spoke of her, he considered adding their names to the very short list of possible suspects. Pulling into the department's parking lot, he settled on moving them to the maybe list.

Entering the building Jack saw Detective Bret Peterson talking to a uniformed officer he didn't recognize. Singleton had placed Peterson in charge of the investigation of the girl found in the alley the night before. Jack crossed the room to where they were standing.

"How's the case coming, Bret?" Jack asked. "Making any headway?"

"Getting there," the detective said. He did not make eye contact. Jack even got the impression that he purposefully looked away.

"Identify the girl yet?" Jack asked.

"Not yet."

"Any suspects?"

"No," the detective said. "But I'm close."

"Close as in you're following some leads?" Jack snapped. "Or close as in you have no clue and would rather stand here talking to this guy?"

"Don't push me, Jack," Bret said, the veins in his neck swelling. "It's my case. I'll handle it."

"You better," Jack said. "She was a real person, Bret. She had a real-life, a real family. And she and her family deserve to have answers."

"I'll give them answers," Bret said. "Now get off my back and go work on your own case. Oh, wait, you aren't on a real case are you?"

"Don't mess this up, Bret," Jack said, ignoring the jab. He looked at the uniformed officer's badge number then up at his face. The officer said nothing, holding his gaze. "What's your name officer?"

"Shaun Travis," the officer said.

Jack nodded, then with one last side glance at Bret he turned away and took the stairs up to the homicide department. He walked through the maze of desks to his own. There was a stack of messages and mail on his in-box. He took the stack and flipped through them until he came to a plain white envelope with his name typed in capital letters across its center.

He set the others down and held the envelope with curiosity. Sliding his letter opener under the flap of the envelope he cut it open with a single motion. Inside there was a single sheet of folded paper. Jack took it out, unfolding the page. His eyes were drawn to the single typed line. In the same capital letters that were on the front of the envelope, the sentence read: SHE IS DEAD BECAUSE OF HIM.

Jack looked around the room. No one was looking his way. He read the sentence again. Scanning the room again, his gaze fell on a detective two desks away.

"Harry," he said holding up the envelope. "Did you see who put this on my desk?"

Harold looked up at Jack and the envelope, "You're kidding, right?"

"No," Jack said.

"I have more to do than watch people putting notes on your desk," the detective said, lowering his eyes to his paperwork.

"Gary," Jack called to another of his co-workers. "Did you see who put this on my desk?"

"I didn't see anything," Gary said without looking up.

"Ben?"

"Sorry," Ben shook his head. "Did you ask Ellen? She brought in the mail."

"Thanks," Jack said returning his attention to the note. He had a good idea Ellen would know nothing about the mysterious envelope.

He studied the six words. Was the she in the note supposed to be Elizabeth? It was possible it was the girl from the alley since he was the original investigator. It was also possible that the note had nothing to do with either case. Without knowing who wrote it or why, it was of no use to Jack. He pulled an evidence bag out of his desk and slipped the note and its envelope inside. Sealing the bag, he dropped it in one of the drawers.

His phone rang and Jack answered it before it could ring again. "Jack here."

"Jack," Kelly Walden said. "Terrance wants to see you in his office."

"What's new?" Jack said. "What does he want?"

"I don't know," Kelly said. "But he doesn't sound happy."

"When has he ever sounded happy?" Jack asked. "I'll be right there."

Jack glanced around the squad room one last time for signs of someone watching him. No one was even glancing his way. He locked his desk and stood, stretching as he did. He still wasn't used to the hours he was working. The chief's office was one floor up and he took the stairs to help get his blood flowing. By the time he reached Kelly's desk, he was more alert and ready to face whatever Terrance had to say.

Kelly told him he would have to wait. Terrance was with someone at the moment. Jack shook his head. It was just like Terrance to demand an immediate audience and not be ready for him. Kelly smiled at him sympathetically and explained there was an unexpected visitor.

The inner office door opened and an attractive woman with an athletic build stepped out, pulling the door closed hard behind her. She turned so she was facing Jack and he saw that it was Terrance's wife, Heather. She nodded at him and he stood.

"Jack," she said. "I never see you anymore."

"I've been working nights," Jack said. "How are you doing?"

"You know me," Heather shrugged.

He did know her. She was one of the few people Jack knew, that seemed to hate Terrance as much as he did. They had spent a couple of evenings, at police functions, drinking and exchanging stories of his shortcomings. It was a lot of fun for Jack, but when all was finished he could go home to his empty apartment. She had to go home with him.

He asked her once why she stayed with him and she answered with a string of vague reasons. She loved him, she had explained. She did once anyway. It was not as simple as packing her suitcase and leaving. There were a lot of problems only Terrance could understand. There was a history she could not dismiss. Once she concluded with, "Besides, who else would have him?"

One evening when Terrance was still a detective, he and Jack worked a case together. It was before they had developed such a disliking for one another. They talked to pass the time while waiting for a suspect to show up at one of his regular hangouts. Terrance talked about his relationship with Heather. According to him, Heather was a bitter, depressed woman who drank too much. She was depressed because she wanted to have children but couldn't. She was bitter because she blamed Terrance for all her problems. Of course, this was Terrance's point of view. He never asked Heather about it.

"We should have a drink sometime," Jack suggested.

"I'd like that," she smiled, although it was so slight Jack almost missed it.

"Soon, then," he said. "For now the chief beckons."

With that, Jack stood and saluted, clicking his heels as he did. This brought a genuine smile to Heather's lips. She leaned in close to speak into his ear. "Careful Jack. Mocking my husband turns me on."

"I wouldn't want it any other way," Jack grinned. "See you later."

Heather left and Kelly announced Jack. He bowed to the secretary before passing into Terrance's office. She smiled and he noted that he was two for two with making the women smile. He wondered how long he could keep it going.

"Jack," Terrance barked before the door had time to close. "What do you think you're up to?"

"I'm investigating a case you assigned me," Jack said.

"Didn't I tell you to report to me?"

"You did," Jack said. "So far I've had nothing to report."

"Didn't I also tell you to stay away from the Mitchells?"

"You told me to stay away from the Governor and his wife," Jack nodded. He really didn't remember the exact wording of Terrance's order but figured the chief wouldn't remember either.

Terrance paused then said, "From now on, you will report to me every day regardless of what you may or may not have. And the order to stay away from the Mitchells will include the entire family."

"How am I supposed to conduct a proper investigation if I can't question the two people who knew the girl better than anyone else?" Jack raised his voice with the question.

"The notes of the original interview are in the file," Terrance said. "That should be sufficient."

"Actually, the notes are crap," Jack said.

"What?" Terrance said.

"There's nothing in your notes," Jack said. "Nothing useful anyway."

"The notes are fine," Terrance said defensively. "You just don't know what you're doing. Besides, it was an open and shut case. We had the guy in a matter of hours."

"The wrong guy," Jack pointed out.

"The right guy," Terrance said. "Just because he's out on a technicality doesn't mean he isn't the killer. You are supposed to be proving he is the guy."

"I'm supposed to be finding the truth," Jack said. "No matter who did it. But you are blocking me from speaking to two of the most important witnesses to the case."

"Stay away from the Mitchells," Terrance shouted. "And that means all of the Mitchells."

"Whatever you say," Jack said, then he added with a sarcastic tone, "Chief."

"Get out of here," Terrance's face reddened. Jack stood and started out the door. Terrance called after him. "And I want reports every day, Jack."

Jack resisted flipping him a bird before the door shut. He smiled at Kelly then left. There were a lot of things he needed to get done. The top of the list was figuring out how to interview the Mitchells before Terrance found out.

16

Jack returned to his desk and started going through the phone messages he had set aside earlier. Most were from Terrance and he quickly dropped them into the trash. There were a few from other detectives, which he sorted according to importance so he could return the calls at his convenience. There were several from a man named Kenneth Truman. Jack stared at the messages requesting him to call back as soon as possible. The name sounded familiar but he couldn't remember where he might have heard it. He placed one of the messages with the others and dropped the rest in the trash. He was not interested in making any calls at the moment and nothing was so important it couldn't wait a little longer.

Jack opened Elizabeth Mitchell's twenty-year-old case file and laid it out next to the new file he had started for the case. His new file was almost as thick as the old one and there was very little they both had in common beyond the name of the victim. He scanned the copies of the interviews Terrance conducted all those years ago. Somewhere in the notes there had to be an answer. If he could find it, then he could work on what the question was.

His phone rang and Jack snatched it up. "This is Mallory."

"Detective, this is Officer Shaun Travis," the voice said. Jack remembered him as the uniformed officer he met that morning. "I am working with Detective Peterson on that girl's murder."

"What can I do for you?" Jack was eager to get off the phone.

"I wanted to let you know we got a positive identification on the girl."

Jack sat up suddenly very interested. "What's her name?"

"Lisa Reagan," Shaun said.

Jack's mind fell into autopilot as he searched his memory for the name. It was another one familiar to him, but like Kenneth Truman,

Jack could not remember where he had heard the name. "Who ID'd her?"

"Her father," Shaun said. "Came in this morning to file a missing persons report on his daughter. Just happened to be her."

"Tough," Jack said.

"No kidding," Shaun agreed. "He asked about you."

"Me?"

"Yeah," Shaun said. "He saw the girl. Gave us her name. Then he asked if you would be working her case."

"Did he say how he knew me?"

"No."

"What was his name again?" Jack asked.

There was a pause while Shaun looked it up in his notes. Then he said, "Charles. Charles Reagan."

A rush of memories flooded Jack's mind. Charles Reagan was the husband of Tracy Reagan who was murdered about ten years ago. She had been so brutally beaten she was almost unrecognizable. The killer had used a small dull knife to make cuts on her body every few inches. It was one of the most sadistic acts Jack had ever seen. Charles was the one who found her.

Terrance was still a detective then, and he and Jack were assigned to the case. The two of them worked closely together for over a month on that one. It was the case that created the rift between them, the reason they still didn't like each other. Terrance wanted the husband for the killing, citing a crime of passion. Jack insisted the man could not have done those things. He was a man who showed more attention to his young daughter's well-being than his own. There was also the fact he had an alibi that could not be questioned. He was in court all day. Charles Reagan was an attorney.

Now, seven years later, violence had reached out and taken hold of the man's family again. The daughter he comforted all those years ago in the wake of his wife's murder had fallen upon the same fate. It was inconceivable. One might conclude the killings were personal and his wife's killer had returned to make Charles suffer again. But that was impossible since Jack and Terrance had captured the wife's killer and the courts had sent him away for life without the possibility of parole.

"Where is he?" Jack asked.

"The father?" Shaun said. "When I left the morgue he was still there. I don't think I've ever seen a man cry like that before."

"He's a good man," Jack said. "Loved his daughter very much."

"You do know him then?"

"In a way," Jack said not elaborating. "Thanks for letting me know."

"I thought you would want to know," Shaun said. "And I knew the chief told Peterson not to tell you anything."

"Then why are you telling me?"

"Hey, he didn't tell me not to tell you," Shaun laughed.

"Thanks," Jack said. "I'll buy you a drink sometime."

"That would be good," Shaun said. "One more thing though."

"What's that?"

"Peterson is trying to pin this on the father somehow."

"Figures," Jack sighed. "Got anything to suggest it was him?"

"No."

"Check his alibi," Jack suggested. "I'm sure it will clear him."

Jack hung up and considered the conversation. It was typical Terrance to assume Jack would want to keep tabs on the case he had to give up. It was also typical Terrance to tell Bret to keep his mouth shut. But that didn't bother Jack. What bothered him was the fact that Charles Reagan's daughter was murdered seven years after his wife. The man would have to be going through a lot right now. He didn't need to be the focus of another investigation. Jack thought about it, but if Charles were at the morgue a half-hour ago he would probably be on the road. He put the decision off until Charles had time to get home.

He returned his attention to Elizabeth Mitchell's case. He re-read page after page trying to find inconsistencies. While he read, images of Lisa Reagan as she was found in the alley invaded his mind. Two young women murdered before they really had a chance to live. Besides both being attractive blondes, they were completely different. Yet, in Jack's mind, he was having trouble separating the facts and the faces of the girls.

Elizabeth was barely seventeen when she was killed. Lisa was twenty. Elizabeth was in high school. Lisa was college aged. Elizabeth came from a family of money and power. Lisa's father, although a lawyer, worked charity cases most of the time, a down to earth kind of man who lived in a moderate house. Governor Steven Mitchell and Charles Reagan would never sit down over a cup of coffee but the two men were connected in a way they would never know. It was a connection no one wanted to have.

Jack was no longer reading but staring at photographs of the crime scene. He became aware of someone standing nearby. Raising his head from his papers he looked into the face of a man with average features and medium build. He was thick but not necessarily overweight and wore a nice suit. His short black hair had streaks of gray throughout. The man's eyes were swollen, his cheeks red, his chin quivering. Jack stood and offered his hand. The man took it. His shake was weak, but he did not let go.

"Charles," Jack said somberly.

"Detective," Charles Reagan responded. His voice was as weak as his grip and his eyes were dull, almost lifeless. "I wasn't sure you would remember me."

Jack quickly directed him to a chair. "I just heard. I'm so sorry."

Charles sat with his eyes on the floor and half nodded, half rocked his acknowledgment. He swallowed hard and looked up at Jack. "Can you find him?"

Jack knew immediately what was being asked of him. "I'm not on the case, Charles."

"Do you know who is?"

"Yes."

"Is he any good?"

Jack hesitated before answering. Charles, always a quick study, caught on fast. Jack grimaced and said, "Okay. I can't promise anything because they have me on another case. But I will look into it as much as I can. See if I can help."

"I would appreciate that," Charles said. "I know my wife would be glad to know the man who caught her killer was looking for Lisa's."

"I'll do my best," Jack said.

"I know you will," Charles said. He sat for a long time, staring into nothingness before excusing himself.

Jack watched him go. How he was going to pull off two investigations without Terrance finding out what he was doing? But then, he really didn't care what Terrance found out.

17

Terrance sat in his office rubbing his temples with his thumbs in slow precise circles. His head throbbed and relief was nowhere in sight. Between his wife at home and Jack at work, he was convinced he would never have another day of peace as long as he lived.

There was an open folder lying on the desk in front of him. On top of the contents of the file was a picture of Lisa Reagan. Not a crime scene photo like the others, this was a head and shoulder shot taken a year or so ago. The first time he saw the girl was when her mother was murdered ten years ago. Now the girl was gone, too. He marveled at how much she had come to look like her mother. A very pretty young woman.

Terrance reached across his desk and pressed the intercom button on his phone. "Kelly, do you have any more aspirin?"

"Sure, Chief," she said. "I'll be right there."

A moment later the secretary entered the office with a glass of water in one hand and two small white pills in the other. She handed them to Terrance who threw the aspirin in his mouth and chased them down with the water. He thanked her and sent her away. Tired and wishing to be alone, he considered going home, but Heather would be there.

They got along once, a long time ago. At least that was the way he remembered it. They had been happy for a number of years. Then he blew it and learned that she was not the type to forgive and forget. Now, he cringed at the sound of her voice. She was always asking him why he was such a screwup. He was Chief of Police and she treated him like a failure.

He received semi-regular visits from her over-sized brothers. They were always trying to get him to tell them why Heather was so miserable. They wanted to know what he had done to their little sister and what he was going to do to fix it. Terrance had tried to fix it, but Heather wasn't interested. Now he didn't care anymore.

He looked at Lisa's photo one more time then closed the file. She was too young to die, but there was nothing to be done about it now. No one would pay for the crime, not the way Tim Waters had paid for Elizabeth's death. He would keep Detective Peterson on the case as long as he could then transfer him to another case. And Jack would work Elizabeth Mitchell's case until the Governor was satisfied that they would never solve the case. The buzzer on his phone sounded and Terrance pushed the intercom button.

"Yes, Kelly," he said. "What is it?"

"The Governor is on line two," Kelly announced.

"Thank you," he said. He sat staring at the blinking light on his phone. He and Steve Mitchell had been friends for years. The friendship started when Terrance stopped Steve's wife for driving while intoxicated. He recognized the woman as the then district attorney's wife and drove her home. He and Steve hit it off that night and remained friends ever since. He answered the phone. "Hello, Steve."

"Terrance," the Governor said. "How's our boy doing?"

"He's working on it," Terrance assured him. "It's going to take time for him to get into the groove. It isn't easy when all you have are photos and reports."

"Okay," Steve said. "I understand. That isn't why I called."

"It isn't?"

"No," Steve said. "We're having a little get together at the mansion tomorrow evening. We'd like for you and Heather to come."

"Tomorrow night?"

"Yes," the Governor confirmed. "Around eight."

"I'm sure we can make it," Terrance said. He was also sure Heather would come down with something.

"Good. Good," Steve said. Then he added, "Why don't you tell Detective Mallory to stop in? I'd like to meet him."

"I'll tell him," Terrance said, "He isn't very social and when he's working a case he seldom takes time off for other things."

"That is good to hear," Steve said. "But let him know I want to see him. That might convince him."

"I'll let him know. I'll see you tomorrow," Terrance said. Telling Jack would have no effect on whether the detective would meet with the governor. Jack wouldn't care if the President wanted to see him. If he didn't want to go, he wouldn't. The problem was the detective would want to see the governor and Terrance would have to let him.

The chief leaned back in his chair and pulled out the file on Elizabeth. He began studying the photos and tried to imagine what the girl would look like now had she lived. He didn't think she would favor either of her parents, but then when he met Lisa he never thought the girl would have grown up to look so much like her mother. He set the photo to one side and took out one of the crime scene shots. It was the way she had been the last time he saw her. He shook his head. It was a shame.

He spun his chair to face his desk fully. He pressed the button on his phone and spoke, "Kelly, could you get my wife on the line?"

"Your wife, sir?" There was hesitation in her voice.

"My wife," Terrance confirmed, then released the intercom button. Kelly knew how Heather treated him and she knew he never called her. He seldom took her calls when she called him. It was only a moment before the secretary announced she had his wife on the line. He waited before picking up the phone. "Heather."

"Having your secretary call me?" she said. "Really?"

"If you would answer when I call, I wouldn't have to," Terrance said.

"What do you want, Terrance?" She said his name with distaste.

"The governor would like us to attend a dinner at his place tomorrow night," he said.

"I'm busy, Terrance," she said.

"Heather," Terrance snapped.

"Ooh," she faked a gasp. "Are you going to get tough on me?"

"Listen," Terrance said, trying to change tactics. "Steve asked for both of us. I'm not crazy about spending an evening with you either, but he asked."

"I don't care, Terrance," Heather said. "He's your friend. You can go without me."

"Fine," Terrance said. "I have to run interference between Steve and Jack anyway. I don't need to watch after you too."

"You're inviting Jack to the governor's," Heather laughed. "That's rich."

"Steve wants to ask him about the case," Terrance explained.

"This could be fun," Heather continued laughing. "You and Jack together. How are you going to manage to keep from killing one another?"

"We'll manage," Terrance sighed.

"I don't know," she said. "I may have to come just to see for myself."

"So, now you're going?" Terrance asked.

"Why not?" she answered. "But I'll have to warn you, I may root for Jack."

"Whatever," Terrance accepted.

"Good-bye, Terrance." She hung up without waiting for a reply.

"Damn," he said, pressing the intercom. "Kelly, get me Mallory."

18

When the coroner called to announce he was preparing to start the autopsy, Detective Peterson sent Officer Travis to observe. He did not go himself, not because he was squeamish, but because he was not interested in hearing what the coroner might have to say. Bret was busy getting the evidence he needed to arrest the girl's father.

Bret never intended to become a cop. He was never interested in helping people, fighting crime, catching bad guys. When it was suggested that he join the force his gut reaction had been to laugh. He still couldn't pinpoint the moment he became convinced. But once he signed up, everything changed.

The first time he put on the uniform people treated him differently. They gave him respect he had never received before. Now, he was a detective. The day he was promoted was not a source of pride as it was for others. It was a doorway to freer days and less work. He brought in his fair share of 'bad guys'. Not as many as other detectives, but enough to keep him out of the crosshairs. As long as the chief left him alone, he did as little as possible.

While Shaun went to witness the autopsy of Lisa Reagan, Bret started working his case against Charles Reagan, her father. There would be those who would argue that no father could do such horrific things to his own child, but Bret had seen it before. His own father had done worse to him and his siblings. It was worse because the man let them live. And they live with those memories every day.

It was easy for Bret to imagine Charles abusing his daughter. After all, the girl wasn't really his daughter. It would even stand to reason that Charles had some involvement with his wife's death seven years ago. Maybe she discovered what he was doing to the young Lisa and threatened to turn him in. He might have hired the man who killed her. Bret might even prove Charles took part in the killing.

He would have to get inside the Reagan house. It was important to find the evidence where it would be the most damaging. Bret decided the lawyer was the type to keep souvenirs. The detective would need to determine where Charles would hide something like that. The obvious place was the bedroom where they would be close at hand. But a man living alone could hide anything he wanted anywhere he wanted without fear of being discovered. Bret would need to take a look around the house to determine the hiding spot.

Bret smiled. It was his favorite part of the job. Nailing someone for a crime. It was like pulling the plug on a person's life when he arrested them. The sense of power was unmatched. At times he got excited just thinking about it. Right now he was having trouble containing his enthusiasm.

19

After repeatedly ordering him to stay away from the governor and his family, Terrance called Jack to tell him he was invited to a cookout the governor was having at his mansion.   Terrance did spend a significant part of the conversation telling him what he could not tell or ask the parents of the murder victim, but the turnaround left Jack speechless.   He was still in a state of shock when his phone rang again.

On the fourth ring Jack answered the phone.   "Detective Mallory."

"Hello, detective," a man's voice said.   "My name is Kenneth Truman."

"Mr. Truman," Jack's mind raced with recognition but could not place the name.   "How can I help you?"

"I've left a number of messages but you haven't returned my calls," Kenneth said flatly.

Jack glanced at the small stack of messages and remembered several were from the man he was now speaking to.   "I keep strange hours.   I haven't gotten to my messages yet."

"I hope you don't mind my calling again," the man said.

"Not at all," Jack assured him.   "Now, how is it I can help you?"

"I need to speak to you," Kenneth said so soft Jack barely heard him.

"Okay," Jack said.   "Tell me what the problem is."

"No," the man's voice was sharp and Jack sensed panic.   "I mean in person.   The phone may not be safe."

Jack rolled his eyes.   He hated the nut cases and the paranoids were the worst, but it was all part of the job.   "Sure.   But can you tell me what this is about?"

"It's about a case you're working on," the man said.   "Very important.   Someone's life may depend on it."

Jack remembered the envelope in his desk with the note about 'her' death being 'his' fault. Kenneth might be the man the note referred to. "I'll tell you what. Tell me where you want to meet and I'll be there."

"Okay," Kenneth said. "North of town there is a state park with a lake. Winchester Lake. On the east side is an area with a group of picnic tables. Are you familiar with it?"

"Yes," Jack answered. "It's a good hour from here."

"Closer to an hour and a half," Kenneth corrected. "Be there at six o'clock. I'll only wait for fifteen minutes. If you aren't there by then, I'll leave. If you don't come alone, I'll leave. Do you understand what I'm saying?"

"I understand you want me to drive to a secluded place alone to meet a man I don't know," Jack told him. "I understand you could be crazy, or a man out for revenge, or both. Not a lot of incentive for me to come out there."

There was a long pause on the other end of the line. The man was breathing, short shallow breaths. Jack waited and tried to put a face to the name. Kenneth Truman rang no bells other than the stack of messages. He then tried to remember if he had ever arrested anyone else by the name Truman; a brother, father, anyone. The name meant nothing to him although there were too many arrests to remember them all.

"You have to come," the panic returned to the man's voice. "I have information that will help you in your investigation."

"How do you even know I'm investigating the case you have information on?" Jack said. "How do you know you aren't supposed to be talking to another detective? What case are you talking about?"

"I can't say," Kenneth muttered.

"There is no case," Jack said. "There is no information. Who are you? Why do you want me to meet you alone?"

"I have information," Kenneth insisted. "And I know you are on the case because someone told me you are."

"Who?"

"A friend."

"A friend!" Jack exclaimed. "Oh. That makes all the difference. Does this friend have a name?"

"No."

"No?" Jack grinned. "You have a friend with no name?"

"They have a name," Kenneth snapped. "I just can't tell you over the phone. Listen, this was all a mistake. Forget I called. You obviously don't care. I'm sorry I wasted your time."

The phone went dead. Jack looked at the phone for a moment and made a quick decision. He sifted through the phone messages on his desk and retrieved the one from Kenneth. He dialed the number and listened to it ring twice.

"Hello?" a weak female voice answered.

"Let me talk to Kenneth," Jack said.

"Who's calling?"

"Detective Jack Mallory," Jack announced. "I know he's there. I was just talking to him."

"You upset him," the woman accused.

"I know," Jack was apologetic. "I'm sorry. Let me talk to him. It'll be okay."

There was the sound of muffled voices and of the phone being passed, more muffled voices and finally the sound of Kenneth's shallow breathing.

"What do you want?" Kenneth was blunt.

"I'll meet you," Jack said. "Six o'clock at the east picnic area at Winchester Lake. And I'll come alone."

"Why did you . . . "

"Don't worry about it," Jack cut him off. "I'll be there. You be there."

"I will," Kenneth said. "And thank you."

"Don't thank me yet," Jack informed him. "If I feel you've wasted my time I'm not likely to be too pleasant."

"I'm not worried about that," Kenneth said. "This isn't a waste of time. It's probably my last chance."

"Last chance?" Jack asked. "Why is that?"

"I'll explain when you get there," Kenneth said. "I have to go now or I'll be late."

The phone went dead a second time. This time Jack hung up as well. He dug the discarded messages from the trash and counted how many the man had left. There were eight in all. This man was either a first-class nut-job, or he thought he had something extremely important to share. Jack hoped the latter was true. He checked his watch. It was already after four-thirty. If he didn't hurry he would be late.

20

It was an hour and thirty-minute drive to the park and if Jack had not had to stop for gas he would have been right on time. The ten minutes he spent at the station was enough to make him concerned whether he would arrive at the park before the deadline the man had given him. It was unlikely Kenneth Truman would leave too soon. He had left eight messages, all with his phone number. It would not be hard to find the man if needed.

It would not necessary though. When Jack pulled into the picnic area it was only ten after six. If the man was true to his word there were five minutes to spare. The detective parked at a vantage point where he could observe all of the picnic tables and much of the wooded area around them.

There were several families gathered at the tables. It was not the secluded location to which Jack accused Kenneth of trying to draw him. He searched for a man among the crowds who was alone, possibly staring back at him. Jack saw no one who appeared to be preparing for a secret rendezvous with the detective. He was beginning to think the man had left early or hadn't shown at all.

There was a rap on his window and Jack turned, half expecting the muzzle of a gun to be pointed at his head. Instead, a bald man stood next to his car slouched over to look at Jack through the glass. The irregular face was not familiar to Jack. He lowered his window about halfway.

"You Detective Mallory?" the man asked.

"Kenneth Truman?" Jack responded.

The man turned away and started walking toward an overgrown area across from the picnicking families. Jack glanced around before shutting off his car and stepping out into the open. He checked his weapon and followed Kenneth, focusing his eyes on the center of the man's back. Kenneth did not look back. He expected Jack to follow.

Kenneth reached the tree line and disappeared behind the foliage. Jack slowed and his hand moved to the handle of his gun. He searched the trees for the strange man but saw nothing. Hesitantly he stepped through the trees pulling his weapon half out of its holster. Emerging from the leaves he stepped into a small clearing. Kenneth was leaning against a tree about fifteen feet away. The man was frail, his hands shook, his eye twitched.

"Hope you don't mind," the man said. "I didn't want to be overheard."

"I don't mind," Jack slid his gun back down into the holster. "What's with all the secrecy?"

"I have to be cautious," the man said. "I've been in hiding for a number of years."

"In hiding?"

"There are some powerful people who would not be happy to know I was talking to you." The man shifted on his feet and stepped forward. "My name is not Kenneth Truman."

"It isn't?" Jack reached for his weapon subconsciously. The man froze. "What is your name?"

"Lance Carpenter," he answered.

"Lance Carpenter?" Jack cocked his head. "Timothy Waters' old friend from school?"

"Yes," he said.

"I've been looking for you," Jack released his weapon. "Why the alias?"

"The people who don't want me talking to you could easily find me if I were using my real name, detective," Lance said. "I don't want them finding me."

"Who are they?" Jack asked. "Why are you so sure they could find you?"

"The governor," Lance said. "And your chief of police. I think they could find me if they wanted to."

"Why do you think they would be looking for you?"

"I know something they don't want me telling anyone," Lance kicked at a stone on the ground.

"About Elizabeth Mitchell's murder?" Jack probed.

"Not her murder," Lance said. "But about Tim."

"What do you know?" Jack asked.

"I know he couldn't have killed Beth," Lance said.

"How do you know?"

"She was alive when Tim left her that night."

"How do you know that?"

"Because I saw her after he left."

"Saw her?" Jack asked. "Saw her how?"

"I went to the house after Tim left," Lance toed the stone again. "To see Beth."

"You were at the house after Tim was?" Jack repeated. Lance nodded. "And you told the police that?"

"I told Singleton," Lance nodded. "He was the detective on the case then."

"What did Singleton say to you?"

"He told me they had a clean case and to keep my mouth shut," Lance said. "I told him Tim was innocent and I could prove it. I was going to tell anyone I could to help Tim. He told me he and the governor could arrange for me and my entire family to have problems."

"What kind of problems?"

"Disappear," Lance said. "Be charged with fabricated crimes. He said he could have the state take my sister's kids away. He told me to leave town and never mention anything to anyone."

"And that's what you did?" Jack asked. "You left town and that was the end of it?"

"Kind of," Lance said. "I thought I would leave for a couple of days. Take some time to figure things out and come back with a plan."

"What happened?"

"I was pulled over on my way out of town," Lance said. "I wasn't speeding so I figured Singleton was going to remind me not to come back."

"Did he?"

"It wasn't him," Lance said. "It was a cop I had never seen before. He asked if I was Lance Carpenter. When I said I was, he shot me."

"He shot you?"

Lance pulled his shirt up to expose a scar in the center of his chest. "Barely missed my heart. I was in the hospital for a month. Luckily the guy took my wallet, I guess to make it look like a robbery. So there was nothing to identify me. When I was able to speak, I told them my name was Jeff Bolton. My family has no idea what happened to me."

"And you don't know the man who shot you?" Jack asked.

"No," Lance shook his head. "He was in a uniform. I assume he was working for Singleton."

Jack sighed. "So, are you Elizabeth's mystery boyfriend?"

"You don't understand," Lance started.

"What don't I understand?"

"Beth was not a 'good' girl, detective," Lance clarified. "Sure, I was dating Beth, but I wasn't the only one. She was seeing another guy that I know of, maybe more. She liked to have fun."

"Were you sleeping with her?"

"No," Lance shook his head. "She wouldn't because of Tim. I figured it was more because of me."

"Why did you go see her that night?" Jack asked.

"She invited me there," Lance shrugged. "Then she dumped me."

"She dumped you?"

"If you can call it that," he said. "We weren't really an item. We hung out together. Went to movies occasionally."

"Did she mention she was pregnant?"

Lance's head snapped up. "She was pregnant?"

"It wasn't yours was it?"

"I told you we weren't sleeping together," he said defensively. "Our relationship wasn't that way. You don't understand."

"I understand you were with your best friend's girlfriend the night she was killed. That makes you a suspect. I also understand that gives Tim a motive for wanting to kill her as well. He may have found out about the two of you. Maybe he killed her and then shot you."

"I would have recognized him," Lance shook his head.

"Maybe you saw the uniform and not the face," Jack suggested. "You wouldn't expect it to be Waters. Or maybe your mind has blocked the image as a defensive measure. Or maybe the whole story is made up and you shot yourself out of guilt for killing the girl but screwed it up and lived. Now you're trying to help Timothy out of the same guilt. Tell me, Mr. Carpenter, where have you been for the last twenty years while your friend was rotting away in prison?"

"I told you," Lance said. "I was in hiding."

"Without a word to anyone?" Jack said. "Some friend you are."

"I tried," Lance said. "I sent some emails to different people. The district attorney, the judge, one of the news channels, the newspaper. I tried all of them."

"And no one came to ask questions?"

"Two days after I sent the emails I got a call at work," Lance explained. "A co-worker lived in an apartment across from mine. He said cops had broken into my apartment and ransacked the place. It was clear one of my emails struck a nerve and they traced the IP or something, so I disappeared again. That's when I became Kenneth Truman."

"How do you know I'm not working for Singleton?" Jack asked.

The man flinched, eyes wide, then he relaxed. "I follow the news, detective. I also still have friends in town. Your feelings about the chief are no secret. My source even told me you were genuinely trying to find Elizabeth's killer. I figured it was time to get the truth out there. Besides, this is probably my last chance to do the right thing."

"You mentioned that on the phone," Jack said. "Why is this your last chance?"

Lance looked up into the trees then back at the detective. "Life is not always fair. Or maybe it is, I don't know." He leveled his eyes on Jack. "I'm dying."

Jack realized then why the man's face was irregular. He had no eyebrows. He was bald and frail. He was fighting cancer. A fight he was convinced he was not going to win.

"Sorry to hear that," Jack was sincere.

"I'm not really," Lance lowered his head. "As far as I'm concerned Lance Carpenter was shot to death twenty years ago in the front seat of a Dodge short bed. And to be honest, I was never fond of Kenneth Truman. The man is a wimp. I think he's getting what he deserves."

"I may need to talk to you again," Jack handed Lance his card. "In case you need me."

"You have my number," Lance said. "Please don't let anyone else know about it. I have a wife and a couple kids. They are having a hard enough time with my illness. They don't need any unexpected visitors."

"I promise," Jack said. "Although someday you may have to come forward."

"I know," Lance said. "But by then I hope it will be too late for anyone to do anything."

"I assume you're saying when you left that night, Elizabeth was still alive?" Jack questioned.

"She was," Lance smiled. "So very full of life. I can't believe that was the last time I saw her."

"Was she expecting anyone else?"

"I don't know," Lance shrugged. "Maybe. She told me to leave the door unlocked."

"Did you?"

"Did I what?"

"Leave the door unlocked?"

"Sure," he said. "She asked me to."

"Okay," Jack offered his hand to the man and they shook. "Thank you. I'll be in touch."

Jack walked to his car and Lance disappeared deeper into the trees. On the way to his car, Jack's mind raced with the information the man had given him. Who had shot Lance? Why had Terrance run him out of town? Who else might have visited Elizabeth Mitchell that night? And most of all, if Lance had left the front door unlocked, who broke the glass by the back door?

21

There was always the chance Lance Carpenter was lying to him. But the man had been in hiding and could have easily remained that way. It was unlikely Jack would have found him under an alias. He had no reason to think the man would not be using his real name. Coming forward and admitting he saw Elizabeth after Timothy Waters left the night she was killed meant risking being a suspect. If he was lying, it only hurt him.

Jack took a drink from his coffee. The murky liquid was lukewarm, but it was better than nothing. He sat in his car with fast-food wrappers cluttering the passenger seat. He was parked across the street from a small apartment building that overlooked the river. It was a nice area of town, quiet and peaceful. The kind of place you would expect to be safe. It was also Lisa Reagan's address when she died.

He was on stakeout, watching everyone who entered or exited the building. He watched passersby: walking dogs, jogging, cycling. Anyone he saw became a note in his mind and on his notepad. He wasn't sure if any of these people were important to Lisa's case. He didn't know where else to begin.

He could not interview people the way he would if it were his own case. He didn't have the time and if word somehow got back to Terrance, the chief would go ballistic. Jack was all for stressing the man out, but there were limits. No, he would not be conducting all the needed interviews. He did have copies of Bret Peterson's file on the investigation. The detective had interviewed the neighbors and the apartment manager. They were all in the file and all pretty useless. Either Bret had not asked the right questions or no one knew very much about the young woman in apartment 3B.

The front door opened and an elderly man stepped out onto the brick steps leading down to street level. He put a cigarette in his mouth and struck a match to light it. After several puffs to be sure the cigarette was lit, he shook the match out and tossed it into the bushes beside the door. He stood taking drag after drag on the cigarette blowing the smoke into the night air. This was the third time the man had come out for a smoke since Jack arrived just over two hours ago.

Dangerously thin, a gust of wind might send the man tumbling down the street. If someone opened the door too fast he would surely land in the bushes with all the spent matches he had thrown there. Jack took a last sip of the coffee then opened his car door and poured the rest onto the pavement. Stepping out onto the street he stretched. His legs were cramped, his back stiff. He approached the man slowly, non-threateningly. The man watched him come.

"Good evening," Jack said when he reached the bottom of the steps.

The man nodded, took another drag on his cigarette and blew smoke over Jack's head.

"I was wondering if I could ask you some questions?" Jack climbed the first step.

"You a cop?" the man's voice was gravel.

"I'm a detective, yes," Jack pulled his badge out and held it up for the man to see.

"Then ask your questions."

"How did you know I was a cop?" Jack asked climbing the remaining steps.

"That what you wanted to ask me?"

"No," Jack smiled. "I was just curious."

"You been sittin' in that car of yours two hours," the man said. "I figured either you're casing the place for robbin' or you're a cop. I figured if you want to ask questions, you ain't here to rob the place."

"You noticed all that, eh?" Jack looked out at the river.

"Yep."

"You notice things all the time?"

"Yep."

Jack pulled a photo of Lisa Reagan out of his breast pocket and held it out to the man. "Ever notice her?"

"Yep," the old man said. "Sweet girl. Damn shame what happened to her. Figured that's why you were here."

"Did she ever have company?" Jack asked. "A boyfriend maybe?"

The man put the cigarette to his lips and inhaled deeply. The tip glowed and burned away down to his knuckles. He released the smoke and examined the butt. Squeezing the end with his boney stained fingers he flipped the butt into the bushes with the matches. "I seen him."

"You saw who?" Jack asked.

"I seen the man who killed her," the man rasped.

"You saw her killer?" Jack turned to face him squarely.

"He came to get her late that night," the man said. "They left together. Next morning he came back. But she wasn't with him."

"Did you tell that to the police?"

"Just did."

"You haven't told anyone else?"

"Just you."

"When he came back without her," Jack asked, "why didn't you call the police then?"

"Figured the girl forgot something and the man came to get it for her," the man shrugged. "He left with a small bag."

"What kind of bag?"

"One of those small carry type bags," the man said. "I don't know."

"Like a suitcase or an overnight bag?" Jack suggested. "Or a duffel bag?"

"That's it," the man nodded. "It was like a duffel bag."

"Any idea what was in it?" Jack asked.

"Now how would I know that?" the man said. He pulled a pack of cigarettes out of his pocket and shook one out.

"What about the man?" Jack continued. "Ever see him before?"

"Yep," the man nodded, trying to light the cigarette.

"You've seen him here before last night?"

"Yep," he said. "Seen him somewhere else too. Can't remember where though."

"Anything distinctive about him?" Jack asked. "Tattoos or scars?"

"Nothing like that," the man said. "But he is old enough to be the girl's father."

"Her father?" Jack questioned. "Do you think it was her father?"

"Nope," the man shook his head. "I knew who her father was. No way that guy was her father."

"Could you give me a description?" Jack asked.

"Medium-tall, well built," the man said. "Good hair, well-groomed. Looked like he came from money, or married it."

"You think he was married?"

"Wore a ring," the man nodded. "Could be a widower I guess, but I doubt it. Only came at night and never stayed long. He had someone expecting him home."

The man gave Jack the rest of the description and Jack wrote it down in his notepad. He was looking for a middle-aged man with brownish hair and square chin. He wore suits that fit like they were tailored and expensive shoes. The old man never got a good look at the stranger's eyes and his skin could be anywhere from pale to well-tanned. Jack took down the man's name and address and handed him a business card.

"If you think of anything else," Jack said, "call me anytime. Leave a message if I don't answer."

"Sure." The man tucked the card in his pocket with the cigarettes.

Jack walked back down the steps and toward his car as the old man stood there smoking, watching his retreat. Jack was almost to his car when the man called out to him. Jack turned to face the man expectantly.

"Remembered one more thing you might want to know," the man's voice made the words hard to understand. "He had an old car. Old sports car. Like a Camaro, but not."

22

Not used to the changed hours, Jack did not sleep well. He tossed and turned until well after three. His mind was racing with questions when he finally drifted off. When the alarm went off at six-thirty he reset it for eight and covered his head with the pillow. The next time the alarm sounded he sat up, rubbed his eyes and fell back to a prone position. An hour later the ringing phone woke him a third time.

"Mallory," he muttered when he answered.

"Jack, where are you?" Kelly asked.

"Home," he responded. "Why are you asking?"

"He's yelling that you're supposed to be in his office giving him an update of your progress," Kelly said. "He wants you in here now."

"Well, I can't come now," Jack said. "Tell him I'm investigating a murder and when I have an update I'll let him know."

"You can't do this to me, Jack," Kelly pleaded.

"I have to be somewhere," Jack said. "I can't stop my investigation because he wants to know that I still don't know anything."

"Jack," she whined.

"I'm sorry," he apologized. "Tell him it's all my fault."

"You tell him," she said.

"What?"

"I'll connect you to his office and you tell him," she suggested.

"I'll pass on that," Jack said.

There was no response.

"Kelly?"

"Jack?" Terrance's voice grated on Jack's nerves.

"Terrance."

"Where are you, Jack?" Terrance demanded. "You're supposed to be giving me an update."

"No update," Jack snapped. "I'm supposed to be investigating a murder. That's what I'm doing."

"I told you I wanted an update every day," Terrance reminded him.

"I am not going to come in every morning to tell you I have nothing new to report," Jack grumbled. "I'll update you when I have time."

"You'll update me now," Terrance barked.

"I've got nothing more to tell you," Jack said.

"What about Kenneth Truman?" the chief asked.

Jack was silent. He was sure he had not mentioned Kenneth's name to Terrance.

"What do you know about Kenneth Truman?" Jack countered. "Do you have someone watching me?"

"Relax," Terrance had gone too far. "No, I am not having you watched. I stopped by your desk to talk to you and saw you had a phone message from a Kenneth Truman. I wanted to know who he was. That's all."

"You never come to my desk," Jack said. "How do you know Kenneth Truman?"

"I told you," Terrance said. "I was already on your floor and thought I would stop by. You weren't there so I came back to my office."

"After going through my messages?"

There was a pause. The blood rushed through Jack's veins. Terrance finally said, "When you get in today, I want an update."

The line went dead and Jack threw his phone on the bed. Terrance hadn't stopped by his desk to see him. As soon as you entered the homicide department you had a clear view of the desk of every detective there. There was no reason to continue across the room to Jack's desk if he wasn't there. Jack was sure Terrance was having someone keep tabs on him. He would have to be careful if he was going to juggle Elizabeth's case and Lisa's.

The call had accomplished something for him. The fog of just waking had been lifted. He was clear and ready to start the day, albeit late. He took a quick shower and dressed. Breakfast consisted of a piece of toast and two cups of strong coffee. There was a lot of ground to cover and he wasn't sure where he wanted to start. He did know where he was going to finish. He had to stop by the governor's place that evening. It was an opportunity he didn't want to pass up. Knowing Terrance, it might be his only opportunity.

The files for both cases were on the kitchen table. The twenty-year-old murder with almost no solid leads. He had a witness who claimed to have seen the girl alive after Timothy Waters left. He had another who saw the girl get into a mysterious sports car. She was cheating on Waters with at least two other men. But there was nothing solid.

Then there was the fresh case. According to the footwork Bret had done, none of the neighbors knew the girl. They couldn't say if she was dating. No one knew if she was home the night she was killed. Only the old man Jack spoke to seemed to know anything. Lisa got into a car with a middle-aged man, who dressed well and drove an old sports car. Again, nothing solid.

Jack looked at the files and a single detail stood out in his mind. Both girls were seen getting into sports cars. Of course, it wasn't unusual for young women to date men with sports cars. Another similarity was the girls themselves. He took out the two head and shoulder shots of the girls. They were both high school yearbook photos, taken when the girls would have been about the same age. The physical difference between the two was clear, but they were both beautiful young women. Both smiled broadly. Both had a sparkle in their eyes.

Jack suspected something more intense behind those eyes. Lisa was growing up without her mother. Elizabeth lived in a family that wasn't exactly perfect. Her siblings did not like her. Her parents did not seem to care. They were too caught up in their own lives to bother with hers. Both girls could have been hurting on levels no one ever realized.

Could it be possible these two girls turned to someone for comfort? Someone they trusted to take care of them, to care for them? The old man at Lisa's apartment building saw her with a middle-aged man. Could it be she turned to an older man for the love she didn't have? Only to find his love was a lure to her death?

Studying the two cases side by side, Jack found himself trying to draw lines between the two. Lisa was killed the day Timothy Waters was released from prison. If Terrance was right and Timothy had murdered Elizabeth twenty years ago, could he have celebrated his release by selecting another random victim? He could be the middle-aged man seen with Lisa. Jack didn't think it was possible. Not because he was convinced Timothy was innocent, but because he couldn't come to accept the idea that Terrance might actually be right.

Timothy didn't have a car twenty years ago, but maybe he borrowed one. Jack made a note to find out who Timothy's college roommate was and what kind of car he drove. He also wanted to find out what kind of car Lance Carpenter drove. There was always the possibility the two friends were in this together and were using each other as alibis. If that were the case it was possible Lance was living under an alias to hide from Timothy, not the authorities. Maybe he was coming forward now out of guilt for not backing his friend twenty years ago.

Jack had not even finished his morning coffee and already his search parameters were broadening instead of narrowing. The detective rinsed his cup in the sink and stretched his frame. Gathering his files together, his thoughts again shifted to connecting the two cases. The possibility the girls were killed by the same man was slim at best and he dismissed the idea. There was no physical evidence to even suggest a link between the crimes. The only similarity was the age of the victims and even that comparison was a stretch. He needed more rest to keep his mind focused and stop trying to merge the cases. Stepping out of his apartment and walking to his car he still had no idea where he was going to begin the day.

23

Terrance sat in his office staring out the window for a long time after hanging up from his conversation with Jack. In his eagerness to find out who Kenneth Truman was, he forgot how he had gotten the name. He wasn't having Jack followed like the detective thought. He was simply having Michelle in communications copy Jack's phone messages for him. Truman's name raised a flag only because there were so many messages from the man. Terrance wanted to know who he was.

He blew it though. Letting Jack know he was checking on the detective, even indirectly, would cause Jack to take extra care to hide what he didn't want Terrance to know. The chief didn't know how he could have made such a huge mistake.

It really didn't matter with Kenneth Truman. He would give the name and phone number to one of the uniformed officers in traffic and have an address in a matter of minutes. He could have a background check by the end of the day with photos. It wasn't as though he didn't have resources at his disposal. The problem was the door to future information from Jack's phone messages was closing. Another mistake like the one he just made would shut it for sure.

He swiveled in his chair and pressed the intercom on his phone. "Kelly, have them bring my car around."

"Yes, chief," she said dutifully.

He sat back then sat up just as quickly, pressing the button again. "And Kelly?"

"Yes, sir?"

"Why don't you take the rest of the day off," he said.

"Really?"

"Why not?" Terrance said. "I'm going to be out the rest of the day. You can have communications take my messages."

"Thank you, sir," Kelly said.

"You deserve it," he said. "I know I've been a pain to deal with lately."

"No," she lied. "You've been fine."

"Nice try," he said. "Now get out of here before I change my mind."

"Yes, sir," Kelly said and the line went dead.

Terrance leaned back in his chair and locked his hands behind his head. There was too much for Kelly to do to let her have the day off, but he knew he could just work her harder until she caught up. The key was in making her think she was getting something at his expense. It was something she would remember, or could be reminded, and would justify a favor at a later time.

Terrance started gathering the papers he was going to take with him. He put them in his briefcase with the files on Elizabeth Mitchell's and Lisa Reagan's murders. He would worry about Kenneth Truman tomorrow. Today he had some people to meet before he saw the governor.

24

Bret knocked a second time and waited for the door to open. He did not allow much time before knocking again. He was getting ready to try again when the knob turned.

"May I help you?" Charles Reagan asked.

Bret held out his badge.

"Detective Peterson," Charles nodded. "I remember."

"I need to ask you some questions about your daughter, Mr. Reagan," Bret said. "And her murder."

"Sure, come in," Charles moved back to let Bret in.

The detective stepped past Charles and began studying the layout of the house. When he heard Charles close the door behind him, Bret turned to the lawyer saying, "That's interesting."

"What's that?" Charles inquired, leading the other to his living room.

"Well, your family has suffered two losses at the hand of violence," Bret observed. "Yet you're still comfortable enough to open the door to a stranger."

"I refuse to live in fear, Detective," Charles said.

"I bet you don't either, do you?"

"Do you have questions about my daughter?" Charles asked, letting his lawyer instincts try to control the direction of the conversation.

"I do," Bret said, staring Charles in the eye for a while before pulling out his small notepad. He flipped the pages until he found a blank one. "What can you tell me about her boyfriends?"

"I can't really," Charles responded. "I haven't met any of her boyfriends. She didn't bring them by to meet me."

"She didn't?"

"No," Charles confirmed. "She didn't."

"How did the two of you get along?" Bret continued. "Any problems between you?"

"No problems," he said. "We got along very well."

"Is that what her friends are going to tell me?" Bret asked. "Or do you want to change your story?"

"Are you trying to imply something, Detective?" Charles' voice raised enough to register although he remained in control.

"Just asking questions, Mr. Reagan," Bret said. "Standard procedure."

"I don't care for your line of questioning," Charles objected.

"I didn't think you would," Bret said. "Now, where were you the night your daughter was killed?"

"I think we're done here," Charles stood.

"I can take you downtown," Bret threatened, "If you prefer."

"Do you have an arrest warrant?" Charles demanded.

"No," Bret said, "but I don't need one to question you."

"Don't tell me the law," Charles snapped. "I know more about the law than you ever will. Now leave or I will have lawyers all over you."

"Don't threaten me," Bret lowered his eyes on Charles. " You don't want to push me, Mr. Reagan. You don't want to do that at all."

"Get out," Charles ordered.

Bret stood. "I'll go for now. But I will be back. You can count on that."

Bret left the house. Hearing the door slam behind him caused him to grin. This would be easier than he thought. And when he finally put the cuffs on this one, he was going to enjoy it. Yes. He would enjoy this one a lot.

25

Armed with new questions, Jack would stop in on Timothy Waters unannounced. He wanted to see Timothy's reaction to a surprise visit.

When he arrived, he parked across the street from the Waters' house and sat in his car sipping a cup of coffee he had picked up at a convenience store. From where he was observing the house appeared to be empty, neither Timothy nor his gray-haired mother passing any of the windows at the front of the home. He finished his coffee, left the car and walked up to the front porch, knocking on the door. He turned his back so they would not see his face through the peephole and waited.

The elderly woman opened the door a crack and peered out at Jack. He turned when the door opened and gave her a huge salesman smile, but the woman recognized him immediately.

"What do you want?" she asked, still fearing the worst.

"I have some more questions for your son, Mrs. Waters," he explained. "Is Timothy here?"

"He's here," she said, not moving. "Why don't you just leave him alone?"

"I can't do that, Mrs. Waters," Jack said. "You know that. He was one of the last people to see Elizabeth Mitchell alive. If I am going to find her killer I have to find out everything Timothy knows."

"You had twenty years to ask him your questions," she accused. "Leave him alone."

"It's all right, Ma." A large arm with the lightening tattoo reached above the woman's head. The hand gripped the door and pulled it farther open. A bare-chested Timothy Waters stood behind his mother. Like his arms, his chest was solid muscle. Another tattoo adorned his right peck. This one was a tombstone with the letters R.I.P. at the top and Beth's name beneath them. Jack couldn't stop himself from staring at it.

"I wasn't allowed to go to the funeral," Timothy explained when he noticed where the detective was looking. "So I had my own."

"I have some more questions," Jack looked away from the tattoo.

"I heard," the man said. "Let's go out back."

The man led Jack to the back door. When he turned away he revealed yet another tattoo that covered the majority of his back. It was an image Jack was familiar with: the scales of justice. Only this image was different from the original. The woman holding the scales had one eye uncovered and she was using the sword to cut away one side of the scale. It was a clear depiction of the kind of justice Timothy received in his trial.

In the back yard, Timothy lit a cigarette as soon as they stopped walking. He turned to Jack and blew smoke out the side of his mouth. He wasn't nervous and Jack did not get the sense the man was stressed in any way. Timothy took another drag.

"You have more questions," he said, blowing out more smoke.

"I have a few," Jack agreed. "Just to fill in some blanks others have created while I was interviewing them."

"Did you talk to her father?" Timothy asked. "Did he tell you how much he hated me?"

"I haven't talked to him yet," Jack said. "But the man thinks you killed his daughter. Why wouldn't he hate you?"

"He hated me long before that," Timothy clarified. "He hated that Beth and I were dating."

"Why do you think that was?"

"Look at this house," Timothy hooked his thumb over his shoulder. "He didn't want that for his little girl. Damn, he expected her to marry money. Didn't matter what she wanted. He wanted her to marry right. And I wasn't right."

"It was easy for him to imagine you killing his daughter," Jack said.

"I'm sure I was the first person to come to his mind," Timothy nodded. "After that, it was a matter of pushing the investigation toward me."

"You think the governor guided the investigation?" Jack asked.

"He was mayor," Timothy corrected. "The police worked for him. Of course he told them to check me out. Probably told them I did it and to make sure I didn't get away with it."

"That's quite an accusation," Jack said. "Have anything to back it up?"

"Typical cop response," Timothy sneered. "I've got the knowledge that I didn't kill Beth and that because they only focused on me her real killer walked away free."

"Which is why I'm here," Jack said.

"You really think you're going to find her killer after twenty years?" Timothy asked skeptically. "Even if you find him, what proof would there be? All the evidence is lost. You won't have anything to convict him with. Face it. Everyone will always think I did it. And they'll all think that because I'm free today, I got away with it. If you can call spending half your life in prison getting away with it."

"Well, I'm still going to try," Jack said. "So, I need to ask you some questions. See if I can't get closer to the truth."

"Go ahead and ask."

"When you left her alone that night," Jack started, "you said she was going to meet someone but you didn't know who."

"That's what I said," Timothy stretched his back and put the cigarette in his mouth.

"What would you say if I told you she was meeting Lance Carpenter?" Jack asked watching the man for his reaction.

"Lance?" Timothy's face contorted. "What makes you think it was him?"

"He told me."

"You're kidding," Timothy said. "You found Lance? He disappeared before the trial." He stopped and thought for a minute, adding things together in his mind. "Did Lance kill Beth? I always wondered why he left."

"He's on my list of suspects," Jack nodded. "Although he came out of hiding to talk to me. If he were guilty he would have probably remained hidden. It would help if you could tell me if he owned a car."

"He drove an old Dodge truck," Timothy thought back. "He was always trying to fix it up."

"A truck," Jack thought aloud. "You know anyone who drove an old Camaro or something like that?"

"Maybe," Timothy said. "It's been a long time. I couldn't give you a name. No one comes to mind."

"Did you ever borrow an old sports car?" Jack asked.

"No."

Jack began flipping through his notepad. He scanned his notes from time to time before continuing his search. He finally stopped and asked, "Can you tell me more about Beth? What kind of girl she was like?"

"How will that help you catch her killer?" Timothy asked.

"I don't know," Jack answered honestly. "Truth is I feel like I'm investigating the murder of two different girls. I hear different things from different people. I wanted your impression of her."

Timothy put out his cigarette and dropped the butt on the ground, smashing it out with the toe of his shoe. "Where do I begin? Beth was a unique girl. She was unlike anyone else I have ever met. Yet, every time I turn around I see her in the face of others.

"She was fun-loving and always happy. We used to sit up all night talking about the great times we would have together someday when we got away from this damn town," Timothy pulled his pack out but didn't take out another cigarette. He turned the pack over and over in his hands. "She was always telling me how much potential I had, you know, telling me I could make it even when I didn't think I could. She was the reason I applied for college scholarships. She was the one who encouraged me to become something better than I was. She believed in me."

"What about parties?" Jack asked. "Did you go to a lot of those?"

"Not really," Timothy shook his head. "I wasn't a partier and Beth was always content to go to a movie instead. She was trying to get away from the other kids at school. She hated them, except for Angela. Beth was a wonderful, sweet girl."

"What about Angela?" Jack prompted. "What was she like?"

Timothy frowned. "At first I liked her. Thought she was a good friend to Beth. But after I got to know her I realized she was a manipulator. She said what she needed to get the results she wanted."

"She lied?"

"All the time," Timothy agreed. "She wasn't even sneaky about it. She'd tell you one thing to get you to do something, then she'd tell you the exact opposite to get you to do something else."

Jack remembered the woman working in her yard. She had not been kind in her description of her best friend. It was possible the two girls weren't as different as Angela suggested. If Jack was to believe Timothy, maybe Angela did know the other boyfriend but didn't want to tell. If it was someone Angela knew, she might want to protect him. Jack would need to check into Angela's husband. He also wanted to know if there was more to Angela's dropping out of cheerleading than she told him.

"I have to say," Jack said, "I have yet to find anyone who thought as much of Beth as you did. One might even get the idea you were making up good things to say to make me think you liked her more than you did."

Timothy nodded knowingly. "Not too many people understood Beth the way I did. That's why she wanted to go away with me. When she was with me she felt wanted, because she was. We could be relaxed and comfortable around each other. I didn't have to pretend to be the big jock and she didn't have to be the uptight rich girl. We were good together."

"The evidence against your image of her is pretty overwhelming," Jack countered.

"What evidence?" Timothy turned on Jack. "What her brother said about her? Or that bratty little sister? Or whatever lies Angela may have come up with? That isn't evidence. It's hearsay. Not admissible."

"Did you know she was pregnant?" Jack was blunt.

The expression on Timothy's face suggested Jack had just slapped him. He did not speak. He only stared at Jack, unsure of what to say or do. He moved his frame to an old lawn chair weathered to the point of near uselessness. He lowered himself into the chair and it creaked under his weight but it held.

"Are you lying to me?"

"No," Jack shook his head. "I spoke to the coroner yesterday. He told me she was about three weeks along. I think she wanted to run away with you so she could claim it was yours. I don't think she was going to tell you it wasn't."

"But . . . .."

"She wasn't as sweet as you thought," Jack said. "She may not have been as bad as the others have told me, but she was no saint."

"Who was the father?" Timothy asked. "If not me?"

"If I were to guess I would say it was the killer," Jack answered.

"You think some guy knocked her up then killed her?"

"I honestly doubt she told them she was pregnant," Jack admitted. "There is the possibility she broke up with them that night and they killed her out of jealousy. They may not have even meant to kill her. They may have become enraged and killed her before they realized what they had done."

"You're saying she had a relationship with this guy?" Timothy furrowed his brow. "Not a one-time thing?"

"I suppose that's another possibility," Jack said. "But that wouldn't explain why she was killed. And Angela told me she called her that day to ask her how to break up with a guy."

"Why would she call Angela for that?" Timothy asked.

"Angela said Elizabeth didn't have a lot of experience breaking up with boys," Jack explained.

"She had plenty of experience," Timothy corrected. "She broke up with the guy she was dating when she met me. She dumped me once. Then she dumped another guy when I convinced her to take me back. Typical Angela. The girl was delusional."

"I see," Jack said. He sorted through his file to be sure he hadn't missed anything and came across the senior picture of Lisa Reagan. He held it out to Timothy. "Ever see this girl before?"

Timothy studied the photo a moment then nodded, "Yeah, I knew her. She was . . . God, what was her name? It was . . . Tammy or Trish? No. Tracy. Tracy Belton. One of Beth's friends from cheerleading. They called her the pretty one if I recall."

"Really?" Jack took the photo back. It was not what he was expecting. Tracy was Lisa's mother's name.

26

Jack drove home and began searching through Elizabeth's file until he came to the picture he wanted. The group shot of the cheerleading squad was black and white. He laid the portrait of Lisa next to it and studied them both. It did not take long to find the girl in the center of the back row with her broad smile. She could be described as Lisa Reagan's twin. She could only be Lisa's mother. Tracy Belton, who would grow up and marry Charles Reagan, who would be murdered at the hands of a sadistic killer. By his calculations, Tracy would have had to have been pregnant with Lisa when this picture was taken.

Jack's eyes moved back and forth from Elizabeth's face to Tracy's. Two young girls, both cheerleaders, both pregnant, both doomed to be murdered. Were there any other connections? Jack had no way of knowing. There was one drastic difference. Tracy's murder had been brutal, nothing like Elizabeth's.

But Jack didn't like coincidences. They mucked up investigations. When there were two similarities in a case there was almost always a reason. It was seldom a coincidence.

But if it wasn't a coincidence that two high school cheerleaders both became pregnant and later murdered there were only two possibilities. Either the man convicted of killing Tracy seven years ago also killed Elizabeth twenty-two years ago, or he didn't kill either one. The evidence was strong in Tracy's case. Once Terrance stopped focusing on Tracy's husband, Charles, the case moved quickly. The conviction came just as fast.

Jack rubbed his forehead. Terrance had found the evidence. Terrance had steered the investigation to a man convicted twice before for assaulting women. He had brought the man in for questioning and gotten a confession before Jack could even get to the station. Jack had been elated to have the killer behind bars. He never questioned any of it. Was Tracy's killer still out there while an innocent man rotted away in jail for her murder? Another Timothy Waters?

Jack sighed. He was going to have to add Tracy's murder to his list of cases. It would mean having three investigations going at once. But he was beginning to believe they were all connected in some way. He had no reason to believe they were, other than a gut feeling. The evidence didn't support the idea. The killings, the murder scenes, and the treatment of the bodies suggested three different killers. Given that two of the victims were friends and two were related made it impossible to not draw lines between them.

He needed to get a copy of Tracy Reagan's file without Terrance finding out. He pulled out his phone then set it down. It would be better to make the request in person and get the file right then. If he gave Terrance too much time to realize what he was doing the chief might block the request. He would have to chance going to the station and hope he didn't run into the chief. Jack was not ready to give an update on his progress.

Traffic was light and Jack checked his mirrors repeatedly for signs Terrance had someone following him. Jack didn't spot anyone but there were a couple of guys on the force who could blend into the background pretty well. He arrived at the station during the shift change and took advantage of the flow of personnel into the building to make his entrance. He broke away from the others once inside and made his way to the basement where they stored older files.

"Jack," the officer inside the cage exclaimed when he saw the detective enter the room. "Haven't seen you down here in a while."

"Well here I am," Jack spread his arms as if to present himself.

Officer Larry Kaninski was what every cop hoped and feared becoming. They all hoped to live to be old cops. They all feared reaching a point in their careers where they were too old to work the streets and too young to want to retire and stay home all day. When asked why Larry chose working the file room rather than living off his pension he would always say, "It beats sitting at home all day staring at a mindless piece of furniture. You've met my wife haven't you?"

Jack took a requisition form and started filling it out. When he was finished he turned the paper to face Larry and passed it to the older man through the cutout in the cage. Larry picked it up and checked it to be sure all the necessary lines were filled in.

"That's an old one," Larry said. "Seven years. That could take me a minute."

"Take your time," Jack shrugged. "I'm in no hurry."

The man looked at Jack over the top of his bifocals. "You're always in a hurry, Jack."

"Old case," Jack pointed out. "No hot trail to follow. I can slow down on this one."

"True," Larry disappeared between two tall shelving units stuffed floor to ceiling with file folders and boxes filled with more folders. Jack did not understand the filing system and hoped he would never have to. He had no intention of working the file room when he was too old to work the street. Or the evidence room. Or any other room. When that time came, he would take his pride and walk away.

"Here we go," Larry returned carrying a folder in his hand. He passed it through the cutout in their cage and wrote a line in his logbook. While he did, Jack thumbed through the folder.

"What's this?" Jack asked.

"That's the folder you requested," Larry explained. "Are you losing it, Jack?"

"No, I'm not the one losing it," Jack held the folder up for Larry to see. "I checked this file in here myself. It was over twice this thick. What's going on?"

"All I can tell you is that's all I've got," Larry shrugged. "Maybe someone else took some things out of it."

"Is there any way to find out who has checked this file out?" Jack asked.

"There's a way," Larry nodded. "But it would take a lot of time to go through the logs. Something like that would have to be approved by the chief."

"The chief, huh?" Jack shook his head.

Everyone on the force knew of Jack's feelings for Chief Singleton. Larry was no exception. "Sorry, Jack."

"That's okay," Jack finally said. "I'll take what's here and hope it's enough."

Jack stepped into the hall and started for the stairs. Before climbing up to the ground floor, he turned down the hall toward the evidence room. He entered and saw Officer Shaun Green in the cage. Shaun had been put on light duty after slamming his patrol car into a tree during a high-speed chase.

"Jack," the officer smiled. "What brings you down to my hell?"

"I thought you were out of here," Jack shook the man's hand through the cutout in the cage.

"I was," Shaun grimaced. "But I made the mistake of telling the captain what a bullshit job this was. So, he put me back down here for another week to teach me a lesson."

"Learn anything?"

"Yea," Shaun smiled. "I learned not to tell the captain what I think."

The two men laughed and Jack took a requisition form. He filled it out and handed it to Shaun. The bored, young officer read the information then looked up at Jack.

"You kidding me?" he said. "This case is seven years old."

27

Jack returned home and placed the evidence box on his kitchen table next to the files for the three murder victims. He lifted the lid and peered inside. His initial fear had been that, like Elizabeth's case, there would be no evidence box for Tracy Reagan's case. With that fear behind him, his concern now was with what evidence would be in the box.

He examined bag after bag of evidence. The woman's clothing was there, stained with blood. There were samples of dirt and fibers found on the floor near the victim. There was a long kitchen knife, which the coroner determined to be the murder weapon. No prints were found on the knife. Hair samples determined to be the victim's were there.

The box was filled with dozens of plastic bags, each containing a small piece of the woman's last moments on earth. At a glance it seemed to be complete. But Jack had worked the case. He had examined the evidence over and over again. At one time he had everything spread out on the very table they were on now. It had been seven years but Jack could remember the two things that bothered him about the case. There was a tissue sample that was never identified. And there was a bracelet Tracy was holding when she was killed that her husband did not recognize. These were the two pieces of evidence that were not in the box.

Jack pulled out the photos of the three women and studied them for a long time. He had so many questions he wished he could ask them. All of them were attractive, evident enough in their portraits. All of them were murdered. Tracy and Lisa were related. Elizabeth and Lisa were killed young. Elizabeth and Tracy were friends on the same cheerleading squad. Lines could be drawn, but no conclusions could be made. The time between each of the murders made the lines very thin.

Checking his watch, Jack saw that time was getting away from him. He was going to have to shower and change for the governor's cookout. If he could get the governor alone he could ask a lot of questions before Terrance would have the chance to stop him. Of course, Terrance would be watching him closely. But that actually made the whole ordeal more interesting. He moved down the hall, undressing as he went.

The shower was hot and Jack leaned into it, closing his eyes and letting the streams of water run down his back until he couldn't take the heat anymore. He dressed casually. He hated suits and didn't think it would be appropriate attire for a cookout, although he had to admit he didn't know what was appropriate when visiting the governor. While getting ready he saw that he had a message on his phone that had come in while he was in the shower. He pressed the play button and waited for the message to begin.

"Jack?" the familiar soft voice called to him. "Listen, Jack. It's Kathy. I need to talk to you. I know I promised not to bother you, but this is kind of important." There was a pause and Jack was about to hit the delete button when she continued. "Well, then, you'll call me won't you? Please, Jack. Okay. I'll talk to you then."

When the message ended, Jack could still hear his ex-wife's voice in the room. They had not spoken in over a year. She insisted it would be easier that way and he agreed only because it was what she wanted. She had never promised not to bother him. He would never have asked her for such a promise.

He scrolled through his contacts until he came to her name. Just before hitting the call button he swiped to clear the screen. He wasn't sure he was ready for whatever it might be. He finished dressing, but could not get her voice out of his head. When he was ready to go it was still early and he sat on his couch, his phone in his hand. This time he hit call.

"Jack?" she answered.

"It's me," he answered. "I got your message."

"Thank you for calling." Her voice was as soft and gentle as it always was. He could always find solace in that voice. He waited for her to continue. "Jack, I need to talk to you."

"What do you need?" he asked.

"Not now," she said. "Not on the phone. Can you come over?"

He was silent for a moment.

"Jack?"

"I'm here," he said. "I'm on my way out right now."

"I know," she said and Jack was taken aback again. "Mr. Night Shift."

"Yeah," he said. "How about tomorrow? I can be there in the evening."

"Could you?" she asked. "I know it's a bother and all."

"No bother," he assured her. "I'll be there around six."

"Isn't that early for you?" she said. "I could wait until closer to your shift."

"No," Jack said. "Six is good."

"Six," she repeated. "I'll see you then. And, Jack, thank you."

The phone went dead and Jack stared at his phone for a while before putting it in his pocket. Kathy was always a strong woman. She did not sound strong on the phone. It had been nearly a year since she had called him. Was something wrong? Was she hoping to try to mend their relationship? He was sure that wasn't it. He pushed the thoughts out of his mind.

He crossed the room to get his jacket from the back of a chair in the kitchen. He looked at the photos on the table, his eyes falling on the portrait of Lisa Reagan. He and Kathy never had children. How different things might be, had they made that choice. His brow furrowed when his phone rang.

He dug it out of his pocket and answered. "Hello?"

"Detective," a man said. "It's Charles."

"Charles," Jack responded, sincerely, "How can I help you?"

"They're after me again," Charles' voice cracked.

"Who's after you?"

"The detective on Lisa's case is suggesting I did it," Charles explained. "He thinks I killed my own daughter."

Jack paused. "Don't worry. I'll take care of it."

"Thank you," the lawyer sighed. "I knew you would help me."

"Charles," Jack was cautious. "How old was Lisa when you met Tracy?"

There was a pause on the other end of the line. Charles finally said, "I loved my daughter, detective."

"I know you did," Jack said. "I'm not doubting that. I need to know when you met her."

"Lisa was six months old," Charles finally answered. "I was charmed by Tracy and then by her daughter. I took them in and loved them with all I had. And now they have both been taken from me."

"I need to ask," Jack continued. "Do you know who her father is?"

"I'm her father," Charles defended.

"I know that," Jack said. "But I need to know if Tracy ever told you who Lisa's real father was?"

"No," Charles sighed. "She was going to tell Lisa when she was eighteen and old enough to understand. She never got the chance."

"Sorry, Charles," Jack apologized. "I didn't mean to upset you further. I just needed to know."

"Find her killer, detective," Charles said. "Do that and you'll have no need to apologize for anything."

28

The governor's cookout was more like the social event of the year. Jack pulled up to the gate at about eight-thirty. When Terrance told him the governor wanted him to stop in to see him, he thought it would be a small affair. What he didn't count on were half the politicians in the state and a virtual list of the who's who in campaign contributors. The guard did not believe Jack was invited. It took showing his badge and a phone call to the governor's assistant to get him inside.

The valet at the door was another nonbeliever as he tried to tell Jack the staff was to park on the street and walk up. To deal with him, Jack flashed his badge and asked for the man's license. After the man complied, Jack said he would return the license when he picked up his car.

By the time he actually rang the bell of the old mansion where the governor lived, as every governor did, it was going on a quarter of nine. The butler who greeted the detective at the door was apparently better informed, possibly due to the phone call from the guard at the gate and did not hesitate to lead Jack through the house to the patio.

The back patio was large, surrounding a long swimming pool that none of the guests seemed to notice. The lawn stretched away forever. It was a beautiful place spoiled only by the people moving about. Everywhere Jack looked he saw small groups of men and women in conversation. The butler gestured for Jack to proceed and turned back into the depths of the house. It was immediately obvious to the detective that he was the only person casually dressed in a sea of suits and evening gowns. The cookout was being catered and even the staff were better dressed than him.

The detective scanned the faces of the guests in search of the governor. The first person he recognized was Terrance. The chief was standing in a half-circle of men, all with an air of bloated importance, holding a drink in one hand and gesturing wildly with the other while talking rapidly.

He spotted the governor and his wife standing at the head of a group of people entranced by the politician's words. On cue they laughed and the governor smiled broadly. Jack rolled his eyes and started through the maze of tables separating him from the couple. He glanced over his shoulder toward Terrance. He was hoping to talk to the governor before the chief knew he was there. Luckily, Terrance was still deep in conversation with the other men in his group.

"Detective Mallory," a voice drew him back. He turned to see Donald Mitchell, Elizabeth's brother, holding out a hand in greeting.

"Mr. Mitchell," Jack accepted his hand in a firm handshake.

"How is the case coming?" the banker asked.

"I'm doing what I can," Jack said. "I've come up with a couple leads."

"Really?" Donald said. "After all these years?"

"It's a matter of knowing where to look," Jack glanced past the man to where the governor still stood talking.

"I'm surprised to see you here," Donald said. "I wouldn't think this would be your kind of thing."

"You would be right," Jack faked a smile. "I was told this was going to be a small gathering."

"For my father," Donald swept his hand to take in everyone, "this is a small gathering. But all of that aside I wouldn't expect to find you here. Are you working?"

"I was invited if that's what you're wondering," Jack said. "Apparently, your father wants to see me."

"That makes sense," Donald sighed. "When Dad wants to see you, he sees you. He probably wants to yell at you. He was upset about my sister."

"Elizabeth?"

"No," Donald said in a dismissive tone. "Virginia. You upset Virginia. Virginia upset Dad. Now, Dad is going to upset you."

"Must be horrible," Jack said.

"What's that?"

"Living in the shadow of your father," Jack suggested. "Was Elizabeth his favorite?"

"My father did not have a favorite," Donald said. "Now if you don't mind I need to greet some real guests."

"You have fun," Jack grinned. "Oh, and Donald . . ."

"What?" the banker turned back to him clearly irritated.

"Just thought you should know," Jack said. "I'm always working."

Donald turned away abruptly and was swallowed by the crowd. For a cookout, this one was very tame. Most of the cookouts Jack attended were primarily groups of cops blowing off steam before they had to hit the streets again. This event was more like a funeral. Everyone stood around speaking in hushed voices. He looked back toward the governor but the man was no longer there.

Jack scanned the crowd quickly to locate the politician, spotting him in a conversation with Terrance. Jack rolled his eyes. The governor would have to wait. He found a bar and ordered a scotch. The bartender poured the drink and handed it to the detective who took a sip. Very smooth. Money can't buy happiness, but it could buy good scotch.

Jack stood in the shadows watching and waiting for an opportunity to catch the governor alone. Spending so many years on stakeouts had taught him the patience to wait for long periods of time for what he wanted. However, in a party this size where the rule of thumb was to mingle with as many people as possible, he did not have to wait long. Terrance and Steve parted and walked in separate directions. Jack hesitated until the perfect moment then stepped up to Governor Mitchell with his hand extended. He didn't like politicians but he had learned how to handle them.

"Governor Mitchell," he said. "So nice to finally meet you."

The governor turned and took the offered hand in a firm shake. The man smiled with teeth showing but Jack got a sense of unease from his eyes. "And you are?"

"Detective Jack Mallory," he introduced himself.

"Oh, detective," the smile faded though not completely. "So good of you to come. Let's talk."

The man put his arm around Jack's shoulder and steered him away from the crowds toward the house. There was a set of french doors nearby and the governor took Jack through them into the office beyond. Jack was relieved to be away from everyone. He was where he wanted to be, alone with the father of the victim.

"Care for a drink?" the governor stepped up to a small bar between two tall bookcases and started pouring from a crystal decanter. He was already pouring the second glass by the time Jack responded.

"Why not?" the detective said. "I can have one." He already had, after all.

"Did your doctor tell you to lay off of it too?" the governor asked, handing Jack a glass.

"No," Jack said. "I'm driving home tonight."

"I see," the governor said. He drifted away for a moment. When he snapped back he said, "How is the investigation coming?"

"As well as it can with the obstacles that are hindering me," Jack said. He drank from the glass. The liquor warmed his throat. He held the glass out to examine the contents.

"Good stuff," the governor said. "You were saying something about obstacles. I can imagine following twenty year old clues would be difficult."

"Yes but the real obstacle is getting to the people I need to interview," Jack said. "Like you."

"Me?" the governor turned. "You can talk to me anytime, detective. I am very interested in getting to the bottom of this."

Jack stopped short of telling the governor about Terrance's orders to stay away from the politician. "That's good. When can I speak to your wife?"

"Is that really necessary?" the governor's tone changed. "I can tell you everything you need to know. There is nothing my wife knows about our daughter that I don't."

"It is necessary," Jack said. "Whether you believe it or not, your wife may know a lot of things about your daughter that you don't. I need to have access to all of the facts if you are truly interested in having all the answers. I can't do that if I can't talk to everyone I need to. You are right about it being hard to follow twenty-year-old clues, Governor. It is even harder when you're denied some of those clues."

The governor stared at Jack a moment, then nodded. "You can speak to my wife, detective. But I want to be there. She was destroyed by Elizabeth's death and she did not take it well when she learned of that boy's release. I won't have you upsetting her even more."

Jack had no intention to allow the governor to be in the room during the interview with his wife but he held his tongue. It would not serve to push the governor into rescinding the chance at an interview. Jack chose to accept what he had and move on.

"Can I proceed with your interview then?" Jack asked.

"Interview?" The governor laughed. "This isn't an interview, detective. This is a party. Call my office in the morning and set an appointment. Then I will grant you an interview. If that goes well, we will discuss a time to speak with my wife."

Jack noted how the promise of an interview with the governor's wife shifted to a 'we'll see' in a matter of seconds. He said nothing. He had already lost ground and did not want to lose any more. The two of them stood silent, the governor wanting to know what Jack thought his wife knew, Jack wondering what the other was hiding. It was a long moment interrupted only when the door to the patio opened.

"Governor?" the chief stepped in glaring at Jack. "Everything okay?"

"Everything is fine, Terrance," the governor smiled his politician's smile. "Jack and I were about to return to the party." He looked squarely at Jack, "Weren't we, detective?"

"Yes, sir," Jack said with just enough sarcasm to make him feel good but not draw attention to it. He nodded at Terrance and walked out. He did not look back to see if the men were following him. He knew they weren't.

He moved into the crowd toward the back door of the mansion. He lowered his head and started shouldering his way through the people who seemed determined to keep him from reaching his destination and ultimate escape from this group of starched shirts and expensive suits. Some cookout. There wasn't even a smoker. A hand latched onto his arm and he tried to pull free of it.

"Jack," a woman said. "Have fun with the governor?"

He looked up. Heather Singleton, Terrance's wife, smiled at him seductively.

29

"Jack," Heather said. "I have been looking for you all evening. I decided you weren't going to be here. Then here you come waltzing out of Steve's office. I had no idea you had an in with the big boys."

"I'm investigating a murder where the victim happens to be his daughter," Jack said. "I'm here so I can meet with him and discuss the case. They won't be inviting me over tomorrow for tea."

"That's good," she smiled. "I would hate to think you were going to become one of them."

Heather gestured to indicate everyone at the party. Jack looked around at the faces of some of the most powerful men and women in the state. There was no doubting the amount of money these people represented. It was the kind of party anyone who wanted to be somebody would want to attend.

"Rich and powerful?" Jack asked. "I don't think you have to worry about me becoming one of them."

She laughed, actually throwing her head back as she did. "They aren't all rich. Or powerful for that matter. Terrance is one of them."

"The chief of police?" Jack shrugged. "You don't think that's powerful?"

"Power is being in control," Heather looked Jack in the eyes. "You think Terrance is in control? I thought you were smarter than that. If Steve wasn't his friend, do you think he would be chief?"

"I suppose not," Jack concluded.

"He wouldn't even be close," she said. "He would kiss Steve's ass if Steve told him to. That's not power. That's Steve's power. Terrance has nothing. He can't even keep you in control."

"In his defense," Jack smiled. "No one else could either."

"Are you sure about that?"

"Positive."

"Why are you here?"

"I told you," Jack said. "I came to question the governor."

"Really?"

"Really."

"So you called the governor and told him you were going to stop by during his party to ask him some questions?" Heather asked.

"No," Jack shook his head. "Not exactly."

"Not exactly?" Heather stifled a laugh. "How about the governor had someone call and tell you to stop by and give him an update. And you snapped to attention and came over. That is power."

"I would not have come if I hadn't wanted to talk to the governor," Jack defended.

"Do you really believe that?" she asked.

"Yes."

She stared at him a moment before nodding. "I think you do."

"I'm investigating the murder of a girl who has now been dead longer than she was alive," Jack glanced back at the house and the room where he left Terrance and the governor. "I didn't want the case but now its mine. So, I'm going to work it like it happened yesterday. That means no one is going to interfere with the way I follow the clues. Not your husband. Not the governor. No one."

"You have clues?" she asked. "After twenty years?"

Jack wasn't sure if her interest was out of curiosity for the case or if she was just bored with the power angle. He paused only a second before answering. "Clues? Yes, I have a few. Nothing too helpful yet. Why do you ask?"

"It surprises me when you can follow clues that are twenty years old," she said. "Of course it also surprised me when they released Beth's killer."

"That's right," Jack snapped his fingers. "You knew the girl didn't you?"

"She was part of the Mitchell family," she sighed. "If you can call it that."

"What do you mean?" Jack furrowed his brow. "You don't consider them a family?"

"Are you kidding?" she laughed. "Jack, look at these people. Do any of them seem the least bit human to you? They all have one thing in common. Money is more important than anything else. It is more important than their family. More important than their own health. Most of the men here have not been to their children's birthday parties in years. If they have children in sports they wouldn't be able to tell you what position they play. They don't care."

Jack checked the crowd of stale personalities again. They were still gathered in groups talking non-stop, though the members of each group had changed in an attempt to mingle. They could be discussing their children's little league games or the performance of the stock market. He got the impression from their expressions that Heather was right. It was all business to them.

"The Mitchell's are the worst ones," Heather continued. "The only thing Steve and Betty think about is the next level of government. I guarantee as soon as the election was over and they found out Steve was going to be governor they started formulating their plan for the move to the Senate or House of Representatives. They never paid attention to their kids. They never knew what they were doing. They're lucky Beth was the only one who ended up dead."

Jack stared at her for a long time, probably too long but she never indicated that it was. Finally he asked, "Can you tell me what Beth was like?"

"Me?" She was caught off guard by the question. "I really couldn't tell you anything about the girl you don't already know, Jack. You'd be better off finding one of her old school friends and asking them. I really didn't know her very well."

"I have already talked to the friends I can find and to Virginia and Donald," Jack said. "Frankly, I feel like I'm getting descriptions of two different people. I was hoping you could tell me about her from a more objective view. You knew her yet maybe not so close as to have a biased memory."

"You want a neutral view." She wasn't asking, but Jack nodded anyway. "Okay. I'll tell you what I know. Beth was a sweet, beautiful little girl. I mean it too. When I met her she was six or seven years old and was the most beautiful thing I had ever seen. I didn't think the Mitchells deserved her. But of course things change. As she got older, she remained pretty, but her sweetness wore off. She became a spoiled brat. Probably trying to get the attention she wanted her parents to give her. She lashed out at them. She did things to upset them. She even broke the law a couple of times."

"I never saw anything in her file about legal issues," Jack's eyes registered his realization even as he said it. "Terrance was a family friend. He made the reports go away."

"Exactly," Heather grinned. "Fact is they became friends because Terrance was willing to make things go away. The first one was a DUI."

"Beth?"

"No, Betty," she said. "That was when we first met the Mitchells. Betty had a few too many, wrapped her car around a tree and Terrance made the whole thing disappear. The next thing I knew, we were having lunch with the mayor."

"You don't like him much do you?"

"Who? Steve?" she snickered. "What's to like? The man is an egotistical ass. He is your best friend as long as you have something to offer him. These people." She swung an arm at the crowd. "They helped put him in office. Do you think that if one of them suddenly lost everything and came to Steve for help that he would give them the time of day? No."

"If he doesn't care," Jack asked, "why is he pushing so hard to solve this case?"

"Are you kidding?" Heather said. "His move from the mayor's office to the governor's office was on a platform of being hard on crime. It all started with Beth's murder. It gave him the edge he needed to win. Now the man convicted of killing his own daughter is walking the streets again. Does that sound like he's being tough on crime? He doesn't want the case solved. He wants that man back behind bars. He wants votes."

"Were there other incidents?"

"What do you mean?"

"After Mrs. Mitchell's DUI?" Jack clarified. "Did Terrance cover up anything else?"

She grinned at that. Jack thought it odd. It faded when she started talking. "Betty had at least two more DUIs. That stopped when Steve finally hired a limo driver to chauffeur her around. Of course, Beth had a couple things. One was shoplifting. Another was a minor in possession. I don't know about Virginia, but Donald had a couple things too."

"Really?" Jack glanced to find the banker in the crowd but couldn't. "He seems so stiff."

"He was a cute kid," she said. "Outgoing and what you might call a class clown. Steve hated it, his humor. 'A man needs to be serious,' Steve would say. But Donald didn't have it in him."

"When did he change?" Jack asked. "When Elizabeth died?"

"No," she became solemn. "Donald and a couple of his friends got caught drinking. They were about sixteen or seventeen. Anyway, Steve was furious. He made Terrance put Donald behind bars for the night. 'To teach him a lesson.' The record was erased but Donald was different after that. He wasn't friendly anymore. He was bitter. Angry. When he heard about Beth's shoplifting thing being swept under the rug he announced he would be going away to college. Far away."

"When I spoke to Donald, I got the impression he didn't like his sister very much," Jack said. "Did he resent her?"

"Until that happened I would have said no," she frowned. "With his parents more or less not there, Donald had always taken the parental role when it came to his sisters. When he left it was devastating to them both. Beth, in particular, did not take it well."

Jack took in the crowd again, this time spotting Donald standing in a small group of aging men. Could the anger he expressed for his sister be a way for him to mask his guilt? Guilt for not being there to protect the younger sister he practically raised? Or maybe for wishing her fate upon her? If in his anger he secretly wished Elizabeth dead, how would he have handled the news when she was killed? Would he blame himself?

Donald smiled at something one of the elder men said. Even as he did, the banker glanced Jack's way. When their eyes met, Donald's smile faded. He turned back to the men he was with. Could Donald have been involved in his sister's death?

30

Jack woke the next morning and his head spun. Heather convinced him he should stay at the cookout and no one came along to show him the way out. The two of them found seats near one of the full-service bars and began insulting Terrance as they had the night they met. It was good, as were the drinks they continued to order until they were cut off. Whether it was Terrance, Governor Mitchell or a very wise bartender, Jack couldn't say. With the morning rays of sunlight breaching the window shades, Jack was wishing, whoever it had been, they had cut him off earlier.

He closed his eyes to the intrusive light, pulled the sheet over his head and rolled away from the window. When he did, he bumped something. His eyes snapped open. All he saw on the pillow next to him was long blond hair. He could not see the woman's face but was positive it was Heather's hair. His head still under the sheet, his eyes moved down the woman's body. She wore no clothing. He let out a slight moan as he closed his eyes and returned to his back. He tried desperately to search his memory of the night before. It was no use. He couldn't remember anything that happened after the bartender told him he couldn't have any more to drink.

Could he have gone somewhere else? Had a drink somewhere else? Maybe picked up another blond woman somewhere other than at the governor's party? Jack clung to that hope as he slung his legs out of the bed and sat up. He did not dare look back at the sleeping woman. But his movements had caused her to stir, her weight shifting on the mattress as she too rose to a sitting position. She let out a moan even more slight than his.

"Where am I? Who are you?" the woman asked. Relief rushed through Jack until her voice registered. Then, "Oh, Jesus. Jack? What happened?"

He turned to her. Heather, disheveled hair and dark rings beneath her eyes, was still a good-looking woman. His sense of panic was reflected in her eyes. She was pleading for him to answer her question. He shrugged and said, "I was hoping you could tell me."

Her hand moved down her body. "Where are my clothes, Jack? What did you do with them?"

"I don't know," he said. "How did you get here?"

She looked at him as if she suddenly understood. Neither of them remembered how they ended up at Jack's place together or how they had come to be naked in the same bed. As for what may or may not have happened between them, they could only guess.

"Jack?"

"Yeah?"

She didn't finish her question. She glanced around the bedroom until her eyes fell on a lump of clothing that appeared to be what she had been wearing the night before. "Where's your bathroom?"

Jack pointed at a door on his side of the bed. The mattress shifted again as she stood. He could hear her feet on the carpet. She crossed in front of him carrying her clothes. He admired her back until the bathroom door closed. When he was alone in the room he rose to his feet and dressed. With a quick glance at the bathroom door he started down the hall for the kitchen. He needed a strong cup of coffee, and he needed it now.

He could remember back in his college days when he would wake up with girls he didn't know or at least didn't know very well. It had been awkward at times though never a complete surprise. Back then getting a girl to come home with him had been the goal. On the very rare occasion the girl turned out to be married, they would simply say their good-byes and she would be on her way. She would return home to whatever problems would arise from her not going home the night before.

But with Heather things were a bit more complicated. She wasn't just married. She was married to the boss. Even if nothing happened between them, how would they explain her not going home after spending an evening talking and drinking together?

The bathroom door opened and there was rustling like she was searching for something. He busied himself with straightening the kitchen while preparing for another awkward moment. When she entered the kitchen she was brushing her hair. Jack stopped short and looked at her for a moment too long. Kathy used to do the same thing in the mornings. She didn't notice or pretended not to.

"Do I smell coffee?" she asked.

"Would you like a cup?" he came out of his trance and reached for a mug before she could reply.

"I take it black," she nodded. "Thanks."

He poured the coffee and held it out for her to take. During the pass, their hands touched. They froze, trying to recall whether it was familiar. Just as quickly, they pulled away and attempted to laugh it off.

"What are we going to do?" Jack asked after they were seated at the drop-leaf table pushed against one wall of the kitchen.

"I'm not going to marry you if that's what you mean," Heather let out a half-laugh.

"That's not what I mean," Jack said.

"I know," she grinned. "Lighten up, Jack. What's done is done." She paused, shifting her gaze toward the bedroom, "Whatever we did."

"Heather," Jack remained serious. "Don't you think Terrance might put one and one together? You spent the entire evening with me. You didn't go home. He isn't stupid."

"I have to disagree with you on that," she said. "Besides, Terrance was staying at Steve's place last night. He told me to call a cab."

"You remember that?" Jack asked.

"He told me that before we got to the cookout," she said.

"Would he call to check on you?"

"You're kidding, right?"

"So, he doesn't know you aren't home right now?"

"No," she said. "He doesn't."

Jack relaxed. It was like a floodgate had opened and with it came the throbbing in his head, a reminder of the evening before. A middle-aged woman, more beautiful than most women half her age, stood in his kitchen holding one of his favorite coffee cups, wearing the same sleeveless black dress she wore the night before. He should be elated. But a mixture of knowing who she was and not remembering anything that happened between them left him confused.

"What do we do now?" he finally asked. He was pouring a second cup of coffee. He gestured toward her with the pot but she waved him off.

"Well," she said, "either we have breakfast or I should be getting home. I understand if you don't want to spend more time with me this morning."

Jack thought back to the conversation he had with the governor. He remembered talking to Donald and later to Heather about the case. The conversation had turned to their mutual dislike for her husband and soon after that he couldn't remember anything more. He glanced at the microwave clock. "I should be getting to work. I have a lot of ground to cover today."

"What a pity," she tilted her head. "I should call a cab then."

"I could drop you off," Jack offered.

"That might not be such a good idea," she smiled.

"True," Jack conceded.

She took her phone from her purse and turned toward the living room. Jack watched until she rounded the corner. Would the events of the night before ever come back to him or would he be wondering about them for the rest of his life? Memory was a strange thing, triggered by the most unusual details at the most unusual times. He walked to the doorway she had passed through and stared at her shape through the back of her dress. She turned toward him surprised to see him there. She smiled.

"What's the address here?" she asked.

He gave it to her and waited while she relayed it to the cab company. She hung up and turned to Jack.

"They'll be here in about thirty minutes," she said.

"No problem," he said. He paused then asked. "Why didn't you take your own car?"

"What?"

"If you knew Terrance was going to stay," Jack rephrased, "Why not take separate cars?"

"My car's in the shop," she said. "And he never drives his baby."

"His baby?"

"That damn car he keeps in the garage," she explained. "He never takes it anywhere. I swear I don't know why he keeps it."

"What kind of car is it?" he asked.

"I don't know," she said. "Some old thing. Are you one of those car men? I just don't understand you people."

"I'm not a car man," he said. "How long has he had it?"

"I don't know," she said. "Seems like forever."

"Is it sporty?"

"What else?" she sneered. "Why do you ask?"

"Just curious," he said. "I need to get ready for work."

He turned away. He needed someone who could look up the cars registered to the chief of police for him. Someone who would not ask questions. Someone he could trust. Only one name came to mind.

31

Larry Kaninski was sitting behind the cage in the file room when Jack walked in. Located on the basement level of the department, the air was heavy with humidity. Larry had his sleeves rolled up to his elbows wiping sweat from his face with a handkerchief. When he saw Jack he stood and smiled.

"Hey Jack," the officer said. "Twice in one week. What's the occasion? I gave you everything on that file."

"Everything was there," Jack confirmed. He had only been there a few minutes and sweat was already forming on his forehead and neck. "What did you do to piss off maintenance? Did they turn the air off?"

"And here I thought my warm disposition was just too much for this confined space," the man grinned. He swiped his face with the handkerchief again. "Seriously though. They said there was something wrong with the air handlers and they're working on it. Of course, that was three hours ago."

Jack nodded then stepped up to the cage. He glanced around to be sure no one else was nearby. "I'm not here for evidence."

Larry leaned forward and said in a hushed voice, "Then why are you here?"

"Do you know anyone up in records?" Jack went with the direct approach.

"I know the same people you know," Larry said. "Why do you ask?"

"Anyone you could get to check car registrations for you?" Jack continued.

"Yes," Larry answered. "But why don't you ask them yourself?"

"Can you trust them?" Jack asked.

With that Larry fell silent for a moment, weighing the question in his mind. He studied Jack's eyes. There was something there but

Larry couldn't place his finger on it. "Who do you want to check on?"

"I have to be able to trust you," Jack said.

"It's me, Jack," Larry held his arms apart in a classic salesman pose. "If you can't trust me, you can't trust your own mother."

Jack hesitated before nodding. "Okay."

"Then what is it?"

"I need a list of vehicles," Jack said, "registered to Terrance Singleton."

"Chief Singleton?" Larry lowered his voice.

Jack nodded again. "He's watching me so I can't do it. I need someone he wouldn't be watching."

"I don't know Jack," Larry said. "I'm getting close to retirement. I can't afford to be fired. I have a pension to worry about."

"I know," Jack sighed. "Listen, forget I asked. I shouldn't ask you to take the risk."

Larry shrugged apologetically and Jack turned to leave. The cage that made up his workplace seemed to close in on the old policeman and he considered how much time he had left to sit inside, rotting away before he could retire. The thought was depressing. He called out, "Jack, wait a minute."

Jack turned around with interest. He approached the cage again with heightened anticipation. "What is it?"

"I might be able to help you out," Larry said. "If you can help me out."

"I don't have any money, Larry," Jack said walking away again.

"No, I don't want money," Larry said. "I mean literally help me out."

"I don't follow," Jack said.

"I want to help you," Larry said. "With your investigation."

Jack stood silent for a moment as what the older man was saying sank in and took hold of him. He wanted out of the cage. He wanted to work a case, even if it was twenty years old and going nowhere. Jack understood why. It would be nice to have another set of eyes and hands in this. But there were also problems that would arise from having the man around. The fact that Jack was meddling in the Lisa Reagan case would be hard to hide from a partner. And there was the most obvious problem.

"No one's going to sign off on that, Larry," Jack argued. "No one is going to want to be responsible for putting you back on the street. And Terrance would blow a gasket if I were using additional resources on this."

"Isn't the chief friends with the governor?"

Jack nodded.

"And the victim was the governor's daughter?"

Another nod.

"I don't think he'd mind an old man like me helping out," Larry said. "Can you at least ask?"

"Okay," Jack said. "I'll ask. No guarantees. Meanwhile, can you get what I need?"

"I'll get it," Larry smiled. "Just get me out of here."

32

"What do you want?"

The man sat in a room the size of a walk-in closet. He slouched in the chair provided for him directing his anger toward his visitor. Jack stood leaning against the far wall choosing not to sit across from the man. Stuart Landerburg wore an orange prison jumper. His arms were covered with tattoos similar to the ones Timothy Waters wore. Jack had not laid eyes on the prisoner in nine years. Not since the trial ended. Not since the day Stuart was convicted of killing Tracy Reagan.

"I need to ask you some questions, Stuart," Jack said.

"Last time you asked me questions I ended up in here," Stuart hissed. "Keep your questions."

"Stuart," Jack tried to soothe the man. "I'm not here to hurt you. It might even help you. Besides, what else do you have to do today?"

"Plenty," Stuart glared. "You're keeping me from my golf game."

"Stuart," Jack continued to use his name trying to make a connection. "Listen to the questions. If you want to answer, you can. If you don't, I'll send you back to your cell and get on with my life."

"Fine," Stuart conceded. "Ask your questions."

"That's more like it," Jack pushed away from the wall. "When you were arrested we had a lot of evidence against you."

"Bogus," the man snapped. "It was all a load of crap. None of it was true."

"Easy," Jack held up a hand. "I need to ask you some questions about the evidence. Like how did the murder weapon end up in your apartment?"

Stuart sat staring at him for a long time. Interrogations were always a struggle. The suspect never wanted to say anything out of fear of saying too much. Jack sighed and sat in the chair opposite the prisoner, making a show of getting comfortable to suggest he was willing to wait the man out.

"Listen," Jack said. "Your home was searched after your arrest and among other things, the murder weapon was found under your kitchen sink. You say you're innocent. So, how did the weapon get under your sink? It's a simple question."

"And you want me to answer it?" Stuart asked.

"I wouldn't have asked it if I didn't want an answer," Jack explained.

"You're shittin' me," the man said glancing around the room for something. "Is this some kind of test?"

"A test?" Jack furrowed his brow. "What kind of test?"

"To see if I'm going to talk," the man frowned. "That's why he sent you isn't it? I mean that's why you're really here isn't it?"

"That's why who sent me?" Jack asked.

"I'm done answering your questions," Stuart sat up straight for the first time.

"You're not done until I say you're done," Jack said. "And I say you're not."

"Ask whatever the hell you like but I'm not saying anything else," the man said.

"You haven't said anything yet," Jack said. "What if I told you I'm trying to help you? Would you talk to me then?"

"Like you helped me seven years ago?" Stuart shook his head. "I'm done here."

"Why?" Jack pressed. "If you're innocent like you claim, this is your chance to tell your side. Why not use it?"

"If I talk to you I'm dead," Stuart said. "Now, let me go back to my cell."

"Fine." Jack stood and opened the door calling for the guard. He closed the door again as Stuart stood. When the convict was close he said, "You know who killed her, don't you?"

"I know who put that knife under my sink," Stuart said.

"Then why don't you tell me who it was?" Jack asked.

The door opened and the guard stepped in. He motioned Stuart toward him and the prisoner complied. Prison had not been favorable to the man. He was thinner than Jack remembered. He walked slightly slouched in his orange jumper. Nothing like Timothy Waters. Just before leaving the room Stuart turned back to the detective.

"You saw the pictures of that woman, right?" Stuart sneered.

"Yes."

"If you knew the man capable of doing that to a woman," Stuart said, "would you want to piss him off?"

33

The night of the governor's cookout, the politician had told Jack he would see him any time. Even so, when he called to set up an appointment, he was surprised when the man's assistant told him that the governor would be free at one-thirty. Not wanting to lose his access, Jack arrived early only to be asked to wait. He sat in the outer office thumbing through pamphlets and watching the secretary take call after call, At first glance Jack thought she was in her early twenties, but after more than forty-five minutes of studying her face and eyes, he was convinced she was in her thirties. Growing bored with the provided reading, he began thumbing through his notes.

He checked his watch every few minutes until it was well after two. Between two of the constant phone calls Jack reminded the young woman of the time. She simply told him he would have to wait and sent him back to his seat.

To his surprise, she announced the governor was ready for him a few minutes later. She pointed him to the door then lowered her eyes to her work. He thanked the top of her head and approached the door. The dark stained oak and brass nameplate reminded Jack of Donald Mitchell's door at the bank. He knocked slightly and, when he heard the governor's voice, let himself in.

"Detective Mallory," the governor greeted him. "So good to see you again."

"Governor Mitchell," Jack shook Steve's outstretched hand. "Thank you for agreeing to see me."

"Well, it's like I said last night," Steve sat behind his desk, a large maple executive style piece. "I want to help in any way I can."

"Yes. You did say that," Jack nodded. "And I hope you meant it."

"Of course I meant it," Steve said. "Where shall we begin?"

"Let's start with you telling me everything you can about your daughter," Jack flipped open his notepad. "Who were her friends?

What did she do with her time? How many boyfriends did she have before she started dating Timothy Waters? That kind of thing."

Steve remained silent for a long time. He was thinking very hard about the questions. Jack suspected the politician would not answer until he had thought out exactly what he would say and what repercussions the answers might have. The questions were obviously not ones he expected.

"Detective," he finally said. "I really don't know what to tell you."

"Just tell me what you know," Jack prompted.

"That's just it," Steve leaned back in his seat letting it recline slightly. "I was mayor then. The firemen were threatening to strike. The plans for the new highway were being challenged and I was working on gaining support for my bid for governor. As ashamed as I am to say so, I don't know the answers to what you're asking. I didn't know my daughter very well. I didn't meet many of her friends. The ones I met, I didn't know their names. I don't know what she did for fun. And as for boyfriends, well . . ." He shrugged.

"Elizabeth's former English teacher said you and your wife were very supportive of her," Jack said.

"Of course," Steve agreed.

"Did you know her grades had been declining before her death?"

Again the governor remained silent. He narrowed his eyes at Jack with an expression somewhere between surprise and anger. Or maybe it was sorrow. Anguish because not only did he not know his daughter well, he knew less about her than he thought he did.

"How is this going to help find Beth's killer?" Steve's voice lost its political charm. The artificial facade drained from his face. "Her grades? Her friends? How will that explain how a man could do what was done to her?"

"Governor Mitchell," Jack lowered his notepad. "Your daughter was murdered twenty years ago. The evidence used to convict Waters is gone. I have very little to go on. What I have found does not point to Waters. It isn't enough to prove he didn't kill her, but there is a possibility he was innocent. Knowing more about her may point me in a new direction, toward the truth. Knowing her friends may not explain anything but there might be someone who knew her who might know something. Maybe not the answer, but a single fact we don't know could be what we need to put it all together."

Steve nodded. "Okay. Let's start again. I'll answer what I can."

Jack smiled reassuringly. "Did you know a friend of hers named Tracy Bolton? She was on the cheerleading squad with Elizabeth."

"No," Steve shook his head sighing.

"Okay," Jack checked his notes, "How about . . . "

"Wait," Steve interrupted. "Did you say Bolton?"

"Yes."

"I knew a Bolton," Steve shook a finger in the air. "Bolton. Bolton. Oh, yes. Oliver Bolton. He was chairman of the board for Clifton Construction."

"Your son-in-law's company?"

"It was his father's then," Steve confirmed. "Bolton had a daughter who disappeared sometime before Beth was killed."

"That was Tracy," Jack said.

"And she was a friend of Beth's?"

"You never met her?"

"If I did, I don't remember," Steve said. "Is there a connection between the girl's disappearance and my daughter's death?"

"I don't know," Jack answered. "I do know that Tracy Bolton was murdered ten years ago."

"She was? That's terrible."

"And her daughter was murdered a few days ago."

"What is this world coming to?" Steve shook his head. "And you think they are connected?"

"I don't know that they are," Jack said. "I have to pursue every possible thread. With someone in your daughter's circle being murdered, I wanted to find out how well they knew each other. I never learned why Tracy vanished. Maybe she knew something. Something that Beth shared with her. Tracy ran, Beth didn't and Beth was killed."

"What could they have known?" Steve asked.

"It's one theory out of dozens," Jack said. "They may be connected. They may not be. That's why I want to talk to Beth's friends. They may know something they were too afraid to tell us twenty years ago."

"I'm sorry I don't know their names," Steve said.

"I know," Jack said. "It would be helpful if I could speak with your wife. To see if she knows anything."

"I will have to check our schedules to see when we're both free," the governor said.

Jack nodded. He considered telling the governor he needed to talk to his wife alone but thought better of it. He didn't want to close that door of opportunity before it ever opened. He said, "I will call you then."

"I'll have my secretary call you," Steve countered. "It will be easier that way. Just give her your card as you leave."

Jack was being dismissed. He thought of the young woman at the desk outside the office. When would she have time to call him? Jack pulled a card out where the governor could see it and started for the door. He turned back almost immediately. "I forgot to ask you about the necklace."

"What necklace?"

"The diamond necklace you gave Elizabeth her senior year," Jack clarified. "I need to know what it might have been worth."

"Detective, I loved my daughter," Steve said. "But, aside from my wife, I never bought diamonds for anyone."

34

"I really appreciate this," Officer Larry Kaninski said a second time.

"I can use the help," Jack nodded. It was much easier to get the almost retired policeman reassigned to him than he thought it would be. As it turned out the captain in charge of the file room was tired of the man. Apparently, Larry was a very forthright individual with a stubborn streak. He was quick to tell people what he thought, whether it was about them, about the job, or about the captain. And he refused to do things the way the captain wanted them done. So, when Jack asked about the possibility of borrowing the old man, the captain was very agreeable.

"You want him?" the captain asked, surprised. "He's yours. Forget procedure. I'll push the paperwork through."

Now, Jack sat at his desk with Larry positioned next to him, bent over to get a good look at the file Jack was examining. Now Jack would have to keep the officer from knowing he was juggling three cases, only one of which was his to investigate. One was even a closed case.

He had received a call from Shaun Travis, the officer working with Detective Peterson on Lisa Reagan's case. He told Jack that they found out Lisa had worked as a waitress in the evenings and had worked a shift the day she was killed. Peterson had no intention of interviewing the co-workers. Shaun was sure Jack would want to know and he was right. Jack intended to conduct the interviews his counterpart was ignoring. He was going to have to get rid of his new help in order to pursue the matter.

"How about that auto registration check?" Jack asked.

"Oh, right," Larry said. "All the cars registered to the chief."

"That's right," Jack nodded.

Larry stared at him for a moment and then chuckled subconsciously. "You are kidding aren't you?"

"No Larry, I'm not," Jack said. "I need you to run the check and get me the results without him knowing about it. I'm positive he's tracking everything I do. So I can't do it."

"Jack."

"You said you wanted to help," Jack said. "This will help."

"Help the investigation or some personal vendetta?" Larry asked.

Jack looked at him sharply. He gave thought to his words before speaking. "Listen. I need to clear up one question about the chief to put my mind at ease. Having that list will put my mind at ease."

"Are you saying the chief is a suspect?"

"No," Jack said. "I'm saying the list of his cars will either make him a suspect or remove him from my list of possibles."

"You're kidding me," Larry smiled.

"What are you smiling at?"

"I never liked Singleton," Larry said. "I'd love to see him hang for something."

"Well," Jack said. "We aren't hanging anybody. Just get the list. Then if you're bored, drive over to Timothy Waters' house and see if he goes anywhere tonight."

"I'm definitely bored," Larry smiled even broader. "I haven't been on a stakeout in years. God, I miss it. Should I report to you if something happens?"

"I have to be somewhere tonight," Jack said, remembering his meeting with his ex-wife. "Just give me a report in the morning. Along with the list of cars."

"Will do," Larry said.

"And Larry," Jack said. "If anything happens, do not intervene. Call backup if needed. Otherwise, we'll deal with it tomorrow."

"Don't worry about me, detective," Larry said. "I may be old, but I'm still a cop. I know how to weigh a situation."

"Sorry," Jack held up his hands. "I didn't mean to imply . . ."

"Don't worry about it, Jack," Larry said. "It takes a lot more than that to offend an old man like me. I'll see you in the morning."

Jack watched as Larry made his way through the desks to the stairway that would take him to the garage and his car. It was good to have someone in his corner, someone to help with all the necessary small details. But Larry was not someone to whom Jack was ready to confide everything. It was risky enough to have the policeman researching Terrance's autos. Telling him about all three cases was not an option. Not yet.

For now, he was on his way to The Super Bowl Bar and Grill. It was a sports bar that specialized in one-dish meals served in large bowls. The grill was a favorite among college kids, especially when any game was playing on the big screen televisions. It was not a favorite of Jack's, who preferred quiet nights in front of his own set at home. Most important, it was Lisa Reagan's place of employment, the last place she was seen publicly the night she was killed.

Jack arrived at the bar and grill as they were opening for lunch. An over-enthusiastic hostess asked how many were in his party and he flashed his badge and asked for the manager. She lost her enthusiasm and disappeared through the dining room in search of the manager. When she returned she informed Jack the manager would be out in a moment and asked him to step aside so she could seat real customers. Jack took a seat in the small row of chairs used by customers waiting for a table.

The manager appeared a moment later with a hesitant smile on his face. Jack rose to meet the outstretched hand belonging to a man no older than Lisa Reagan had been. Jeremy Ulman's jaw was clenched and he repeatedly scanned the faces of those who watched from a distance. Even as Jack explained the purpose of his visit, Jeremy seemed to be looking for a friend in those faces.

"Do you have a problem?" Jack snapped, pulling the man's attention to him. "Is there a reason I'm talking to the side of your head?"

"No. No," Jeremy assured him. "I'm just, well, you know."

"No, I don't know," Jack said. "Why don't you enlighten me?"

Jeremy glanced around again. Jack was about to lose it when the man turned back to face him muttering something about company policy.

"What are you talking about?" Jack asked. "What policy?"

"The one about dating employees," Jeremy whispered. "As a manager, I am not supposed to date employees."

"Why are you telling me?" Jack said. "I don't work for your company."

"Because," Jeremy whispered again, "I was dating Lisa Reagan."

Then Jack understood. It was not a friend Jeremy Ulman was looking for in those faces that were watching. He was looking for an enemy.

35

A half-hour later a disgruntled assistant restaurant manager entered the Super Bowl Bar and Grill. Jack flashed his badge in the man's face, saying he was going to be questioning Jeremy downtown and would be back to question others when he was finished. The assistant manager pointed out the time, that business would be rolling soon and Jack told him to be prepared to step in where needed. The assistant frowned but said nothing.

Jack took Jeremy to his car, sat him in the front seat and turned to face him. He stared at him a long time, knowing this would make the nervous man even more nervous.

"Aren't we going to go?" Jeremy croaked. He cleared his throat, embarrassed. He pointed out the windshield. "Downtown, I mean."

"No," Jack shook his head slightly. He couldn't risk Terrance finding out he was interviewing witnesses on Lisa's case. "We aren't going downtown."

There was a long silence and Jeremy shifted uncomfortably in his seat. His hands shook as he tried to find somewhere to put them, finally settling for locking his fingers together and placing his hands between his legs. He watched Jack while trying not to make eye contact. The detective watched him intently. He noted every drop of sweat and every twitch. When he was ready, Jack spoke low and calmly.

"What are those people in there going to tell me about you and Lisa Reagan when I start asking questions?" Jack gestured to the restaurant.

"I don't know," Jeremy said, his head bent down to his interlocked fingers.

"Then why don't you tell me before they do?" Jack said. "That way there'll be no confusion."

Jeremy nodded as if deciding he was doing the right thing. He adjusted his frame to face Jack, giving one last glance at the building behind him before speaking.

"Let me start by saying I didn't kill Lisa," Jeremy said.

"Never said you did," Jack pointed out. "Is there a reason I should think you did?"

"No," Jeremy said. "I just wanted to get that out. You know. Before everything else came out."

"Everything else?" Jack asked.

"About me and Lisa," Jeremy explained.

"Tell me about your relationship," Jack said. "Why is it her father didn't seem to know about you?"

"No one was supposed to know," Jeremy said. "It is . . . "

"Company policy," Jack finished. "You mentioned that. So, if it was against company policy and you are obviously concerned, why did you date her?"

"Are you kidding?" Jeremy said, smiling honestly for the first time. "If you ever met her, you wouldn't have to ask that."

Jack thought back to the young girl cradled in Charles Reagan's arms ten years ago. Jack remembered noticing even then how beautiful the girl was, how much she looked like the photographs of her mother. It was easy to see why a young man might want to risk a lot to spend a little time with her.

"What was she like?" Jack asked. "Lisa Reagan the person. I know her father, but I never really knew her. What kind of person was she like?"

When Jeremy spoke of Lisa, he talked about a woman full of life. He spoke of a woman of intelligence and spirit. She was contagiously happy and was always planning for the future. She was ready to meet life head on and go wherever it might take her. As Jeremy described the woman Lisa Reagan was, Jack did not envision Lisa Reagan's face. He saw Kathy, his ex-wife.

Jeremy finished and sat looking at Jack expectantly. Jack studied the young man's face and replayed the words in his mind. He compared the words to those Timothy Waters used to describe Elizabeth Mitchell. They could have easily been the same. If not for the twenty-year span, they could have been the same person.

"When did things change?" Jack asked.

The smile, ever present while Jeremy talked about Lisa, faltered. Jack had not been sure, only playing a hunch, until he saw the waver in Jeremy's eyes. Jack leaned in.

"When did things change?" he repeated.

"It wasn't like things changed," Jeremy said.

"Something changed," Jack insisted. "What was it?"

"It wasn't what," Jeremy sighed. "It was who."

"Who?" Jack questioned.

"Yeah," Jeremy nodded. "Who."

"Explain," Jack pressed.

"Well this guy showed up at the restaurant one night," Jeremy said. "He asked to be seated in Lisa's section. Then while she's waiting on him, he tells her that he used to know her mother."

"Lisa's mother?"

"Right," Jeremy nodded. "Of course, Lisa's skeptical because her mom was killed a few years back. So, the guy tells her some things about her mom and proves he knew her. Lisa asks how he knew she was at the restaurant and he tells her he's been keeping an eye on her. That freaks her out. This guy could be some kind of nut. Then he drops it on her."

"Drops what on her?" Jack asked.

"He looks her in the eye and tells her that he is her father," Jeremy said. "Says he got her mother pregnant when she was in high school and she left town. He spent all these years looking for Lisa, his long lost daughter."

"I thought he had been keeping an eye on her," Jack said.

Jeremy stopped, thought about it and said, "He did, didn't he?"

"What did he look like?" Jack asked.

"I never saw him," Jeremy shrugged. "The first time he came in, I was off. Lisa told me about it later. Other times, she never mentioned he was there until he was already gone. I tried to watch and see who she talked to but couldn't ever tell if it was him."

"He came in more than once?"

"He would come in from time to time and they would talk," Jeremy said with less enthusiasm. "She started having less and less time for me. We still saw each other every once in a while, but she was busy a lot."

"Any reason why?"

Jeremy held his fingers up like quotation marks. "She was getting to know her father, she said."

"Was she getting to know her father the night she was killed?" Jack asked.

Jeremy's eyes widened as if everything suddenly made sense. He started nodding slowly. "You don't think he was her father do you?"

"I don't know," Jack said. "But I'm reasonably sure getting to know him was not the best thing for Lisa."

36

None of Lisa's other co-workers could add anything to Jeremy's story. Most did not know Lisa was dating anyone. The few that suspected something between Lisa and the manager did not have first-hand knowledge, only gut feelings. As for the stranger who asked to be seated in Lisa's section, only a couple of the waitresses saw him, but neither had seen him for some time. They both described him, but the descriptions did not match one another. By the time Jack left the restaurant the evening crowd was starting to pour in and time was getting short for Jack to make his appointment with Kathy.

His ex-wife still lived in the house they had selected together when times between them were still good. He had liked the large family room where he planned to spend many relaxing days, she had liked the huge walk-in closets she planned to fill with as many clothes as was humanly possible. Today, the family room was mostly bare as the only furniture Jack took with him when he moved out came from that room. Though he could not see the closets, he knew they were no fuller than the day he left. Kathy lost her joy of shopping somewhere along the way.

They stood in the living room in awkward silence. There was a grin on Kathy's face that suggested a mixture of confusion and uncertainty. Jack slid his hands into his pockets, pulled them out and rested them on his hips then finally locking them behind his back.

"Can I get you a drink, Jack?" Kathy asked, already moving to the small table that served as her liquor cabinet. "I have some bourbon here."

"That would be great," he said to her back. There was something different about her. The way she moved, the way she acted. He could be imagining it but he didn't think so. She was different.

"I want to thank you for coming," she said, handing Jack the drink she had poured. She held her own drink close to her chest, moving it only to take occasional sips.

"I told you I would always be here for you," Jack smiled sheepishly. "So, here I am. What is it you want to talk about?"

She didn't say anything at first. She smiled at him warmly and stood silent as if gathering her thoughts. When she seemed satisfied, she tilted her head and asked, "Jack, do you remember the vacation we took our third year of marriage?"

It was Jack's turn to stand in awkward silence. Of all the things he had thought she might want to discuss, this had not made the list. He had not thought of that time in their lives in ages. He opened the floodgates and let the memories come. Jack nodded his head. "Sure. Florida. We spent a week walking up and down the coast searching for seashells and drinking cute little drinks with fruit and umbrellas in them."

Kathy's smile broadened and she moved to the couch where she sat in the corner pulling her knees up to her chest. She rested her chin on her knee. "Remember the waiter at that beachfront bar? The one from Jamaica or somewhere like that?"

"You mean 'Whut ken uh gechya?'", Jack laughed.

"That's him," she laughed. "That was the best week."

"It was, wasn't it?" Jack agreed.

"I think about it all the time," Kathy said.

"Really?"

"Jack?"

"Yes?"

"I need new memories," she said, her smile fading to something sadder.

"New memories?" Jack asked. "I don't follow."

"I need to do something different," she said focusing on her glass. "I need to make a change. It's been two years."

"What are you saying, Kathy?" Jack tried to catch her gaze but she looked away. "You want to take another vacation?"

"No, Jack," she looked at him finally. "I've met someone. He's a nice man. He's around when I . . . I mean he has a normal . . . Oh, Jack."

"He's not a cop," Jack clarified. He set his drink down. "I guess I should be going."

"Jack," she said.

"Listen," Jack turned to her. "We aren't together anymore. I knew someday this was going to happen. You'd move on without me. You don't have to explain. We were good once. That was a long time ago. You deserve something better."

"Jack," she said again. "You know I love you, Jack. But I need someone who is there. I need to give this a chance."

"Don't worry about it, Kathy," Jack said. "It isn't like I haven't been on a date or two myself."

She appeared hurt for a second, but it faded quickly. She rose from the couch and stepped toward him. He did not move so she wrapped her arms around his chest and hugged him. He let his arms envelop her and hugged her back. They stayed like that for what seemed like a lifetime before moving apart. He walked to the front door and she followed him a couple paces behind.

From his car, he looked back at the woman he had once planned to grow old with. She leaned into the open doorway with her hands pushed into the pockets of her pale blue jeans. He once promised to always be there for her. He never imagined a time would come when she wouldn't need him.

37

Larry Kaninski was sixty-one years old, too young to retire but far too old to be pulling sixteen-hour days. His wife of thirty-eight years was furious with him for agreeing to stake out Timothy Waters' house, furious with Jack for asking him to do it, and furious with the bag boy down at the grocer for not putting her eggs in her sack when she checked out. To Larry, furious, not just angry, was his wife's normal state. So the opportunity to spend a quiet evening sitting in his car was not an assignment, it was appealing.

It had not always been like that. For years he and Rhonda had been the happiest couple on earth. He couldn't wait to get home from work. She couldn't wait for him to walk through the door. Even when they found the sickness that would someday take her from him, they were of high hope. They went through the first round of treatments side by side. They would fight it to the end. The second round of treatment was harder but they still thought they could win. By the third round it was obvious they were losing the battle and Rhonda was losing her mind. Not insane. She simply wasn't herself anymore. She slipped into this other, bitter woman. At first Larry thought she was simply giving up and taking it out on him and the world. When the doctors told him that wasn't the case, that the illness had reached her brain and was causing the changes in her personality he was glad to know she had not given up. But on that same day, he did. He could not fight anymore. Instead, he fell into a mode of taking care of her the best he could and waiting.

That was when he began to show his age. He could no longer keep up with his partner and declared himself unfit for the streets. His partner, who knew Larry and Rhonda's history, understood and helped him with the transition. What Larry didn't know was how stir-crazy he was going to get sitting in that cage every day. He wanted to work and was very happy to have the chance to do just that.

On the passenger seat next to a ham and cheese sandwich he had made in case he got hungry was a manila folder containing the information the DMV gave him on Singleton's cars. Larry was proud of himself for getting the list and he was excited to talk to Jack about what he had learned. Unfortunately, Jack had his meeting and Larry had his stakeout so that conversation would have to wait until morning. He hoped, after staying up late, he didn't oversleep in the morning.

It wouldn't be so bad if something would happen. He had been sitting in his car watching the Waters' house for over two hours and in all that time nothing changed. The lights that were on remained on and the lights that were off remained off. It was as if there was no one home. But there was a car in the drive and Larry had a sense that there was someone in the old house.

He wasn't sure how long he should wait before calling it a night. He wished he had asked Jack before. There really wasn't much point in watching if no one ever appeared in his line of vision. It was easy to assume, then, that there would be some sign that it was time to go. Observe the man come home and all the lights go dark and you can say he's in for the night and go. Observe him come out and follow him to some unknown location where he commits a crime, then call in backup. But sitting and staring at a house that may or may not be empty, when do you say enough is enough?

He reached for the sandwich, laying it gently on his lap. He unfolded the foil he had carefully wrapped it in earlier. He flattened the corners of the foil one at a time until he was satisfied they would not curl back up to scratch his hands while he ate. He took a large bite and chewed. For thirty-six years his wife had made his lunches. This sandwich he made himself. It just wasn't the same. Wasn't the same at all.

He thought he saw a shadow cross one of the windows. Setting the sandwich back on the foil and slipping it over to the passenger seat, he took a pair of binoculars he had brought for just this purpose and focused them on the house. The dimly lit window grew inside the lenses of the binoculars and Larry could see the shade was pulled. Any shadow he would have seen would have been someone walking between the window and whatever light source was on inside. He watched intently for a moment and, seeing nothing, scanned the other windows of the house. Each time he came to one with the shade not drawn, he tried to focus the lenses inside the dark house. Nothing was moving and he began to question whether he had seen anything or if his mind was playing tricks on him.

He put the binoculars down and picked up his sandwich again. He took a large bite, savoring the flavor. He took a drink of the soda he brought along. It was warm but still tasted good. He figured part of the reason everything tasted so good was because he was happy to be on the street again. Being locked up in that cage had dulled his senses.

He watched the house as he took his next bite, and again saw something. He brought the binoculars up to his eyes and focused on the same window he thought he had seen a shadow before. This time, as the view in the lenses sharpened, he had the answer he had been trying to get since his arrival. The shade was open, the room was visible and Larry could see an elderly woman sitting in a cushioned chair. She wore a pair of glasses and her head was bent to a book she held in her hands. Had she opened the shade or had her son done it? He cursed himself for not keeping a better watch.

He tried the other windows again, searching each with newfound enthusiasm. He was determined to know if Timothy Waters was in the house before calling it a night. He wanted something to report to Jack. He did not want to go into the office and tell him he watched the house all night and had no idea if the suspect was even inside. The other windows produced nothing new and Larry refocused on the reading woman.

He would watch her, he concluded. At some point, if Timothy were in the house, she would surely say something to him. So he settled back with the binoculars trained on the woman's face. He reached blindly for his sandwich so he could eat while he watched. It was in that moment, with the binoculars in one hand and his sandwich in the other, he heard the crack behind him. Just outside his open window, it was like a twig breaking beneath the weight of someone's foot.

38

The bars closed early that night. At least that was the way Jack saw it when the bartender told him he would have to go. Last call had gone by unnoticed by Jack who cursed under his breath, paid his tab and staggered out the door. Only a couple of blocks from his place, he was glad he left his car at home because as tired as he was he would have been very tempted to try to drive.

He had known the time would come when Kathy would want to remarry and start a family, maybe have a couple of kids. It was what she wanted from the very beginning before his career started getting in the way. He had known she would not sit alone in that house forever. But somehow he wasn't ready to hear it. He wasn't ready to give up. He had hoped when the time came, it would be him she remarried.

A couple of teens drove by, honked their horn and yelled at him. He could hear them laughing above the roar of the engine long after they had disappeared. Laughing at him. Everyone would be laughing at him soon enough when they learned that he just sat there as the greatest woman he ever met rode off into the sunset with . . .

She had only said he wasn't a cop. She never told him what the man did for a living. A normal man. Oh God, if he was a defense attorney Jack might have to shoot himself. But then, she tried to stay away from legal types after they separated. Too many of them knew Jack. No, it wasn't a lawyer.

What kind of man would Kathy consider normal? In his line of work, he came across all types of people in all types of professions. Unfortunately, not many could be classified as normal. To Jack there was no 'normal' anymore, just different degrees of abnormal. The last man he knew who he would consider being normal was his own father.

Michael T. Mallory worked Monday to Friday from eight-thirty to five. He came home every day and took a half-hour nap before dinner. He ate methodically and spoke to Jack's mother only briefly about his day. He said little to Jack and Jack said little in return. While Jack was away at college, he received a call from his mother. Mike Mallory had a heart attack at his office and died at the age of forty-eight.

It was the funeral that surprised Jack more than anything else in his life. Over five hundred people showed up to give their last respects for his father. There were so many flowers Jack and his mother donated most of them to the church. Enough people brought food to the house they could have eaten for an entire year. Most of it went to a homeless shelter in town. With him away at school there was no way his mother could have eaten it.

To this day, he had no idea why so many people came to the funeral. He did not know most of the people. Did not know where his father would have met them. Jack guessed they had come from his office. A very large office, indeed. He smiled a bit. There were two things he always intended to ask his mother before she passed away but never did; what his father did for a living and what the T. in his name stood for. Someday, he supposed, he would have to use his skills as a detective to find the answers to both those questions.

His apartment complex stood in the center of a long street in a light commercial district. Even at the late hour there were quite a few people out. Cars raced by and he ignored them. Most of the pedestrians gave him a wide birth not wanting to antagonize a man of his size and obvious foul mood.

So, it was to his amazement when he approached the entrance to his apartment complex that a group of Hispanic teens stepped to block his path. He stopped and looked into the five young faces, each looking back at him with a combination of anger and boredom. He showed his badge and a couple of them allowed fear to slip into their expressions but they did not back down. Jack focused on the one he determined to be the leader.

"I suggest you all leave while I still have time to forget your faces," he said.

"We'll leave," the leader said in a thick south of the border accent. "But first, you'll give us your money."

"We can't mug a cop, man," one of the boys said.

"I'd listen to your friend," Jack said, never taking his eyes from the leader's. "You mug a cop, you think everyone's going to forget about it?"

"Just shut up and give me your money," the leader said. "I ain't afraid of you. You're drunk. I can smell you from here."

"Okay, then," Jack held his hands up. "I'll give you my money, then you go."

"Yeah, okay," the leader said.

Jack nodded to indicate a point beyond the boys. "Is he with you?"

The boys turned to look at the darkened shadows under the trees that made up the small courtyard in front of Jack's apartment. There was no one there. They turned back to face Jack's pistol. Jack held it to the leader's head. One of the boys turned and ran.

"How fast can you run?" Jack asked the leader. The remaining four boys turned and ran as fast as they could. Jack watched them to be sure they did not return. He put his weapon away and continued his walk home. He struggled with the lock on his door before finally gaining entry. He slid the deadbolt on the door in case the boys had followed him home with plans of revenge. He left the lights off, preferring to feel his way to his room in the dark. The only glow was the light on the microwave.

He pulled his phone out of his pocket and set it on the counter, noticing that there were two notifications of missed calls and messages. He hadn't realized the bar had been loud enough for him to miss the ringing.

Pressing the play button on the first message it began with a period of silence before Kathy's voice came over the small speaker. He was not ready for a pity speech or apology or whatever she might be calling for. He hit the stop button and made his way to his room. He took his jacket off and tossed it over a chair. He kicked his shoes against the wall then let his body fall onto the bed fully clothed. The next time he opened his eyes, it was morning.

39

Jack heard screaming and bolted upright in bed. His head spun and the light from his window caused his eyes to shrink into their sockets. What he thought had been screaming he quickly identified as his phone. The clock told him it was after ten and he moaned. He rolled to the edge of the bed and answered the phone.

"Mallory," he said in a low hoarse voice. He examined his wrinkled clothing and grimaced. He did not remember walking home the night before. The altercation with the teens was forgotten.

"Jack?" Kelly asked. "You okay?"

"Yes, Kelly," Jack said. "I'm fine. What's up?"

"You need to get in here, Jack," she said. "He's talking about having your badge."

"That's new," Jack said. "Tell him I woke up sick but will be there soon."

"If I tell him that," Kelly said, "you better look sick when you get here."

"That shouldn't be a problem," Jack said examining himself in a mirror. "Nope. No problem at all."

He stood, swayed and caught hold of the chest of drawers in time to keep from falling. He steadied himself before walking to the bathroom, stripping off his clothes as he went. After a quick shower he started feeling half human again. As he stepped out of his apartment, his phone rang again. He hesitated, not recognizing the number. He was going to let it go to voice mail, but answered at the last moment.

"Mallory," he said flatly.

"Mallory, where have you been?" the man said. "I called you last night. Left a message."

The memory of two messages on his phone came back to him. The first had been Kathy and he had not listened to the other.

Apparently he should have. As that sank in, it occurred to him he didn't know who he was talking to.

"Who is this?" he voiced his thought.

"It's Officer Travis," Shaun said.

"Shaun," Jack said. "I wanted to thank you for the information on Lisa Reagan's place of employment. I learned a lot."

"Well, that's good but that's not why I called," Shaun said. "Was Kaninski working for you?"

"What do you mean?" Jack asked.

"Larry was shot last night," Shaun said. "I was pulled off the Lisa Reagan case to work on Larry's."

"He's dead?" Jack asked.

"Sorry, Jack," Shaun said. "I need to get some information about what he was doing for you."

"Who's the lead on this?" Jack asked.

"I am," Shaun said.

"You?" Jack raised his voice. "You aren't even a detective."

"I know," Shaun agreed. "But I can handle this."

"Where was he shot?" Jack demanded.

"He was in his car," Shaun answered. After a pause, he gave Jack the address.

"Shit," Jack exclaimed. "Water's house."

"What?"

"Never mind," Jack said. "I have to go to the office. I'll talk to you later."

"Jack," Shaun said. "If you know something you have to tell me."

"Shaun," Jack said. "I'm really not in the mood. I'll talk to you when I'm ready."

He hung up and jogged to his car. He had an idea now why Terrance wanted to see him. He obviously learned about Larry and was ready to blame Jack for the whole mess. Had Terrance found out Larry had checked into his auto registrations?

Larry was killed outside Timothy Water's house. Timothy had opportunity and motive. But Jack didn't think the man would be stupid enough to kill a cop and leave the body in the vicinity of his house. It wasn't the best neighborhood. Thirty years ago it was home to poor families who managed to scrape up a loan for a small house. Now it was mostly elderly couples trying to hold on to what they had. The houses were aging, in need of new roofs and paint.

The youth in the area were up to no good because the residents couldn't do anything to stop them. It wasn't uncommon for the police to make drug arrests on the same street where the Waters' lived. A dealer, seeing Larry camping out in his car, could have gotten nervous and decided to be proactive. Jack wanted to delve into the details, knowing he already had too much on his hands.

The station was unusually silent as it always was after one of their own was killed. No one spoke to Jack as he made his way up to Terrance's office. When he reached the outer office Kelly started to say something but Jack raised a hand to stop her, moving quickly past her to the door to the inner office. She rose from her seat trying to protest but it was too late. He opened the door fast and pushed it open hard enough for it to bounce off the wall before swinging back closed. Terrance, already on his feet, turned sharply to the intruder.

"Jack . . ." he started in his attack tone.

"What the hell is going on, Terrance?" Jack demanded.

Confused, Terrance cocked his head to one side. "Who gave you the authority to change a man's assignment? An assignment that got him killed."

"His captain authorized it," Jack snapped. "Now, tell me what you're up to."

"You're lucky I don't take your badge," Terrance yelled. "You got one of my men killed, Jack. You're the one who should be explaining what you're up to. Can you do that? Can you explain to me why you got one of my men killed?"

"Like you care," Jack snapped. "It's like you don't want these cases solved."

"What are you talking about?" Terrance said. "I want them solved. And it would help if you would finish yours instead of creating new ones. They tell me Kaninski was killed in front of Waters' house. I want him for this one and for Elizabeth Mitchell. Get me the evidence, Jack."

"You put Bret on Lisa Reagan's case and now Shaun Travis on Larry's case," Jack argued. "You can't tell me an idiot and a green uniformed officer are going to solve these cases."

"I assign who I've got where I need them," Terrance said. "They'll get what they can."

"He was a cop," Jack snapped. "What they can isn't good enough."

"He was an off-duty cop," Terrance said. "He gets Travis."

"Off duty?" The blood began throbbing in Jack's temples. "He wasn't off duty. He was on a stakeout."

"He wasn't authorized to be there." An air of authority came to Terrance's voice.

"Wasn't authorized?" Anger came to Jack's. "I authorized him."

"And you weren't authorized to assign him," Terrance said.

"Don't you pull that crap," Jack lowered his voice to a threatening tone. "You know he was on duty. You know his wife qualifies for the benefits due to the widow of a cop killed on duty. You can't deny her that."

"I can and I will, Jack," Terrance said. "That's all there is to it."

"I'll let the press know how you're treating a fallen officer," Jack said.

"And I'll let them know you sent Kaninski on a stakeout he was too old and too out of shape to handle," Terrance said. "You got him killed so you could go see your old lady."

Jack was about to attack Terrance on his moral standing. He was about to tear into the man for his ineffective handling of his position. Then it clicked in his mind what Terrance said. "What did you just say?"

"You got Kaninski killed," Terrance said.

"How did you know I was meeting with Kathy last night?" Jack asked.

"I didn't," Terrance said firmly, but his eyes were swimming as though he was trying to remember what he had said.

"You said I got him killed so I could see my old lady," Jack reminded him. "How do you know where I was last night?"

"You must have mentioned it," Terrance insisted.

"No," Jack shook his head. "I didn't tell anyone about that. You're having me followed aren't you?"

"Don't be ridiculous," Terrance dismissed the accusation. "Why would I have you followed?"

"I don't know," Jack admitted. "But I intend to find out."

"It's going to be hard for you to find out why I'm doing something I'm not even doing," Terrance said. "Maybe I should have your badge."

"Take it and the press gets everything," Jack said.

"Gets everything?" Terrance said. "What, Jack? What are you going to give them?"

"Try me," Jack said and started out of the office.

"Jack," Terrance called after him.

The detective hesitated, wanting to continue out of the room but something in the way Terrance called his name made him turn back. When he did the chief was standing behind his desk, a yellow folder held in his hand for Jack to see. The folder was covered with a dark spray pattern as if someone had splattered juice on it. It wasn't juice. It was Larry's blood.

"What is this, Jack?"

"A folder, Terrance," There was venom in Jack's voice now.

"Not any folder, Jack," Terrance said. "The folder from Kaninski's front seat when he was killed. Do you know what's inside?"

"Cut the crap, Terrance," Jack said walking up to the desk with his hand outstretched. The chief put the folder in Jack's hand and Jack took it from him. He opened it and studied the single page inside. At the top was Terrance Singleton's name. Below it was a list of four vehicles registered to the chief. They included the Mercedes E 350 the chief drove, Heather's BMW 540i, a GMC SUV and a boat trailer. Jack stared at the list, not at what was there but rather at what was not there. There was no sports car of any kind, new or old. To Terrance, he said, "Shouldn't this be in evidence?"

"No, it shouldn't be in evidence," Terrance yelled. "I had it brushed for prints. That's all that was needed. But tell me something, Jack. Why did Kaninski have a list of my registered vehicles in his car?"

"I was following a hunch," Jack said.

"A hunch?" Terrance repeated. "About me and my cars?"

"You know me, Terrance," Jack shrugged.

"Yes, Jack," Terrance lowered his voice so Jack had to strain to hear him. "I know you. And I know what you're up to. Now that you've gotten one of our officers killed, I suggest you stop playing around and get some evidence on Timothy Waters. Put him away before he kills another cop."

"You think he killed Larry?"

"Get me the evidence," Terrance repeated the order.

Jack started to argue, thought better of it and turned away from the chief. He walked to the door, turned the knob and pulled to reveal Kelly sitting at her desk. Before letting the door close behind him he called back to Terrance. "Did the governor own a sports car twenty years ago?"

"Get out of here," Terrance yelled. Jack let the door shut.

40

Detective Bret Peterson hated Jack Mallory. It wasn't a disliking of the man. It was pure hate with every ounce of his being. In his mind this was not a petty thing or irrational at all. To Bret, hating Jack was as natural as, well, breathing.

It started years ago when Jack joined the force. Bret had donned his badge three years prior to Jack, but in the field Jack showed promise. Jack had a natural talent for reading scenes and gathering information, something Bret had to work at and still didn't get right more often than he did. On more than one occasion Bret found himself taking a backseat to this younger, less experienced officer. In the end Jack made detective four years before Bret. His resentment of Jack ran very, very deep.

It was a source of satisfaction when the chief took the Lisa Reagan case from Jack and gave it to him. Jack was so possessive with his cases. And to give Elizabeth Mitchell's case to him was icing. He loved watching Jack getting frustrated and right now the detective was as frustrated as Bret had ever seen him.

But then, the Kaninski case came up. Bret was furious that such a high-profile case was given to Officer Travis. Bret was the first on the scene. That alone made the case his. And second, Shaun was still in uniform and supposed to be helping with the Reagan case. He didn't need help but it was nice having someone to do all the footwork for him. After all, he had a lot to do. He didn't have time to interview all the people connected to the case. Even worse was the fact that he would be obligated to watch over Shaun's progress on his investigation.

Bret pulled into a diner and looked around before going inside. Sitting in a booth toward the back, he ordered the meatloaf platter and a cup of coffee. When the coffee came he used sugar and cream to turn it to a light shade of brown before drinking the sweet liquid. Waiting for his lunch he sat with his head resting in the palms

158

of his hands. He stayed like that thinking about what he would be doing that afternoon to fill his time. He would have to go back to Lisa's apartment building and interview a couple of her neighbors he missed the first time. And there were a couple of errands he would need to attend to. It was going to be a late day. He really wished Shaun could handle the interviews.

The waitress set his meal in front of him and he did not acknowledge her. He started in, eating quickly as he had learned to do while living in a household with a father who could become violent at the flip of a switch. He was oblivious to his surroundings, so it was a surprise to look up and see a man standing in the aisle pointing a gun across the counter at the cashier. The man was demanding money, promising to shoot if they did not comply. A moment later the filthy man was gone, carrying a to-go bag full of bills and change. Bret finished the last few bites of his meal and laid a ten on his table. It was enough to cover the bill, no tip. Casually, he left the diner before the squad car arrived. He was a homicide detective. He didn't have time to deal with robberies.

41

Jack's phone rang and he pulled it out to answer. He checked the screen and saw that the number was blocked like so many of the county numbers were.

"Mallory," he answered.

"Detective Mallory," the man said. "This is Warden Finnegan at the prison."

"Yes, sir," Jack said. "What can I do for you?"

"You came to visit one of my prisoners a few days ago," the warden said.

"Stuart Landerburg," Jack confirmed. The man convicted of killing Tracy Reagan. Jack was convinced now that he had not committed the crime and knew who did. But he wouldn't come clean during the interview. Was he having a change of heart? "Does he have more to say?"

"Afraid not," the warden said. "Landerburg was stabbed to death last night."

"He what?" Jack said. The last thing Landerburg said to Jack was about his fear of upsetting the real killer. "How did it happen?"

"I was hoping you could tell me," he said. "You came to talk to him. The next day we get a court order to give the man some added privileges. Made it look like he was getting favors for cooperating."

"What kind of favors?" Jack asked.

"More yard time," the warden said. "Common room time. Library privileges. All areas that gave him more exposure to the general population."

"You think it got him killed?"

"That's exactly how it happened," the warden said. "Some of the prisoners staged a disturbance and when it was over we found Landerburg dead in the back of the library. Was hoping you could tell us who he ratted on so we could narrow down the suspect list."

"He didn't rat on anyone," Jack said. "Didn't give me a name. Didn't give me anything. I didn't request anything for him."

"Really?" the warden said. "With the timing I thought for sure it was you."

"Sorry I can't help," Jack said.

"No problem, detective," the warden said. "We'll just have to find his killer the hard way. Thanks for your time."

"Oh, warden," Jack said. "What judge issued the order? I could ask him who requested it for you."

"That would be good of you detective," the warden said. "Just a second. I have it right here. Oh, yes. Here it is. A Judge Paul Watson. Do you know him?"

"Yes, sir, I do." It was Terrance Singleton's brother-in-law.

42

Officer Shaun Travis joined the police department six years ago with the idea that he would be chasing bad guys and following clues to apprehend criminals. He spent the first five and a half years of his career writing speeding tickets and directing traffic. Occasionally he would be called to a domestic violence or public intoxication, but generally he did very little of what he always hoped he would be doing. About six months ago, after repeated requests, he was assigned to work with a detective, to learn the ropes. Unfortunately that detective was Bret Peterson, the laziest detective Shaun could remember ever meeting. The man did absolutely nothing. He sent Shaun out to do his work without direction. Shaun struggled to do what needed to be done without messing things up. His only learning was what he taught himself through doing, and through the mistakes he made.

He wanted to learn as much as he could so he would have enough knowledge to succeed if ever given the chance to do so. He wanted to be ready to take on his first solo case and prove himself to everyone. What he didn't count on was that his first opportunity, his first solo case, would come far sooner than anticipated. He wasn't ready. But the worst part of the whole arrangement was the case. Larry Kaninski was someone he had known, a fellow officer and a good man. He wanted the killer caught more than anything but he was sure he wasn't the man for the job. Some day he would be, but not now, not today.

In spite of his doubts, he stood in the garage staring at Larry Kaninski's car where the lab had put it after they were finished with their examination. The doors were covered with a fine powder where they had dusted for prints. There were two wooden poles about the thickness of pencils protruding from the seat to show the trajectory of the bullets that killed the officer. The sight, with the darkened cloth of the seats where Larry's blood had stained them, was depressing.

Shaun stood next to the car slightly forward of the driver's seat where the strings and rods left by the crime lab showed where the shooter must have stood. He shaped his hand like a gun and pointed it through the open window. He stood like that, staring for a long moment. He stood. He stared. And he frowned.

The bullets that had taken Larry Kaninski's life passed through his chest and into the seat behind him. That meant the killer was standing in Larry's full view when they shot him. Larry's service revolver was still in its holster when he was found. How does a seasoned veteran cop let a killer walk up and shoot him without trying to defend himself? It was true he was watching the Water's house and it would not be too difficult to get close to a man looking through a pair of binoculars. But the binoculars sat on the dash of the car. If he were looking through them when he was killed they would have been found in his lap or possibly even on the floorboard. It was unlikely Larry would take a bullet to the chest then reach up to set the binoculars on the dash. If he could do that he would have dropped them and gone for his gun.

So the killer was standing in front of his victim and there was no sign of any attempt to defend against the attack. Either the killer was very good and Larry had no time to respond, or the killer was someone Larry did not see as a threat. The former was possible because of Larry's age and the fact he had spent the last several months pulling light duty in the records room. The latter was enough to send a chill up Shaun's spine. For Larry not to recognize the man who approached him as a threat in Waters' neighborhood would almost have to mean Larry knew the man.

A 9-1-1 call alerted police of shots fired and a possible homicide. Detective Peterson was the first on scene. He had been listening to his scanner when the call came in and happened to be nearby. According to him, Larry was dead when he arrived and there was no sign of anyone else. There were no shell casings on the ground near the car. Either a revolver was used or the killer cleaned up after himself. Shaun cringed at the thought of a man standing in the middle of the street and shooting someone, then taking the time to find and pick up the shell casings. Could anyone be that brazen?

Bret's theory was that Timothy Waters exited his house through the back, shot Larry and returned to the house. Shaun's problem with that scenario was that there was no way Larry would have let the suspect get that close to him. Also, Timothy would have to climb over two fences without alerting the neighbors. And he would have to return the way he came or chance being seen entering his house after the shooting. Last, there was the 911 call. The records show that the call was placed from the Waters' house. The woman who placed the call could only be Timothy's mother, and bad or not, she wouldn't turn in her own son.

But if it wasn't Timothy, what was the motive? It wasn't robbery. Nothing was taken from the scene. Even if they panicked when they found out they had just killed a cop, they would have taken his gun. It was too valuable on the street not to. There were no signs that Larry's body was even touched let alone searched. The killer shot him and left. Shaun hoped it wasn't anything as simplistic as a random act of violence with no motive. Cases like that were nearly impossible to solve.

His phone rang and Shaun pulled it out to answer.

"Can you talk?" the voice asked.

"What?" he responded.

"Can you talk?" the voice repeated. "Are you alone?"

"Yeah," Shaun said. "Who is this?"

"It's Mallory," Jack said. "You're working Larry's case."

"Yeah," Shaun confirmed. "Just started."

"What have you got?" Jack asked. And Shaun told him.

43

Terrance held the folder in his hand a long time after Jack left before finally letting it tip down and fall into his trash can. He did not have it dusted for prints as he told Jack. He probably should have, if for no other reason than to find out what moron in the D.M.V. gave out his information. He really couldn't understand what relevance the cars he owned now would have on Elizabeth Mitchell's murder. It would make more sense to know what cars he owned twenty years ago. But those records were lost years ago.

He couldn't believe Jack asked him if the governor owned a sports car at the time of Beth's death. It was definitely not the kind of thing he wanted Jack doing. His resolve to keep Jack away from Steven was strengthened. Terrance had promised the governor he would see Timothy Waters back in prison. Asking questions like that might make Steven wonder if there were suspects other than Waters. Terrance wasn't in the mood to start answering questions about the investigation. Especially when he couldn't get Jack to tell him what he's up to.

The phone buzzed indicating Kelly needed him. He reached across the desk and pushed the flashing button.

"What is it, Kelly?"

"Your wife is here," she said.

Terrance let out an exasperated sigh. Heather was not what he needed right now. He considered sending her away but that would only delay things.

He pushed the button again, saying in a defeated tone, "Send her in."

A moment later the door opened and Heather pushed her way into the office. She sneered at Terrance before closing the door behind her. Crossing the room she sat in one of the chairs across from her husband, crossing her long legs.

"And to what do I owe this pleasure?" he asked.

"Cut the crap, Terrance," Heather said. "You know why I'm here."

"I didn't even know you were coming," he corrected. "How in the world would I know why you were here?"

"A big, important detective like yourself should be able to figure it out," Heather feigned awe.

"I'm not a detective," Terrance said.

"I've heard that before," Heather's lips curled into a devious grin.

"Do you need something or did you just come to piss me off?" Terrance asked.

"Oh, no," Heather said. "The pissing off is a benefit. I actually do need something."

Terrance waited a moment, then said, "Well, what is it?"

"I was thinking," Heather uncrossed and recrossed her legs. "Fact is, I'm not getting any younger."

"You came down here to tell me that?"

"God knows you aren't getting any younger," she added.

"What does any of this have to do with anything?"

"It occurred to me that someday you are going to actually get old." She spoke as though she was discussing the upcoming weather.

"Heather," Terrance said. "Will you get to the point? Please?"

"Someday you are going to retire," she continued. "Someday you won't have a job to come to every day."

"That's a long time off, Heather," Terrance said. "Right now I wouldn't bet on me living long enough to retire. You and this place are killing me."

"We can only hope," Heather said. "But the fact remains that if you do live long enough, you will have to retire someday."

"Yes," Terrance agreed. "Someday, very far away, I will have to retire. I don't see why you care. Someday. Who cares about someday? What is it you want, Heather? Tell me so you can leave and I can get back to work."

"How can you not care about the future?" Heather asked, sincerely confused.

"I gave up caring about the future a long time ago," Terrance said. "You took care of that for me."

"You can't blame me for your mistakes," Heather snapped, a burst of anger that surprised and relieved Terrance. It was more what he was used to.

"What do you want?"

"When you retire, you are going to be at home more," Heather said. "Sure you'll find things to do, things to get you out of the house. But the fact is you will be home more."

"So?"

"So," Heather said. "When that day comes I don't want to be there."

"And?"

"And," Heather said. "I think it's time we got a divorce."

44

With the Waters' house to his back, Jack stood on the porch looking across the street to where Larry's car was parked when he was killed. Shaun stood next to him pressing the doorbell every couple of minutes. No one came to the door. Shaun opened the screen door and stepped inside its swing radius to prevent it from closing. As he did, Jack spun around with his hand balled in a tight fist and hammered on the door. The sound was solid and loud. Shaun thought he heard wood crack in the frame or maybe the door itself.

A moment later the door opened and an angry Timothy Waters stood inside looking out at them. Recognition of Jack did not lessen the tension in his muscular body. He demanded, "What are you doing?"

"We rang the bell," Shaun said. "You didn't answer."

"Bell's broken," Timothy pushed the button and nothing happened. "You've got no reason to hit my door like that. You've disturbed my mother."

"Well, sir," Shaun said, "We just . . ."

"Let's get to the point," Jack interrupted.

"You're here about that dead cop across the street," Timothy said.

"The emergency call came from this house," Jack confirmed.

"My mom called," Timothy nodded.

"Did she see it happen?" Jack asked.

"No," Timothy shook his head. "She didn't see anything."

"You?"

He nodded.

"Can we come in?" Jack asked.

Timothy stepped to one side and allowed the two of them to enter the house. They followed him through the house and out the back. They acknowledged his mother when they saw her and she eyed them suspiciously, still believing Jack was there to take her son from her again. Outside, Timothy lit a cigarette and began blowing smoke toward the sky.

"What did you see?" Jack asked when they were settled into a small triangle.

"Well, I spotted him early in the evening," Timothy said. "Just sitting in his car watching us. I looked out again about an hour later and saw he was still there. So I put the shades down in my mom's room and in the living room so she could watch her shows without being spied on. But I kept the rest of the house dark after the sun went down. I don't care for being watched. I thought he might leave if he thought I wasn't here."

"But he didn't," Jack said.

"Nope," Timothy inhaled a long drag and let the smoke roll from his mouth. "He kept sitting there watching the house."

"And you got tired of it," Jack suggested. "You went out the back here and over the fence there. By the time he knew you were on him, it was too late."

Timothy glared at him. "No. Wasn't nothin' like that. I started watching him."

"You watched him?"

"Put a chair in the back of a dark room and sat back and watched him," Timothy shrugged. "Wanted to see who would give up first."

"But he didn't give up?"

"No."

"What did you see?"

"This man showed up," Timothy said.

"A man showed up?" Jack asked.

"That's what I said," Timothy answered. "He appeared out of nowhere."

"Nowhere?"

"You going to keep repeating me?"

"What did this man look like?" Shaun asked.

"Kind of tall," Timothy said. "It was a long way and it was dark."

"That's it?" Jack asked. "He was 'kind of tall'?"

"He was dressed nice," Timothy added. "I remember thinking he was there to replace the first guy."

"You thought he was a cop?"

"Sure, at first," Timothy nodded. "No one else around here dresses that way."

"What did he drive?" Jack asked.

"Never saw a car," Timothy said. He took another drag on his cigarette and held it before letting a long stream of smoke escape his lips. "He came from the trees across the street. Left the same way."

"So, he appeared from the trees and came up on the car," Jack summarized. "Then what happened?"

"He shot the guy," Timothy said. "What do you think happened?"

"Well," Jack said. "We know Officer Kaninski was shot. What we don't understand is why he never went for his weapon. Not exactly a great neighborhood. We can't figure out why he would let the killer get so close to him without pulling his weapon."

"Get close to him?" Timothy chuckled. "He let the man get close to him. He let the man walk up to him and stand there talking to him for a while. It looked like they knew each other. That was another reason I thought the second guy was a cop. They talked for a while, acted real chummy."

"They talked?"

"That's what I said," Timothy said. "That's why I was so surprised when the second guy shot him. I guess he was surprised too."

"You think they knew each other?" Shaun said. "Not a stranger asking for directions or something like that?"

"They talked too long for that," Timothy said. "To me, it looked like they knew each other."

"After the shooting, what happened?"

"The guy left through the trees like I said," Timothy took a quick drag on his cigarette. "And I told mom to call 911."

"He didn't kneel down to pick up shell casings?" Jack asked.

"No," Timothy shook his head.

Not picking up shell casings told Jack the weapon used was a revolver, a fact the crime lab would confirm soon enough after they ran the slugs from the scene. But Jack felt better when he could be a step ahead of the lab. Finding the weapon, or the shooter would be a much harder task. Any step he could take without the help of others was good.

"He did do one thing I thought was strange," Timothy brought Jack from his thoughts.

"He did something strange?" Jack asked. He wasn't sure he heard right.

"Yeah," the man's nicotine-stained fingers held the last bit of his cigarette to his lips and he inhaled all he could. When he finished, he held the butt between his thumb and forefinger. With a quick flick, the butt flew into the yard. "He reached into the car. Pulled out some papers or something."

"A yellow folder?" Jack's interest was sparked.

"Could have been," Timothy nodded. "He looked at them, took something out and tossed the rest back into the car."

45

The diner smelled of grease and smoke. The clatter of forks on plates and spatulas on the grill filled the air. Jack sat across from Shaun with a burger in one hand. The officer was testing the BLT he ordered with a curiosity not usually given to sandwiches. He had never seen greasy lettuce before. Yet between two questionable slices of toast he was looking at just that. Not a little grease on lettuce. It was greasy lettuce.

"You should eat that," Jack said between bites. "You'll need the energy."

"Uh-huh." Shaun wasn't convinced.

"Tell me what you think about Waters," Jack said, taking a large bite.

"If you take him at his word," Shaun continued to study his sandwich as he spoke. "It sounds like someone Kaninski knew came to the stakeout with the sole purpose of killing him."

Jack swallowed hard. "And if you don't take him at his word?"

"Then you have a recently released killer trying to cover his tracks so he doesn't end up back behind bars." Hunger finally won out and Shaun started eating.

"You get any feel for where the truth falls?"

"My opinion?" Shaun looked up. "Or my evaluation of the facts?"

"Both."

"The facts point to Waters," Shaun explained. "He had motive and opportunity. And if he was guilty of the killing twenty years ago then he has the capability to do it again."

"But?"

"My opinion is he wouldn't be so stupid as to kill Kaninski in front of his own house," Shaun said. "I also don't think he would have had his mother call 911 if he had done it. And why even mention the mysterious yellow folder?"

"Mysterious?"

"There was no folder in the car," Shaun said.

"You haven't heard about the folder?" Jack asked.

"No," the officer said. "You have?"

"Let's just say I'm not surprised you haven't." Jack pointed at Shaun with his half-eaten burger.

"What do you know about it?"

"I know what was in it," Jack said. "Or at least I thought I did. Evidently there was more in it before Larry was killed."

"Do you think he was killed for what was in the folder?"

"I think he learned something someone didn't want him to tell," Jack wiped his hands on his napkin and took a drink from his soda. "And if that's the case it means he died because of what I asked him to find. I intend to find out what it was."

"You forget," Shaun said.

"What?"

"This is my case," the officer clarified.

"Larry was working for me," Jack argued. "You can't stop me from following the leads I find."

"You have the Elizabeth Mitchell case," Shaun pointed out. "And I know you're following up with the Lisa Reagan case. When are you going to have time to work another case?"

Jack opened his mouth and let it close. Shaun didn't know he was looking into Tracy Reagan's case again and Jack wanted to keep it that way. He said, "Okay. But I want you to keep me up to date. And if you have questions, call me. Do not call Bret. Do not call Terrance. Call me."

"Any advice will be appreciated," Shaun agreed.

"And one more thing."

"What's that?"

"This guy obviously has no problem shooting cops," Jack said. "Don't take anything for granted. Don't turn your back on anyone. Keep your weapon at the ready and be prepared to use it. Possibly on someone you know."

"You think you know who it is, don't you?"

"I have ideas," Jack confirmed.

"But you're not going to tell me."

"I don't have any concrete evidence."

"Did Larry know who you thought it was?"

"He did," Jack nodded.

"And now he's dead."

"Now he's dead."

"Sounds to me like you may be on the right track," Shaun said.

"But without proof," Jack said, "I've got nothing."

"If Larry knew who the suspect was," Shaun thought aloud, "why would he let them get that close? He didn't even have his weapon ready."

"Maybe he thought he was safe because he was a cop," Jack suggested. "Or since they were in the middle of the street. I don't know."

"Maybe it wasn't who you think," Shaun offered.

"Maybe," Jack conceded. "But if it wasn't, why is Larry dead?"

"Waters said the killer took something out of the car," Shaun said. "Maybe Larry found out something you didn't know. Maybe he stumbled onto the killer and the killer shot him for it."

"All I have to do is figure out what was taken from the folder," Jack said. "Should be easy."

Jack's phone rang and the detective set his burger down to answer, "Mallory."

"Jack," a woman said. "This is Sergeant Tinneyson."

"What can I do for you, Susan?" Jack said. Susan worked the front desk at the station. She had been there as long if not longer than anyone else on the force and she could handle herself in any situation. She had a special talent for handling people. In all the years Jack had known her, he couldn't remember her ever calling him.

"There's a woman down here who wants to see you," Susan said.

"I'm working," Jack said. "Tell her I'll be back at the office at three."

"You need to get down here now, Jack," Susan said in the matter-of-fact tone she often saved for out of line suspects. "She's not very happy with you, and the chief wants to lock her up. I'm not locking her up, Jack."

"What did I do to her?" Jack asked.

"She says you got her husband killed," she answered.

"Oh, my God," Jack closed his eyes. "Mrs. Kaninski."

"No," Susan said. "I know Larry's wife. This isn't her."

"Then who is it?" Jack asked already rising from his seat.

"Says her name is Winona Truman," Susan said.

"Truman?" Jack tried to scan his memories. "I don't know a Truman . . ."

Even as he said the name it occurred to him who it was. Kenneth Truman was the alias Lance Carpenter had hidden behind for the past twenty years.

46

Shaun watched Jack leave the restaurant with the phone pressed to his ear. He used his finger and poked at his BLT. Would it be possible to wipe the grease away with his napkin before the detective returned? He looked out the window to see if Jack was still on his call and saw that the detective's car was gone. With a heavy sigh he pushed his plate away deciding it was the best way to not clog his arteries. He collected his ticket and made his way to the register to pay.

Being called away was not surprising to Shaun. Detectives received new cases all the time. In this instance it was unlikely Jack had received a new case. There was no way they would assign him another homicide so soon. A lead maybe? He would have liked to tag along, watch Jack at work, maybe learn a thing or two.

When Shaun asked to train as a detective, he requested to work with Jack. It was disappointing to be assigned with Bret who was known throughout the department as a lazy man with no clue how to solve anything. It was also known that he was in the chief's pocket and was assigned trainees so he wouldn't have to work too hard. It was a sore spot between the chief and the department.

Shaun was glad to have the opportunity to work with Jack even if it was unofficially. He never dreamed he would have his own case so soon. And such an important case was overwhelming. He wanted to do it right. He wanted to be able to say he closed his first case.

It bothered him that Jack hadn't named his possible suspect. Whoever it was would be the obvious main suspect in Larry's death as well. With both of them digging for clues, it would be much easier to get the proof they both so desperately wanted.

The midday sun was bright and Shaun put his sunglasses on as he walked to his car. He wasn't sure how to proceed. He had no suspects other than Timothy Waters and he was inclined to follow

Jack's opinion that the man would not have done it. What he needed was a good motive for someone to want Larry dead. The missing folder Jack mentioned might give him some clues, but it was apparently removed from the scene before he got there. This brought up the question of who removed it and why.

The witness said the killer reached into the car where Larry sat dying of his wounds and pulled out the folder, took out part of the contents and threw it back into the car. It would have been faster to take the folder with him. He could easily discard what he didn't want when he wasn't standing on the street next to the man he had just killed. Maybe that was what happened and Timothy was mistaken or lied about what he had witnessed. That would explain why there was no folder at the scene when Shaun arrived.

Bret Peterson was the first to arrive on scene after the shooting had been called in. If the folder had been there, it was possible the detective found it. But where was it? Why wasn't it in evidence? What reason would he have for removing it?

Shaun pulled into traffic and fell into pace with the other drivers on their way to, or back from, lunch. He needed to know what was inside the folder. It was the only thing in the investigation resembling a motive for the shooting. He turned north, following the car in front of him absently. When he realized he was on the road leading to the lab he decided that was where he needed to go. He would pick up the findings from the tests they had run and while he was there he would find out if any of the techs had seen the mysterious folder before it vanished.

If that proved fruitless he would start questioning the people who he was convinced knew more than they were saying. Jack was one of them, and Bret. He would talk to Timothy Waters about what he saw. There must have been more. No one can sit and watch a murder and get as few details as Timothy gave them. He was going to get to the bottom of this case if he had to work on his own time.

Pulling into the parking lot next to the lab Shaun parked in a shaded spot. Opening his door he let it swing a little too much and it bounced gently off the SUV in the space beside him. He cursed and got out of the car, slammed the door shut and knelt to examine the other's door for marks. Finding nothing, he straightened his frame and walked briskly to the entrance.

He followed the corridor to the lab office where he identified himself and asked to speak to the coroner about Larry. He was told to wait and he paced the hall for almost half an hour. The receptionist called his name and directed him to a back office where he would meet with the coroner.

The small office was cluttered with stacks of papers, although the desktop was clean and organized. The one chair opposite the desk for the occasional visitor was home to a stack of large envelopes clearly marked as x-rays. Shaun considered moving them to the desk but decided to stand while he waited for the coroner to appear.

It was only a few minutes before the coroner walked into the office, passing Shaun without a glance and dropping a folder in the center of her desk with an audible thud. She was a stout woman with a broad forehead exaggerated by her hair being pulled back into a tight bun. Her facial features were set in a permanent scowl which deepened when she acknowledged Shaun was there. She glanced at her watch and raised an eyebrow as if to let him know his time had begun.

"What can I do for you, detective?" she asked in a thick German accent.

"Officer," Shaun corrected.

"What?"

"I'm not a detective," he explained. "It's Officer Travis."

"I am very busy," the coroner said. "I really am not concerned with your rank. Do you need something? Or did you come all the way down here to explain the difference between officer and detective?"

"No, ma'am," Shaun said. "I need to know if you learned anything from the Larry Kaninski autopsy."

"Well," the coroner huffed. "I learned that there are two entrance wounds in his chest, two exit wounds in his back. I learned that the cause of death was suffocation because the bullets collapsed one of his lungs and crushed his trachea. I know what he had for dinner and I know that he was only a short time away from a massive heart attack. What is it you want to know?"

"I want to know what time he was shot," Shaun said. "How far away was the shooter standing when he pulled the trigger. And I want to know why he never went for his own weapon."

The coroner paused, the heat draining from her face. She took a breath then said, "I can help you with the first two. The other one is up to you."

"Fair enough," Shaun said.

"The wounds suggest close range," the coroner said. "The trace lab is working his clothes to check for gunpowder residue. As far as when he was shot, I would say it was close to midnight. I'll know more when I run a few more tests."

"Thank you," the officer said. "One more thing."

"What would that be?" the coroner asked.

"You say he suffocated?"

"Yes."

"How long would that have taken?"

"A couple of minutes, maybe more," the coroner said.

"Don't you think he would have tried to call for help?" Shaun asked. "Or at least fought for air?"

"I'm sure he would have."

"Was there any indication that would suggest he did that?"

"No," she answered, "there wasn't."

"Okay," Shaun said. "Thank you for your time."

The coroner retreated to the hallway, leaving Shaun alone in the small office. He stood for a moment staring at the single folder in the center of her desk. When Larry's killer had reached into the car to take the folder, the old cop would have still been alive. Did he reach out and touch his killer? Did he plead for help? What Shaun wanted to know most was if Larry was shot at midnight why did the 911 call not come until almost one in the morning?

47

Jack entered the station and crossed to the front desk where Sergeant Tinneyson sat with an air of authority meant to intimidate. She was speaking with a distraught mother demanding to know why her son had been arrested. Susan was firm yet patient with the woman, finally convincing her that it would be best for her to sit and wait until more information was available. The system moved slowly. Behind the woman stood a man waiting his turn to speak with the sergeant. Jack stepped in front of him, despite his protests. Susan pointed to the far corner of the waiting room where a woman in her late thirties sat sobbing audibly. Jack approached her slowly, trying to imagine how she had been able to drive herself from her home to the station.

"Mrs. Carpenter?" Jack said, sitting in the seat next to her.

Her eyes swollen she said, "Truman. My name is Sandy Truman. My husband was Kenneth Truman. And if you are Detective Jack Mallory, you killed him."

"Excuse me?" Jack said. "I didn't kill anyone."

"You may as well have," she said.

The anger in her voice was overpowered only by the anguish. Jack understood both emotions. Using the softest tone he could muster, he said, "Why don't you tell me what happened."

"He went to meet with you is what happened," she shouted, the anger taking center stage. "He trusted you and you betrayed him is what happened."

A large uniformed officer standing guard over the room started toward them but Jack waved him off. The woman scowled, digging through her purse until she finally withdrew a tissue. She wiped her eyes and blew her nose before wadding the tissue up and squeezing it tightly in her hand.

"Mrs. Truman," Jack said. "I did not betray your husband. I never mentioned Kenneth to anyone. But I can tell you I want to find out what happened. I want to put his killer in jail. To do that I need you to tell me what you know. Everything you can."

Her scowl was still set, but tears formed in the corners of her eyes. She wanted to scream, to let her emotions go and take it out on everyone within range, especially the detective. But she felt Jack's sincerity. She wanted to hate him. She needed to hate him. She drove all this way to let him know how much she hated him. Now, she couldn't do it.

"Ken was a good man," she said, her voice timid, the venom gone. "He was hiding something from me from the day we met. I knew that. I accepted it. He never talked about his past or his family. But at night, sometimes, he would talk in his sleep. Just words really. Not sentences. He would say names I didn't know. Or mention places we had never been to. It was part of him I knew nothing about. But it was okay because I knew things were good between us."

"When did you learn the truth about his past?" Jack asked.

"We were watching the news and a story came on about this convicted killer being released because of lost evidence," she said. "Ken became very excited. At first I thought he was upset because the system was putting a killer back on the street. For the first time he talked about something from his past. He explained that the man was someone he used to know and that he was innocent and deserved to get out."

"Did he tell you everything at that point?" Jack asked.

"No," she shook her head. "A couple nights later a man, I think a police chief or something, was on the news saying they were going to find the evidence to put the man back behind bars where he belonged. After that Ken became enraged. He kept saying he couldn't let them do it again."

"Did he say what he meant?"

"No," she sighed. "That was when he told me his real name and he told me about what happened. He told me he was going to help his old friend. That's when he called you."

"Your husband told me he knew that Timothy Waters was innocent because he met with Elizabeth after Tim that night," Jack said. "Did he tell you why he waited twenty years to come forward to help?"

"I asked him about that," she said. "He told me he was scared. He had been hiding so long, living under a different name for so long, he was afraid of what would happen if he went back. But knowing his friend was out of jail, Ken couldn't stand by and let them put him back in."

"What did your husband say when he returned home the night he met with me?" Jack asked.

"He said everything was going to be okay," she laughed a little, involuntarily. "He said he felt he could trust you. He said you were going to help his friend."

"Was he a good judge of character?"

"Usually," she said.

"Do you trust me?" Jack asked.

"My husband is dead, detective," she said. "I don't feel very trusting."

"I can understand that," Jack nodded.

The front doors opened and two uniformed officers guided a large man wearing handcuffs into the station. The man pushed and pulled against his captors, shouting obscenities as they went. For a brief moment the prisoner broke free and started for the exit. One of the officers overran him and used his own body weight to slam him into the wall. After that he was being dragged down the hall by the two officers as well as another who came to help.

"Let's get out of here," Jack suggested. "I'll buy you lunch and we can talk."

"Talk about what?"

"Whoever killed your husband did it to keep the truth from coming out," Jack said. "I need to know everything he told you about Timothy Waters and the killing that put him behind bars. I need to know if he told you anything about the people he was hiding from. And I need you to tell me the circumstances behind his death."

"I will answer your questions. And I do need to eat," she said as they stood. "But I'll meet you there."

"I could give you a ride," Jack offered.

"I'm not getting in a car with you, detective," she said.

"Why not?"

"When my husband was killed," she said. "He was talking to a cop."

48

Terrance stepped onto the curb in front of one of his favorite bars. The only thought on his mind was that Heather wanted a divorce. After all these years of wondering why they were still together, she had finally asked to end things. He was at the bar to have a drink, but he wasn't sure if it was to celebrate the future or to mourn the past. It really didn't make a difference. Either way, he would be drunk by last call.

Heather had put him through hell for years. Not being able to have children had embittered her toward him. She blamed him for having a low sperm count or just not being available. That was years ago. They never went to a doctor for the truth. They just grew distant. They hadn't touched one another in years. They seldom even spoke, and when they did it was in anger.

The secrets between them tore them apart. Yet it was those very secrets that became the truths that never allowed them to ever be completely free of one another. Things had finally reached the point where enough was enough and Terrance was considering getting out. Recently everything began to spin out of control. Had Heather sensed that and thrown in the towel before he could? How would things between them be going forward?

"Terry!" the bartender called out as Terrance pushed his way through the door. "It's been a while."

"Hello, Jon," Terrance acknowledged, selecting a seat at the bar. "It hasn't been that long has it? A week or so."

"I thought it was longer," Jon smiled, setting a glass in front of him. "The usual?"

"Yes," Terrance nodded. "Make it a double."

"No problem," Jon poured scotch over ice. "Special occasion?"

"You know me," Terrance grinned slightly. "Every day is a special occasion."

Jon laughed and moved down the bar to help a couple just sitting down. Terrance sat sipping from his glass and staring at his reflection in the mirror that covered the wall behind the hundreds of bottles of alcohol. He looked into his own eyes and noticed for the first time how sunken they were. He was tired. Tired of the lies, tired of the path his life had taken. He wasn't sure if divorcing Heather would be a fresh start or the end.

"Can I get you another?" Jon asked.

Terrance lowered his eyes to his glass and was surprised it was empty. He didn't remember finishing it. How long had he been there? He checked his watch and started to stand. Then he settled back down, looked Jon in the eyes and said, "Why not?"

Jon dropped a couple more cubes of ice in the glass. The bottle appeared and he poured another double. Terrance lifted the glass and examined the amber liquid.

"How long have I been coming in here, Jon?"

"Well, let's see," Jon scratched at his chin. "I bought the place from Howie, what was it, seventeen, eighteen years ago? And I was tending the bar for almost ten years before that. I think you've been coming at least that long."

"Over twenty-five years," Terrance contemplated. "That's a long time. A quarter of a century."

"Hard to believe," Jon nodded.

"In all those years have I ever seemed happy to you?"

"Not tonight," Jon said. "That's for sure."

"I'm serious," Terrance said. "Have you ever considered me to be a happy man?"

"Not exactly happy," Jon admitted. "Although the last few times you were in here you were close. Then you come in tonight pretty much worse than ever."

"That's what I thought," Terrance said.

"You know," Jon added, "most people who come in here, come to get away from their lives, forget about the outside world for a bit. I don't get an upbeat crowd. Look around you." Terrance looked. "Not exactly a happy group."

"My wife wants a divorce," Terrance said without knowing he was going to say it.

"I didn't even know you were married," Jon responded. "I'm sorry, man."

"Don't be," Terrance waved the sympathy off. "It's been a long time coming. Besides, I think it's a good thing."

"Well in that case, congratulations," Jon smiled. "How about another drink on the house to celebrate?"

"That would be nice," Terrance said.

Jon poured and moved away to help the rest of his customers. Terrance watched the ice cubes spinning inside his glass. He lifted the drink and held it in front of him, peering through the liquid. Then, with a smile, he raised it above his head as if to toast an old friend at his wedding.

In a strong voice that brought eyes around to him, he said, "To Lisa."

49

Sitting in his living room, Charles Reagan cradled a cup of coffee in his hands as if he was trying to use it to stay warm. No comfort was being derived from the cup nor the drink inside. Charles was using the cup as a means to occupy his hands. He sat squarely in his chair with sharp angles and deep lines carved into his face. Across from him, Detective Peterson sat jotting notes onto a folded piece of paper that may have once been a grocery list.

"I don't understand why we have to go through this again," Charles finally said, clearly uncomfortable with the detective's return. He wanted to talk to Jack Mallory. "I've answered all these questions before."

"Well, this is an ongoing murder investigation," Bret explained. "It's a little suspicious that both your wife and your daughter were murdered. Don't you think?"

"What are you implying, detective?" Charles' hand tightened on the coffee cup but he could not disguise the tension in his voice.

"I'm not implying anything," Bret said. "I'm saying it's suspicious."

"They caught my wife's killer, sir," Charles said. "And as far as I know the man is still in prison."

"Well, maybe he didn't act alone," Bret suggested. "Or maybe he was hired. There are lots of possibilities, as there are in your daughter's death."

"You can't be serious," Charles said. "What reason would I have for wanting my daughter killed?"

"I never said you," Bret grinned mischievously. "But since you mentioned it, maybe she saw something all those years ago. Maybe she was going to let the truth out."

Charles stared at the man in front of him. It was the same type of talk he heard after his wife was killed. He could never dream of harming his wife then nor his daughter now. Seven years ago he was the focus of scrutiny, a suspect in a crime he could not even imagine. Now, with his daughter killed as well, he was beginning to be the focus again. Meanwhile, the real killer was walking around as if nothing happened. It was enough to send him over the edge.

"Sir," Charles said through clenched teeth. "Do you have children?"

"No I don't," Bret did not look up from his notes.

"Then I suppose you can't imagine what it's like to lose a child," Charles said. "Someone you watched grow up. Someone you read to at night. Someone you taught how to talk and walk and helped with her homework. Someone who, when she called to say, 'Hi, Dad', made a difference in your day. There is no way I could have hurt my daughter. I couldn't do what was done to her."

"You could have hired someone," Bret said.

"It is inconceivable to want one's own daughter harmed."

"Yet," Bret said. "She, in fact, was not your daughter."

"She was!" Charles yelled. He set his coffee on the table next to him to avoid spilling it, or possibly throwing it. "She was as much my daughter as she was her mother's. More than the man who got her mother pregnant all those years ago."

"Do you know who her father was?" Bret asked.

"No," Charles said. "Maybe you should be looking for him."

Bret laughed, a short snorting sound. "I'll do that. But that won't help you, Mr. Reagan."

"What are you talking about?"

"I have proof you were involved in your daughter's death," Bret said.

"Proof?"

"And before I'm done," Bret leaned forward menacingly, "I'll have proof you had something to do with your wife's death as well."

"What proof?"

"Now, I can't tell you that," Bret said.

"I loved my daughter," Charles said. "Why are you doing this to me?"

"Because you're a killer, Mr. Reagan," Bret said. "And it's my job to put killers behind bars."

"Are you arresting me?"

"Not yet," Bret said. "But I suggest you cancel any plans to leave town for, say, the next twenty years or so."

The detective stood and walked out the front door leaving Charles sitting in his living room where he and his family once spent long hours together. A portrait of the three of them, the last taken before his wife's murder ten years ago, hung above the couch. He stared at the image of his wife's eyes wishing she were there for him to talk to. He shifted his eyes to those of his daughter, so young and innocent. The portrait revealed a happy family untouched by the violence that would soon destroy them.

A tear rolled down Charles' cheek and he wiped at it with a finger. The damp spot held his attention for a moment. He raised his hands to his face and began to sob.

50

Having already eaten lunch with Shaun, Jack ordered a cup of coffee and a piece of cherry pie. He convinced Sandy Truman to order the chicken salad, arguing that she needed to eat something. When the food arrived she finally began to relax.

"Tell me about yesterday," Jack said, wanting to know what the last hours of her husband's life had been like, from her point of view.

She finished chewing the bite of salad she had taken. It took a while and Jack considered if it was because she was stalling.

"He was in high spirits in the morning," she said. "All those years of hiding, of looking over his shoulder and lying about his past were finally coming to an end. I guess he was right. He just didn't know how they were going to end."

"How was he with you?" Jack asked.

"We spent the morning together. It was the best day we had since learning the cancer had returned," Sandy said. "He opened up to me, telling me about his family and growing up, all those things I've been wanting to know forever. He's such a, was such a sweet gentle man. I was sure his childhood couldn't have been bad enough to make him want to hide it, but I knew he had a good reason for keeping it to himself. I figured he would tell me when he was ready. And to hear him talk about his family tore at my heart. He missed them so much. He was so excited about being able to see them again."

"Did he tell you anything about Timothy Waters?"

"He had a lot to say about Tim," She nodded. She paused, wanting to get it right. "They were best friends. He felt so guilty about not coming forward years ago. Early on it was fear for his life. Then it was uncertainty. In the end I think he was so used to our life he didn't know how to go back."

She stopped, her eyes focused on an undetermined point somewhere over Jack's shoulder. Jack waited for her to continue, trying to sort through his thoughts. When she still didn't say anything more, he waved down the waitress to replenish his coffee. With his cup refreshed, he cleared his throat and asked, "Did he tell you anything about what Timothy was convicted of doing?"

"No," she shook her head. "He never got that far. He was just beginning to talk about it when the doorbell rang."

Sandy's eyes drifted away once more. Sadness overwhelmed her and tears began to form.

"The doorbell rang," Jack prompted. "What happened then?"

She turned to Jack searching his face for something so intensely he became uncomfortable.

"He was talking to me about his past," she said. "Things he hadn't shared with anyone for two decades. He wanted to talk about it. He was smiling. So, he opened the door without looking to see who it was. I couldn't see who was there, but I saw the expression on his face. His face fell. The smile gone. He said, 'May I help you, officer?'. There was no response. Not one I could hear anyway. I started to step up to the door to see what was going on when I heard the shots. Two of them, very quick. Ken stood there and I thought they missed. Or maybe they weren't shots at all. Then his knees buckled and he fell. I ran forward to try to catch him, but it was too late."

"Did you see the shooter?"

"No," she shook her head.

"He didn't come in?" Jack asked. "To be sure your husband was dead?"

"No," her head shook again. "I screamed Ken's name and rushed forward. I didn't even think about someone being there, someone who could have shot me as well. By the time I thought about it and looked, there was no one there. All I saw was the car driving away."

"You saw the killer's car?" Jack shifted his weight so that he was leaning toward the woman.

"Just the back," she said, putting his hope to rest with the knowledge that she would not be able to identify the make or model.

"Oh," Jack sighed. "What about the color or anything unusual?"

"Nothing comes to mind," she said. "We live in the country and our driveway is long. I saw the car as it was turning onto the road."

He smiled slightly at Sandy and handed her his card. "I have to go. If you think of anything else call that number."

She looked at the card as if she were trying to make sense of it. She raised her eyes to his but didn't say anything. He stood and dropped a twenty on the table for his coffee and her lunch. He thanked her for what information she provided and started to walk away.

"Detective," she called to him.

He turned back. She was standing beside the table gathering her purse. Others in the restaurant eyed him with caution.

"I do remember something," she said, moving toward him. "About the car I mean."

"What's that?"

"All I saw was the back, like I said," she explained.

"Yes?"

"I remember the taillights," she said. "They weren't modern. They were old."

"Old?" he repeated. "Like something from twenty years ago? Or old like something from the sixties?"

"The sixties, I guess," she said. "I'm not too good with cars."

Jack stood silent for a moment trying to think of the one question that would jog loose the memory she didn't know she had. He considered the story Sandy told him. He was disturbed by the idea that Lance Carpenter's killer might have been a policeman. It was especially upsetting since it had apparently been a patrolman who shot him twenty years ago. It gave credence to the idea that the man who failed to kill him the first time may have come back to finish the job. And that meant the killer found him after twenty years of hiding. Either the killer was very lucky or somehow Jack led him to Lance.

A chill crawled up Jack's spine at the thought he might have had a part in Lance's death. He never imagined anyone would make the connection between the name Kenneth Truman and the young friend of Timothy Waters. There was no doubt in Jack's mind now. Terrance had asked about the man who left so many messages for him. Either the killer was dressed like a cop or Lance recognized the man on his porch as a cop. Of all the cops who had been on the force for twenty years, only Terrance came to mind.

The phone in his jacket rang and Jack pulled it out of his pocket. He excused himself to her and answered the call with a huff, "Mallory here."

"Jack?" Shaun asked.

"Yeah," he responded. "What do you need?"

"I need to talk to you about something I learned," Shaun said.

"What is it?" Jack's eyes remained fixed on Sandy.

"I'd rather not discuss it over the phone," Shaun said.

"Okay, then where do you want to meet?"

"How close are you to Waters' house?"

"Fifteen minutes," Jack said.

"I'll be there in twenty," Shaun said.

"See you then," Jack said. "What's this about?"

There was silence, leaving Jack to question if he had lost the connection. Then he heard Shaun say, "I found another witness."

51

Timothy Waters stood in his mother's living room looking through the window at Shaun Travis, who seemed to be searching for something he lost. Timothy did not remember the man's name but knew who it was. He came to the door when he first arrived claiming to have more questions. At Timothy's request, his mother told the young officer that her son was not available. She refused to say he wasn't home. She had never been able to lie to people. But what she said was enough to satisfy Shaun, who disappeared for a time while he walked up and down the neighborhood. He reappeared a few minutes ago to perform his painstaking search of the ground beneath his feet.

Watching through the window reminded Timothy of being back in prison. He had watched countless guards over the years walking the halls between cells, searching the cells themselves and leading prisoners in and out of lockup. After twenty years behind bars he was finally free, but he was no freer than he had been six months ago. He was a prisoner in his own home. The only differences were his mother and the view outside his cell.

He was not completely honest when this officer asked his questions earlier. He and the detective working Beth's case asked a lot of questions, just not the right ones. It really didn't matter what Timothy said. He was going to be a suspect the moment the man in the car was killed. That was the way the justice system worked. Innocent until considered guilty and then always guilty after that. First to be questioned. First to be considered. First to go to jail.

Even in prison, things worked in this manner. Timothy had been surprised to learn the way the prison ran. It was like a city inside. Leaders and followers. Jobs and rewards. It paid to play the politics of the inmates. He learned that from his first cellmate. The man was in his early sixties when Timothy arrived. He was serving a life sentence for murder, an accident the man explained. No one was supposed to be hurt.

His name was Maximillian Normanburger. He insisted on being called Max and nothing more. Timothy agreed and never called him anything else. A lot of the inmates called him 'old man' or 'long-timer', but even they had a respect for him. Max taught Timothy how to stay out of trouble and how to stay safe behind bars. He introduced him to the leaders and made sure Timothy was accepted. Because of Max, Timothy never had to experience the things he saw other new prisoners suffer.

Max was a thief by trade. A very good thief. Timothy thought the man was exaggerating and boasting a bit too much, but years later he was able to do some research and found that Max was as good as he said he was. He was hitting houses, mansions really, in five different neighborhoods. He spread the hits by time and districts so well that it was months before the connection was made that it was the same man doing all the jobs.

Of course, things changed or he wouldn't have become Timothy's cellmate. It was the last job he would do although he didn't know it at the time. He cased the house for several weeks and had the man's routine down to exact minutes. The homeowner was so predictable Max became careless. He showed up and did not verify that the man's car was gone from the garage. It was bridge night and the man was always gone.

When Max entered the house after disabling the alarm, he strolled through the house to see what he was going to take before he started working. On the second floor, while he was examining a painting to determine if it was real or a fake, he heard the man walking up behind him. He turned as a golf club swung down at him, ducked just as the head of the club grazed his temple, then rushed forward to tackle his attacker. Unfortunately, the homeowner was a very small, frail, almost ghostly man. Max hit him hard and knocked the wind out of him. A rush of triumph surged through him until he realized the man was not moving from the place he landed.

Max examined the man and found there was no heartbeat, no pulse. He was dead. It was determined later that the impact of Max's shoulder into the man's chest had triggered a heart attack. So Max, who called the police and waited for them to arrive, was convicted of murder and sentenced to life in prison. That was thirty-six years before Timothy moved into the upper bunk of cell 223.

The night Timothy lay in his bunk and told Max the story of Elizabeth, the old man listened intently without interrupting. Timothy told of his relationship with the young girl. He explained the plans they had made. He told of how they spent the last evening of her life, not knowing it would be the last time they would spend together. And finally he told how she was found the next morning, the investigation that followed and the trial that lead to his conviction. When he finished they lay in silence so long Timothy thought his cellmate had fallen asleep.

"You know," the man said finally. "I've been in this place a very long time. I've seen cons of all walks of life. Some were okay. Some were bad. Some were really bad. But most of them insisted they were innocent. But listening to you, I have to say: This is the first time I ever believed it to be true."

They never spoke of it again after that. Max taught Timothy how to survive in prison until he became too old and Timothy became something of a bodyguard for his teacher. Max referred to him as the son he never had and Timothy called him 'My old man'. When Timothy's father died, Max comforted him. When Max died two years later, Timothy cried silently all night.

Now, watching Officer Travis through the window, he wondered if he would be going back to prison for yet another murder he hadn't committed. He lied to the cop, something else he learned to do while in prison. Now he waited to see if his lie would be found out. If it were it would be hard to explain. It would probably land him in jail. He regretted that. But it was a lie he had no choice but to tell.

The truth was Timothy had gone out to the car and had a look inside. The man was still breathing and tried to speak to him. But he died before saying anything. The man was able to put a hand on the folder lying on the passenger seat. When he released his last breath, Timothy opened the folder and removed one of the pages. He wore gloves, leaving no prints.

That page was in his hand now and he wished he could go back and leave it in the car. He wanted the police to know it existed, at least the two working the case. That was why he told them the killer had taken it, to let them know there was something to find. But he couldn't give it to them without incriminating himself. He wasn't sure why he wanted them to know, but he thought it was important. He remembered being asked something by the first detective that made sense when he held up the single page.

He looked down at it. The county letterhead was at the top. To the right was a simple 'page 2'. Halfway down the page was the name, Terrance Singleton, with an address. Beneath that was the registration information for a 1972 Barracuda.

52

Jack was pulling up behind Shaun's car when his phone rang. It was the governor's assistant telling him that the governor and his wife had agreed to meet with him the following morning. His first instinct was to say he would have to reschedule. He did not want to meet with them together. Fortunately, he kept himself in check and accepted the time. Jotting the appointment down in his notes, he would worry about getting them apart when he got there.

Shaun was standing in the street walking in a grid pattern appearing to be searching for something. He nodded a greeting to Jack and started for the sidewalk. Jack exited his car and met the officer there, glancing toward Timothy Waters' house as he had done several times since he arrived.

"What's this about a new witness?" Jack asked.

"I was going door to door and found a witness who had not been home during my first run through the neighborhood," Shaun explained as he led the detective to a house several doors down from Waters'. "You should hear what they have to say."

Standing side by side on the porch Shaun rang the bell. They only had to wait a few minutes before a small middle-aged woman opened the door. She was hesitant at first but when she saw Shaun she smiled and let them in. They settled in her living room where she offered them drinks and cookies. Jack declined but found the woman unwilling to take no for an answer. He ended up with a cup of coffee and a plate of macaroons. Shaun had tea and sugar cookies.

"Eat up," Deloris Green smiled broadly.

"I need you to go over what you saw the other night," Shaun took a bite of cookie. "I need you to tell Detective Mallory what you told me."

"Detective Mallory," she held her hand out in front of her. "So nice to meet you."

"Nice to meet you," Jack said not sure what she expected him to do with her hands. He chose to ignore them. "Now what is it you saw?"

"Eat your cookies," she said, lowering her hands to her lap.

Jack took a bite, examined the cookie and returned it to the plate glancing at Shaun who shrugged.

"Mrs. Green," Shaun coaxed. "You told me you saw what happened to the man the other night. The man in the car."

"Awful, just awful," she shook her head as if to loosen the memory.

"What was it you saw, ma'am?" Jack asked.

"The man sat in his car for a long, long time," Deloris said.

"And then what happened?" Shaun pushed.

"Then the other man came," she smiled. She stood and left the room. Jack looked at Shaun who raised a finger to indicate Jack should remain patient. She returned with a coffeepot and filled her own cup and topped off Jack's as well even though he hadn't drunk any yet. She set the pot on the small table next to the chair she then sat in.

"You were saying something about another man," Jack tried to get her on track.

"The other man was evil," she said. "Do you want more tea?"

"No thank you," Shaun said. "Tell us what the evil man did."

"He was evil," she turned sharply to Jack, narrowing her eyes. "He came from out of nowhere. You sure you don't want more tea?"

"I'm sure," Shaun waved a hand over his glass.

"When you say he came out of nowhere," Jack asked, "do you mean you didn't see where he came from?"

"He just appeared," she whispered. "Out of thin air."

"Okay," Jack sighed.

"Tell us what the man did after he appeared," Shaun coached.

"He talked to the man in the car," she smiled and nodded. "Talked to him a long time."

"How long?" Jack's interest was renewed.

"A long time," she repeated.

"And then what?"

"Then boom," she clapped.

"Boom?" Jack asked.

"Boom. Boom," she clapped twice.

"Are you saying the evil man talked to the man in the car then shot him?" Jack asked.

"Boom," she clapped again.

"What is this proving, Shaun?" he turned to the officer.

"There's more," Shaun did not take his eyes from the woman. "Mrs. Green, after the man shoots, after the booms, what happened?"

The woman leaned forward in her chair. "The evil man walked away into darkness."

"Into darkness?" Jack threw his hands up.

"And when the evil man was gone the angel came." She closed her eyes and raised her face upward and smiled. "The angel came."

"The angel?" Jack leaned forward. "What does that mean?"

"The angel came for the man in the car." She opened her eyes and looked at Jack as if he were stupid. "He came and reached into the car and took the man's soul with him."

"He took the man's soul?"

"Yes."

"What did his soul look like?"

"White as the stars."

"And where did the angel go once it had the man's soul?" Shaun pressed.

"He went to the dying house," the woman began to cry. "The dying house needs the soul."

"Did you see the angel clearly?" Jack asked.

"You can't look an angel in the face," the woman shrieked.

"Jack," Shaun grabbed his arm. "That's it. She doesn't know anymore."

The two of them stood and excused themselves. Leaving the half-eaten cookies and full drinks on the coffee table they showed themselves out as the woman cried. They locked the door as they left.

"What good was that?" Jack lashed out at Shaun. "She didn't tell us anything. And she could never take the stand. Why did you call me here for that?"

"She told us two things," Shaun corrected.

"What are you talking about?"

"She told us there were two men at that car the night Larry was killed," Shaun pointed out. "The first one talked to him before shooting him. And she told us Timothy Waters lied to us."

"Lied to us about what?"

"The soul was white, Jack," Shaun said. "like a piece of paper. And which house on this block would you call the dying house?"

Down the street there was one house with a dead lawn and shriveled bushes. One house in need of a new roof and a paint job. The dying house belonged to Timothy Waters' mother. According to the woman, Timothy had not killed Larry, but he had taken the other page out of the file.

53

Terrance was parked in the half-circle drive in front of his house with the engine running, as he had been for almost an hour just watching. He wasn't sure what he was watching for. The house was dark and had been since his arrival. He would have thought Heather was not there if her car wasn't parked in front of the garage. The flat gray sedan issued to him by the department was quiet as most department cars were. A team of mechanics in the garage worked hard to keep them all in top shape so they would be ready to give that little extra when duty called.

Terrance hated the quiet.

He associated the quiet with his life. The sterile, meaningless life he had lived. He became a cop to make a difference. He worked hard to achieve the position where he could actually make that difference. Yet, what had he done? Not much that he could be proud of. His father used to call it 'existing just to exist'. It was what his old man did. And it was what he wanted to avoid doing himself. But ultimately that was all he was doing.

Every day had become a means to get to the next and in many ways there was no motivation even to do that. The only reason to carry on was for a marriage he was unhappy to be in. Now even that was ending. Many would think divorcing a woman like Heather would be a good thing and at first thought Terrance would be inclined to agree. The problem was it wouldn't be that simple.

There were too many loose ends to walk away, too many secrets between them to be forgotten or ignored. They would have to address them, those things they never spoke of. They would need to come to agreements, provide assurances.

He shut off the car and climbed out of the seat, stretching his legs and back. Years had passed since his days of stakeouts. The last hour reminded him why he didn't like them. He lifted his briefcase from the passenger seat and fumbled with his keys while he walked to the front door. He wondered briefly if Heather would have changed the locks, but wasn't sure what the point would be in that.

The key turned smoothly and he pushed the door open, letting it swing freely on its hinges. Inside he turned back and closed the door quietly. He pressed against it to be sure it latched. The familiar click announced his success and he slid the deadbolt into place. Dropping his keys into his pocket he walked through the entry hall toward the kitchen.

"I thought you weren't coming in."

Terrance jumped. Heather was sitting in the corner of the living room veiled in darkness. The sound of her voice was so startling he lost hold of the briefcase, dropping it to the floor with a loud thud. He spun his head to locate her shadowy form in the chair next to the window.

"Jesus, Heather," he exclaimed. "You scared me half to death."

"You sat out there a long time," she observed.

"I was thinking," he bent down to pick up his case. "We should talk."

"Talk?" she laughed. "You've been watching our marriage spiral into oblivion for twenty years and now you want to talk?"

"There was no spiral, Heather," Terrance said. "It plummeted."

"And who's fault was that?" she quipped.

"Let's not get into an argument about blame," Terrance sat across the room from her. "We need to discuss certain things. Issues that need to be resolved, resolved in a way we can both live with."

"We've been living in separate rooms for all this time," she grinned. "Why should I expect us to both live with anything?"

"Can we just get through this?"

"I'm listening," Heather tilted her head toward him.

"Well, there's the obvious," Terrance crossed one leg over the other.

"There is," Heather nodded. "And you can be sure I won't say anything and I'm sure you won't."

"You know there's more to it than that," Terrance said.

"Terrance," Heather sat forward, a sliver of light catching her face. "We know there's more, but we also know we can't write rules for every little detail of our divorce. There's too much. Let's leave it at we say nothing."

He wasn't sure what he expected or even wanted. A contract was out of the question. Some things were best left unwritten.

Promises between two people who didn't trust one another were pointless. What it came down to was fear. The fear each had of the other and the information the other had in their possession.

"Fine," Terrance gave in. "You don't talk. I won't talk. Life will go on as it always has. Only we won't live together anymore."

"We have separate bedrooms," Heather said. "We keep different hours. We haven't lived together in years. The difference will be that we can finally move on with our pathetic little lives. You can find some young floozy to settle down with and I can . . . well, I can do whatever the hell I want to do."

"What about Paul?" Terrance asked. "Is he going to accept this?"

"He will if I tell him," she said. "He's my brother. He'll support me in whatever I want. You know that."

"And B.J.?"

"If I tell him it's my idea, he'll accept it," she assured him. "We're all getting too old for these games anyway. As long as nothing unexpected happens everything will be fine."

"Nothing will be fine, Heather," Terrance frowned. "That line was already crossed years ago."

"When this is all over, you should really think about taking a vacation," Heather said. "You seem rather stressed."

"I wonder why?" Terrance said.

"You trying to blame me for your problems?" she asked.

"You are my problem," he responded.

"I'm hurt," she feigned pain.

"Whatever," he stood. "I'm going to get some rest. I'll take tomorrow to pack my things. Will you file soon?"

"I'll find a lawyer tomorrow," she said. "No point in wasting time."

"Stay away from that one guy," Terrance said. "What was his name?"

"Friedman?"

"That's the one," he nodded. "He'll just rip us off."

"I was thinking of Snyder," she said.

"He'd be good," he nodded again. "I'm going up."

He started out of the room. As he reached the base of the stairs he looked back at the woman he had married a quarter of a century ago. "It's funny."

"What's that?" she looked up at him.

"This is the first civil conversation we've had in twenty years."

54

A large framed man, Bret hated sitting in cars for long periods of time. If he were going to be cramped he would rather be in his own vehicle rather than the piece of junk the department issued him. But tonight there was no choice. The warrant he had requested would be ready to serve in the morning and he was going to watch Charles Reagan's house just in case.

Surveillance was the part of the job he hated the most. It was so boring to sit and wait for something that may or may not happen. He didn't like reading and unless there was a game on, he never turned on the radio. On more than one occasion he dozed off. Once he slept while his suspect drove away to commit another burglary. He didn't know the man was gone until he returned with his haul.

He wouldn't fall asleep this time. He had enough caffeine in him to keep him going for days. He had a thermos of coffee and an ice chest full of sodas. His only problem would be if he needed to go to the restroom before the night was over, which was likely. That was one of the reasons he was parked next to the largest evergreen in the area. It was thick enough to shield him from the street if he wanted to get out and stretch his legs or relieve himself.

He reached for another can of soda and popped the top. The night was young and there was no point in taking any chances. Falling asleep in your car, even in a nice neighborhood like this, could be a ticket to ending up like Larry Kaninski. He pushed against the seatback angling it so he could stretch his legs and watched the house.

The ring of his cell phone surprised him. He checked the caller ID and raised an eyebrow. The surprises never stopped.

"Hey," he said after pressing the talk button. He listened for a while nodding his head even though no one could see him. "You sure about that?"

Again he listened. He was never one to talk much. He talked even less when he was on the phone. He took a drink from his soda and continued listening. After a time he said, "That's not such a good idea."

He waited.

"I know what you're saying," he said. "But come on. We aren't talking about a traffic ticket. You can't sweep it under a rug."

He waited some more. This time he was shaking his head.

"I still don't think it's a good idea," he said. "I just . . ."

He listened.

"I understand," he said. "But . . ."

He rolled his eyes.

"Well, what did he say?"

He waited.

"I think...," A motion in the direction of the Reagan house caught his eye. "Listen, can I call you later? I have to go."

He shifted impatiently.

"I'm working," he said. "I have to go. I'll talk to you tomorrow."

He hung up the phone and dropped it into his pocket. He never took his eyes off the distraction that had stolen his attention from the call. It was the opportunity he was hoping for. Charles was climbing into the driver's seat of his car.

55

The knock was solid, forceful. The two men stepped back and waited. When the door opened they were ready for anything. What they were greeted with was the elderly Mrs. Waters.

"Mrs. Waters," Jack greeted. "We need to talk to Timothy."

"You just missed him," she said.

"Missed him?"

"He left a few minutes ago," Mrs. Waters said.

"Do you know where he went?" Jack asked.

"No," she answered. "Just said he needed to go."

"And you have no idea where he went?"

"No idea," she shrugged.

"Mrs. Waters," Jack looked past the woman to the interior of the house. "If you know where he is you really should tell us."

"I told you I don't know," she repeated.

"Did he say when he would be back?" Shaun asked.

She turned to him as if noticing him for the first time. She looked him over then said, "No. He didn't."

"You wouldn't tell us even if you knew." It was not a question. Jack made the statement out of frustration.

"I would not," she admitted. "You boys ruined his life. Put him in prison all those years for killing that girl. I don't know why, but he loved her. He could never have hurt her. And now you're back looking for him again. I won't help you. No, sir."

"Mrs. Waters . . .," Shaun started.

"Forget it," Jack interrupted. "She's not going to tell us anything."

"So we just drop it?" Shaun turned on Jack. "We don't even try to find him?"

"Oh, we'll find him," Jack said. "He lied to us. He looked us in the eye and lied. And for that, we'll find him."

"What if we don't find him?"

"He watched someone shoot Larry," Jack said. "He watched and then rather than call for help, he went out to that car and stole something out of it. If he had called right away, Larry might be alive today. For that I'll hunt him down."

"You're wrong," Mrs. Waters said.

"I'm what?"

"Your friend," she said. "He would not be alive today."

"How do you know?" Jack demanded. "Every minute counts. Every minute he sat in that car bleeding without help on the way. He might have lived."

Mrs. Waters shook her head. "We didn't wait to make the call, detective. I called while Tim went out there. I didn't wait for him to come back."

"Why did he go out there at all?" Shaun asked. "He disturbed a crime scene. That alone is a crime."

"He went out there to see if he could help the man," she said. "Tim is a good man. He was more concerned about that stranger's life than he was about going back to prison."

"He took something out of the car, ma'am," Jack said. "How did that help Larry?"

"I don't know anything about that," she said.

"Mrs. Waters, what did he take?" Jack insisted.

"I don't know."

"Don't know?" Jack asked. "Or won't tell?"

The lines in her face were deep crevices that made her appear older than she was. Twenty years she waited for her son to return to her. Twenty years she cried herself to sleep after praying for miracles that were not answered. At least not until now. She would not survive her son returning to prison, even for a short time.

"I know Timothy didn't kill Larry," Jack assured her. "We have a witness who saw another man do it. We don't want Timothy for this. But if he saw something, or if he's in possession of evidence that will help solve this case, I want to see it. I need to see it. I won't arrest him if he gets it to me. But if he destroys that evidence, I will come after him. I will put him away on any charge I can come up with. If he makes it possible for a killer to walk away, I will hold him responsible."

Jack glanced at Shaun who only raised an eyebrow in response. Jack turned away and started back to his car. Shaun followed, jogging to catch up. Behind them, Mrs. Waters shut the door to the outside world that had been so cruel to her.

"And how do we find him?" Shaun asked trying to keep pace.

"If I know Timothy Waters," Jack said. "We won't find him."
"Then all that was for nothing?"
"No," Jack grinned. "He's going to find us."

56

The convenience store was almost empty and the cashier nodded to Charles as he entered. The bright lights of the business stung his eyes but he ignored it. He moved along the walls and finally into the alcove promising restrooms. In the end he found himself standing next to the front counter waiting for the cashier to finish with another customer.

"May I help you?" The flatness in the man's voice was notable.

"I'm looking for a payphone," Charles explained.

"Outside," the man said.

"Outside?"

The man pointed out the large window that spanned most of the storefront. At the far edge of the glass was a single payphone. Charles let out a low chuckle. He had walked past the phone on his way in. Without a word he left the store and approached the phone. He picked up the headset and put it to his ear to be sure there was a dial tone.

Searching his pockets he tried to remember where he had put the card. He retrieved it from the breast pocket of his shirt, smoothing it out between his fingers. He drove his hand into his pocket in search of change. He pushed two quarters into the slot and waited a moment before starting to dial. He pushed each number deliberately. When he finished he listened to the hypnotic ringing as he waited.

"Mallory," Jack announced himself.

"Detective."

"Yeah," Jack said. "Who is this?"

"Charles Reagan," Charles said.

"Charles," Jack became more cheerful. "What can I do for you?"

"Did you talk to Detective Peterson?"

"No," Jack admitted. "I'm sorry. I've been so tied up I forgot, but I will."

"Detective . . ."

"Listen, Charles," Jack interrupted. "I'm in the middle of something right now, can I call you back?"

"I'm at a payphone," Charles said.

"A payphone?" Jack said. "Where are you?"

"A gas station," Charles answered. "I think my phone may be bugged."

"Why would you think that?" Jack asked.

"He told me he was going to prove I killed Lisa," Charles' voice cracked. "He said he could and would. He's coming after me, Detective."

A car pulled up, its music blaring so loud the sidewalk vibrated beneath Charles' feet. He turned toward the sound and saw a group of teens exit the car as the sound stopped. They were talking loudly and roughhousing. One of them bumped into Charles and they all filed through the doors to the convenience store without a word of apology.

"Charles?" Jack said. "You there?"

"Yes," Charles said flustered. "Sorry."

"When did you talk to Peterson?" Jack asked.

"Earlier today," Charles said.

"And he said he was coming after you?"

"He said he's going to arrest me," Charles confirmed.

"Damn," Jack said. "Listen, Charles, I know this guy. I know how he thinks and I know how he works. I didn't expect him to move so soon. I'm sorry about that. Now that he is acting though, he'll act fast. They'll be searching your house in the next couple of days."

"There's nothing there for them to find," Charles said.

"All the same," Jack continued. "Is there somewhere you can stay? Maybe a motel? Pay cash and use a fake name until I get this cleared up."

"They can't run me out of my home, detective," Charles said. "I've lost everything else. They can't take that from me."

"Just for a few days," Jack suggested.

"No," Charles insisted. "I have nothing to hide. I will not give them a reason to validate their claim by running and hiding. I only came here to make this call to let you know what was happening without alerting them that I spoke to you."

"Charles . . ."

"I hope you can help me, Jack," the lawyer said. "I really do. But I can't sit in a motel waiting for you to give me the signal that it's safe to go home. To go to my own home. I can't."

"I'll make some calls as soon as I can," Jack promised. "With any luck we'll have a couple days. I'll fix it."

"Thank you." There was an audible change in Charles' voice as he strained to keep control.

He hung up the phone. His hands were shaking. He pushed them into his pockets to hide them from the rest of the world and walked to his car. Unlocking the door, something he did nearly every day, proved to be an unexpected challenge. Secure in the driver's seat, he rested his forehead on the steering wheel and contemplated what Jack had told him.

They would search his house. It was not that he had anything to hide from them or even the idea of them trying to blame him for his daughter. The problem he had was these strangers going through his wife's and daughter's things. It was all he had left of them and he did not want them to be violated that way. He would need to do something to protect them.

He backed out of his space and turned the car toward home. It occurred to him he may have been followed and he studied the drivers of the cars he passed. No one looked like the detective. But then, he was trained to follow people and probably knew how not to be seen. And there was nothing to say the detective wouldn't have someone else follow him.

He slammed a fist into the steering wheel. Sneaking out of his house at night to make phone calls, looking over his shoulder for tails, rushing home to hide his most cherished possessions, he was sick of how he was being made to feel. He was a lawyer. He would fight back his way. In the morning he would file a harassment suit against Detective Peterson and the police department.

57

"Damn," Jack snapped his phone closed and dropped it into his jacket pocket.

"What's up?" Shaun asked from the passenger seat of the car.

"Peterson is going after Charles Reagan," Jack explained. "The man takes his time doing everything and on this, he's in a hurry."

"Yeah," Shaun said. "When I was working the case with him he kept saying he needed to get the case wrapped up as soon as possible."

"Must be trying for a promotion," Jack said. "The man has been a third detective for years. Should have never made detective in the first place."

"That's the impression I got from working with him," Shaun agreed. "He never did anything. He didn't want to work the scene. He didn't study the evidence that I ever saw. And he hated writing reports. I really wasn't sure what he did."

"Nothing," Jack chuckled. "That's all he does."

The two men sat in the front of Jack's car parked almost exactly where Larry's car was parked when he was killed. They were not trying to hide the fact they were there. They were not slouched down in the seats or speaking in hushed voices. From time to time they got out and stretched their legs.

They were silent for a while. Shaun finally broke the silence by asking, "Do you really think he'll come back?"

"The man was in prison twenty years," Jack said. "He has nowhere to go, no other family, no friends. He'll be back."

"But isn't the fact he has no friends and no other family a risk?" Shaun asked. "I mean wouldn't he have an easier time disappearing than say a man with a wife and a couple kids?"

"Yeah, sure," Jack nodded. "But you seem to forget one thing."

"What's that?" Shaun asked.

"The only family he has in this world, the only person who stood beside him all the time he was in prison," Jack pointed, "lives in that house right over there. He'll be back. She won't let him leave her after twenty years of trying to get him home."

"Even if it's to keep him from going back to prison?" Shaun suggested.

Jack hesitated, considering what Shaun was saying. Given the choice between never seeing him again or seeing him returned to prison, would Mrs. Waters encourage her son to run? Of course she would. Jack had been foolish to think he could outguess a man like Timothy, wronged by the system that should have protected him, faced with the possibility of history repeating itself. It would be natural for him to think the system would fail him again, natural for him to conclude his only alternative was to vanish.

"You may be right," Jack exhaled.

"Then what do we do next?" Shaun asked. "We can't sit here all night."

Jack did not answer. His eyes were focused on the house where Timothy Waters grew up. It was an average structure for an average family. Twenty years ago Timothy, the son of a working-class family, was dating the daughter of the mayor. He sat forward, a thought coming to mind.

"No one has ever asked Mrs. Waters about them," he offered.

"About who?"

"About Timothy and Elizabeth," Jack clarified. "No one ever asked Mrs. Waters what she thought about her son's relationship with Elizabeth Mitchell. No one ever asked her what she thought might have taken place the night the girl was killed. Hell, they never even asked her to confirm Timothy's story about what time he got home the night of the murder."

"You think she would remember anything after all these years?" Shaun asked.

"I'm positive," Jack said. "A piece of information that could have kept him out of prison? I bet she could tell you everything about that night."

"Why don't you ask her?"

"I'm going to," Jack said. "First thing in the morning I'm going to find out everything she knows, including where her son is."

"That won't be necessary." The voice came from outside the car.

Being startled, complicated by images of their own ideas of what Larry Kaninski's last moments were like, both men went for their guns.

58

When the phone rang Terrance opened his eyes and stared at the ceiling in darkness. It had been years since he had been a detective on call. The only reason he received late calls now was for major problems; natural disasters, plane crashes and the like. He rolled his head and saw that it was one o'clock in the morning. He rolled the rest of his body and reached for the phone after the third or fourth ring.

"Who is this?" he said, gruffly.

"Mallory," Jack said.

"What do you want?" Terrance asked. "Do you know what time it is?"

"Crime never sleeps," Jack quipped. "We need to talk."

"Then talk," Terrance barked. "I want to get back to sleep."

"I mean in person," Jack explained.

"In person? Are you insane?" Terrance sat up. "It's one o'clock."

"Right," Jack said. "I'll be there in half an hour."

"Did you not hear me?" Terrance yelled. "This can wait until morning."

"No," Jack argued. "It can't."

"What is this about?"

"I'll tell you when we get there," Jack said.

"Tell me now," Terrance demanded. "And who is we?"

"See you in thirty," Jack said.

The line went dead and Terrance sat on the edge of the bed staring at the phone. He cursed and dropped it on the nightstand. Sliding out of bed he grabbed his robe and threw it on. Stepping into his slippers, he left the room and started down the stairs. He glanced at Heather's door as he went.

They had maintained separate rooms for a number of years now. She apparently had not heard his phone or if she had, she

214

was ignoring it. Late-night calls were never good. The last one he received was the worst. But he would never have to worry about that again. He was flooded by sadness. He shook it off and descended the stairs to the main floor, not stopping until he came to the kitchen.

The light was bright and he squeezed his eyes to let them adjust. He wanted something to drink. He couldn't make coffee because the caffeine would keep him up the rest of the night. He couldn't have alcohol because Jack might get the impression he was drinking to calm his nerves; that he had something to hide. He settled for milk. He stood in the living room, where he and Heather had been talking just a few hours ago, looking out the window into the night. What could Jack want to talk to him about that couldn't wait until morning when civilized people talked?

Headlights arched across the room momentarily flooding Terrance in its harsh light. The clock read a quarter 'til two. Terrance still stood in the window, his eyes half-closed from exhaustion. His empty milk glass sat on the end table beside him. He did not move until the car stopped and the lights went out. Both front doors opened and he squinted to make out the passenger. To his surprise the passenger was Jack. He looked for the driver but they had moved out of view.

There was a soft knock and Terrance crossed the room to answer. Opening the door he turned on the porch light to assure a good view of the men. Recognition did not take long.

"Travis, what are you doing here?" Terrance questioned.

"I'm working with Jack," the officer answered.

"Since when?" Terrance attacked. "The last time I checked you were on two different cases. The last time I checked I had not assigned either of you partners. Has that changed?"

"No, sir," Shaun responded.

"Lay off, Terrance," Jack added.

"Lay off?" Terrance turned on the detective. "You come to my home in the middle of the night with another officer who should be working a separate case and tell me you're working together and you want me to lay off?"

"Then we understand each other," Jack said.

"Understand?" Terrance's voice raised. "I knew you were nuts Jack, but this is a reach even for you."

"Tell me about your car," Jack said.

"My car?"

"I don't remember you always answering questions with questions," Jack said. "Yes, your car."

"What about my car?"

"You own a '72 Barracuda," Jack held up the vehicle registration. "Looks a lot like some of the old Camaros."

"So?"

"We want to know about it."

Terrance stood defiantly shifting his eyes form Jack to Shaun. His blood was beginning to boil and his head was throbbing. "Are you telling me, detective, that you called my home at one o'clock in the morning, waking me up, to ask me about a '72 Cuda?"

"Yes."

"And it never crossed your mind to wait until morning?"

"Never did," Jack shrugged.

"I suggest you think about it now," Terrance growled.

"We're here now," Jack reminded.

"And you're leaving," Terrance yelled. "Now!"

"What is the Cuda Club?" Shaun asked.

"What?" Terrance's head snapped in the officer's direction.

"At the bottom of the registration there's a handwritten note," Jack explained. "It just says 'Cuda Club'. We were wondering what that meant."

"If you must know, the Cuda Club is a social group for people who own Barracudas," Terrance said. "What do you mean a handwritten note? Didn't you get this from the DMV?"

"No," Jack answered. "Actually this is the paper removed from Larry's car the night he was killed."

Terrance was silent for a moment. "How do you know? Where did you get it?"

"Timothy Waters gave it to me," Jack answered. "He says Larry handed it to him before he died."

"Waters killed Kaninski?" Terrance asked.

"No," Jack said. "He went out to check on Larry after the shooting. Larry gave him this."

"And you believe Waters?" Terrance asked. "Why would Larry give him the registration for my car? What purpose is there in that?"

"How long have you owned the car, Terrance?" Jack asked.

"I bought it over thirty years ago, Jack," Terrance sneered. "What does that have to do with anything?"

"I have a witness that says Elizabeth Mitchell was seen getting into a sports car a few days before her death," Jack said, "and another who saw Lisa Reagan get into an old car that was 'like a

Camaro'. I'm guessing when I show her pictures she's going to tell me the car she saw was the 'Cuda."

"Are you accusing me of something here?" Terrance's face reddened. "Are you seriously suggesting I'm a murderer?"

"We're not accusing you of anything," Jack held his hands up. "But we believe this paper is why Larry was killed."

"He was killed for this?" Terrance said.

"We believe so."

"But Waters didn't kill him?"

"No."

"Then how did he get the paper?"

"We told you," Jack said.

"Yeah, yeah," Terrance nodded. "Larry gave it to him. My problem is that if Larry was killed for this piece of paper, why didn't the killer take it? That is if Waters wasn't the killer."

59

Charles sat in his kitchen eating two eggs. They were supposed to be over-easy but he had broken the yolks and cooked them too long. He had not eaten a good egg since his wife was killed. Lisa had done a fair job the times she tried but now she was gone as well. He missed them; but not because of his breakfast. He missed having them in his life. He missed holding them.

The doorbell chimed and Charles set his fork down, folded the newspaper and went to answer the door. He checked the peephole and saw Detective Peterson standing on the porch. There were a number of uniformed officers with him as well. Charles sighed before disengaging the deadbolt.

"Detective, I didn't expect to see you again so soon," Charles said upon opening the door. The truth was he had expected the man to return as soon as possible. It was for that reason Charles spent most of the night packing away his private things that reminded him of his wife and daughter. These photos and mementos were now safely tucked away in a storage facility he used to keep old files from his law practice. Peterson would not include this in any search warrant he might have.

"We have a warrant," Bret said as if responding to Charles' thoughts. "You will need to vacate the premises."

"Yes, well," Charles said. "I need to get my jacket and keys."

"Officer Jordan will accompany you to get your things," Bret smiled. To the uniformed officer beside him, he said, "Inspect anything he wishes to take with him."

The officer nodded his understanding before escorting Charles to the kitchen where the lawyer pointed at his sport coat and briefcase. Jordan patted down the coat and handed it to Charles then lay the case on its side to open. The latches snapped and Charles voiced his protest, as there were private case files inside. Jordan noted the protest then searched the case paying little attention to the files. Satisfied, he closed the case and slid it to Charles.

On the way out Bret eyed Charles suspiciously. He followed them to the front door and stood on the porch as Charles descended the stairs. As the lawyer reached the side of his car, Bret finally spoke.

"The car stays here," he called out, holding up the warrant. "It's included."

"I have to go to work," Charles said.

"Officer Jordan," Bret said.

"Yes, sir?"

"Please see that Mr. Reagan gets to his office," Bret ordered. "Then report back here."

"Yes, sir." The officer led Charles to his patrol car and opened the rear door for him. As Charles sat in the back seat he watched Detective Peterson turn and disappear into his home. He remembered the last time he had sat outside watching a detective pass through that door. It was when his wife was murdered and the detective in charge came up with damaging evidence to prove Charles was guilty.

60

"They're in my house right now," Charles said when Jack answered his phone.

It was the third time he had dialed the number. Jack and Shaun were with Timothy Waters and did not want to interrupt the questioning. But the persistence of the caller finally grated on Jack's nerves and he answered with a harsh greeting not overlooked by Timothy.

"Who's in your house?" Jack asked, confused.

"Detective Peterson and his goons," Charles answered. "They showed up with a warrant and are searching my house."

"Charles?"

"Yes," he faltered. "I'm sorry. I . . . detective, they're searching my home."

"Christ, he's moving fast," Jack said more to himself than anyone.

"I don't have anything to hide," Charles said. "But they're in there. And I would have to be crazy to say I wasn't nervous."

"Listen to me Charles," Jack said. "I'll be there as soon as possible. I'm with some people, but when I'm done here, you're at the top of the list. Okay?"

"Jack," Charles' voice sounded hollow and distant. It was the first time he had called Jack by his first name. "I feel like it's seven years ago all over again."

"And seven years ago everything worked out fine," Jack reminded him. "And everything will be fine this time too. I'll be there before you know it."

"I'm at my office," Charles said. "I couldn't sit there and watch again."

"That's good," Jack said. "Get some work done. Take your mind off what's going on. I'll take care of it and before you know it things will be normal again."

"They'll never be normal again, detective."

"I'm sorry," Jack sighed. "I just meant . . . "

"I know what your meant, detective," Charles said. "I wish it were true."

The line went dead and Jack closed his eyes. When he opened them again, he turned to where Shaun and Timothy were waiting.

"Now where were we?" he said, rejoining them.

"You were asking me why the killer didn't take the paper when he shot your cop friend." Timothy was in a defensive stance. The three of them stood in his mother's backyard. Smoke trailed after the cigarette in Timothy's hand. "But to know that I would have to know the killer, or at least what he was thinking. And I don't. Hell, I don't even know why the paper is so important."

"It's a registration," Shaun said.

"I'm not stupid, officer," Timothy said. "I read it. But so what?"

"It implicates the owner as a possible suspect in a murder investigation," Jack offered.

"Detective Singleton?"

"Chief Singleton," Shaun corrected. "Yes."

"You think Singleton killed Elizabeth?" Timothy stared hard at Jack.

"Not that investigation," Jack said.

"I thought you were working Elizabeth's case," Timothy said.

"I am," Jack said. "Shaun here is working another girl's case."

"But you're together," Timothy said. "So there's a connection. And if he killed this other girl, then he might have killed Elizabeth too."

"There's no proof he knew Officer Travis' victim," Jack held his hands up. "It could be nothing at all."

"And how does all this tie in to me and your cop friend?" Timothy cocked his head.

"It gives you motive," Shaun responded.

"Motive?" Timothy asked. "What motive?"

"You gave us the paper that implicates Singleton," Shaun said.

"Let's go," Jack said.

"What?" Shaun turned to the detective.

"We've taken enough of your time," Jack offered Timothy his hand. Timothy did not take it.

"Jack?" Shaun protested.

"We're leaving," Jack turned away, leading the way out of the yard.

Inside the car Shaun barely let the door close before he started to argue his opinion of leaving in the middle of questioning. Jack let him vent. When he was finished Jack started the car.

"You done?"

"For now," Shaun grumbled.

"What was Waters' motivation for killing Larry?" Jack asked.

"The registration," Shaun said matter-of-factly.

"To what end?"

"To be sure it got into your hands," Shaun said.

"That's where the problem is," Jack said. "How would Timothy Waters know Larry had the registration? And even if he did, we already had it. Why kill Larry to take it and give it back?"

"But if someone else killed him for the registration," Shaun said, "why would they leave it behind?"

"Exactly," Jack pointed at Shaun.

"Exactly what?"

"If the killer didn't want the paper," Jack said, "he didn't kill Larry to get it. So, the question is: What else did Larry know?"

61

After Jack and Shaun left, Terrance did not go back to bed. Between Heather announcing she wanted a divorce and Jack questioning him about the car, he was wired. Sleep was out of the question so he dressed and put on a pot of coffee.

He went out to the freestanding garage, entering through the side door. In the center of the garage was his Barracuda covered with a tarp. He pulled back the cover and looked at it for a moment before replacing it. There were some empty boxes in the garage somewhere. It was time to start packing his things for the move. Where he was going to go had not even crossed his mind. He moved things around while he looked for the boxes and was amazed at the amount of junk he had collected over the years. Most of it he would leave behind.

Jack was getting close to the truth, or at least was heading in the right direction. It was only a matter of time before he figured things out, Terrance guessed. Everything would change when that happened.

He found the boxes in a corner behind sets of tires he had removed from the sports car over the years. He couldn't remember why he didn't get rid of them. He took four of the boxes and left the garage. He would fill them and put them in the car then get more if he needed them. There wasn't really that much he wanted to take with him. He had a sudden desire to keep it light. In his youth he lived by the philosophy that you should only own what you could carry with you in case you needed to move in a hurry. The things he had accumulated over the years far exceeded that. It was time to go back to the past.

In the house, he carried the boxes up to his room two at a time. On the second trip he was startled to see Heather at the top of the stairs watching him. He didn't say anything. When he was halfway up, she did.

"What did Jack want?" she asked.

"I didn't know you were up," he said.

"I was," she said. "Now, what did he want?"

"He was asking about the 'Cuda," he said.

"Why?"

"He likes old cars. I don't know," Terrance snapped. "Ask him."

"He comes out in the middle of the night to ask about your car and you don't ask why?"

"It doesn't matter," he said. "Whatever he had in his mind, he doesn't anymore. You know how he is when he gets an idea, he has to follow it through until he's satisfied. Then he moves on."

"Why would he be interested in your car?"

"Heather," Terrance said. "I don't know and I don't care. He's gone. And if you'll let me get by I'll get packed so I can go as well."

He stepped past her and went to his room shutting the door behind him. Heather stared after him for a long time before returning to her own room. She crossed the room glancing out the window to the garage as she passed. She used to love that car. But now it was a reminder of the way things used to be and would never be again. She needed to get back to sleep.

Terrance tossed the empty boxes onto his bed and started pulling clothes out of drawers and dropping them in. He took only those items that fit, ignoring the things he had saved in hopes he would lose the extra pounds he had been putting on. He took his favorite ties, leaving the ones Heather had given him when they were still civil to one another. His shoes and belts went in the bottom of one box. His clock and the various necessary items that littered the tops of his dresser and nightstand went on top. When his closet and drawers were mostly empty and the awards and personal pictures were removed from the walls, he stood in the center of the room looking for things he might have forgotten. There was nothing he could see.

Of the four boxes he brought up for the job he had only filled three. It surprised him. There were still things in the room, but nothing he wanted. He would take the other box to the office downstairs. He didn't think he would need much more than that for everything he would want from there. He lifted one of the full boxes and left the room. These boxes would go in the 'Cuda before he started on the office.

He managed to get down the stairs, across the lawn and into the garage before he remembered he did not have the keys with him. He set the box next to the car and returned to the house. Grabbing the keys and another box he followed the same path out again. In the garage he set the second box on the first and pulled the keys out. Slipping the appropriate key in the lock he opened the trunk. He had a mechanic do all the work on the car including tires. He had not opened the trunk in years. When he looked down into the car's storage compartment he saw, shoved to the back, a dusty purse. It was an expensive purse in its day. Terrance stared at it for a moment in disgust.

He lifted the boxes one at a time and dropped them into the trunk. Then with one last glance at the worn, aged leather handbag, he slammed the lid. After twenty years he still could not forgive himself for what he had done.

62

Jack dropped Shaun at his car and steered his own toward Charles Reagan's home. He was confused why Peterson was moving so fast on the case. It was unlike him to do anything fast. Maybe Singleton was behind it somehow. He was sure Peterson didn't have the clout to get a judge to sign off on a search warrant like this so soon.

When he pulled up to the curb, he was surprised by the sheer number of department vehicles there. With that many cars and vans, the house must be crawling with people from top to bottom. It was definitely overkill and with that many people searching the house, there were too many chances for errors or just sloppy work. In this case, Jack hoped it would work in Charles' favor.

He stepped out of his car and presented his identification to one of the uniformed officers guarding the perimeter. He purposely chose an officer he did not know in case Peterson had given orders to keep him off the premises. He was allowed to pass without incident. By the time he reached the front door of Charles' home, he spotted Peterson through a window talking to some of the officers inside. Jack stepped in, catching Peterson's eye immediately. The detective waved the others away and moved to intercept Jack.

"That's far enough," he held up a hand. "We're collecting evidence here."

"Looks to me like someone opened all the cages at the zoo," Jack smiled. "How many people do you have working this place?"

"Jack, what are you doing here?"

"Heard you were searching the house," Jack shrugged. "Came to see if you needed any help."

"Yeah, right," Bret said. "Why are you here?"

"I'm here to find out how you got a judge to agree to waste tax dollars and manpower searching the house of an innocent man,"

Jack became very serious. "I'm here to ask you why you don't get off your ass and do some real investigating so you can catch the killer instead of harassing one of the few decent men left in this city."

"Your decent man killed his own daughter," Bret yelled. "He bludgeoned her to death and threw her body away like it was trash."

"You know he didn't do it," Jack yelled back. "You know, yet here you are anyway."

"I know he didn't do it?" Bret said. "And how would I know that? Because he said he didn't? Jesus, Jack, are you that naïve?"

"Charles Reagan is not capable of doing this crime," Jack said.

"I think he is," Bret said. "He is very capable. He's done it before. I think he killed his wife seven years ago."

"We caught his wife's killer," Jack challenged. "He's already in prison."

"An accomplice who took the fall," Bret argued. "Reagan was there. He helped. And after I get him for this case, I may go after him for the other."

"He had a solid alibi the night his wife was murdered," Jack said through clenched teeth. "You can't change that."

"Don't be so sure," Bret sneered.

"What's that supposed to mean?"

"You'll have to wait and see, Jack," Bret said. "Now get out of here. You're contaminating the scene."

"Your scene was contaminated the second you brought all these people into this house," Jack said. "This is ridiculous. Do you even know how many people you have in there? Does Chief Singleton know?"

"You don't need to worry about my case," Bret scowled. "Now get out of here."

There was a commotion inside the house and the two detectives were drawn away from their argument by a series of shouts and camera flashes. A woman in a lab coat stepped through the door carrying a long object in gloved hands. She held it up so the men could see it was a bat. She brought it to Bret and set in on a table next to him.

"We found this in the front closet," the woman said. "It's been wiped down but there are traces of blood."

Bret put on a pair of latex gloves and lifted the bat. He looked at it closely from all angles then gripped it as if he were going to swing. He turned to Jack and pretended to swing the bat at him, stopping inches from his head.

"You see, Jack," he said. "Even you can be wrong."

63

Heather watched from her bedroom window as her husband of twenty-eight years carried boxes from the house to the garage. She knew he was putting them in that car of his. She never understood why men put so much into their cars. They put time and money into keeping the thing in good condition but put little or nothing into their marriage or life. The irony being Terrance was now packing his life into the car.

The other irony was that if it had not been for the car she and Terrance would never have met. The first time she saw him was at a car show leaning over the hood of the Barracuda polishing it with a rag. She was the passenger of a similar car and they stopped to talk to Terrance, who was only twenty years old then. She was struck by his charm and the way he talked about life with so much hope for the future. It was not long before she was the passenger in his car.

Terrance was cursing below and Heather could imagine him trying to open the front door with a box in his arms. The hope that was such a huge part of their lives when they were young was gone now. It slipped away from them a long time ago. She was a big part of the reason. She criticized him at every turn for everything no matter how small and insignificant. She knew it now, and truthfully, part of her knew it then. She worked hard to break the habit she had spent a lifetime developing. No matter how hard she tried, she couldn't stop. It was the way she grew up.

Her mother had been a hard woman to live with. She and her brothers were the target of criticism all their lives. Each of their fathers was criticized from the day they moved in until the day they walked out. None of them ever married her and because they were not the type of men to care about kids, they never returned. Men came and went. And after each would leave, their mother would become worse, blaming her children for driving her lovers away.

Terrance came into view carrying what appeared to be an exceptionally heavy box. Heather watched him make his way across the lawn and into the garage. When she couldn't see him anymore, she moved away from the window and lay on her bed. She stared at the ceiling for a while. She was surprised to be experiencing emotions. She and Terrance hadn't really been a couple for years but the prospect of ending their marriage left her with a strange sense of loss.

She would have to talk to her brothers. They were very protective of her and would be quick to conclude that Terrance had chosen to move out on his own. It would be difficult to convince them that she had made the decision herself. She told them countless times she would never let Terrance go. She made it clear she intended to make his life miserable as long as she could. They would not believe she changed her mind. They might even conclude he was threatening her.

As much as she had come to hate and despise her husband, she could still remember when he was good to her. He was the only man, other than her brothers, whoever treated her as a real person. And it was her fault that everything changed.

Not being able to have children was the catalyst. They tried and tried but she was not able to get pregnant. That was when she started being more critical of Terrance. Even after they found out she was barren, she took it out on him. In truth it was one of her mother's many boyfriends who was to blame. He had sneaked into her room one night and raped her. He told her that if she ever said anything to her mother he would kill them both.

Heather turned up pregnant. Her mother told her she was a tramp and took her to a man who took care of the pregnancy. He also took care of any future chance she might have to be a mother. She would not tell her mother who the father was. She was afraid the man might keep his promise to kill them. But after her brothers insisted she finally told them about the rape.

The boyfriend did not have a job and the next morning while their mother was at work, Heather's brothers attacked the man while he slept. Her brothers were teens and big for their ages. They gave him such a beating he passed out. They thought they had killed him. While they discussed whether they should call the police or try to get rid of the body, the man came to, gathered his things and left through the back door. They never saw him again. They never told their mother what happened. She assumed the guy, like all the others, got bored with her and left.

The garage door opened and shortly after, the low rumble of the Barracuda's engine rattled the windows. He was really going. She couldn't blame him. It was what she wanted and she was relieved it was happening. They had long ago passed the point of reconciliation.

As the sound of the engine faded into the distance she closed her eyes and started to drift off to sleep. Then her eyes snapped open and she sat up suddenly. She still did not know why Jack was interested in the Barracuda, but it was going to look suspicious that Terrance moved it the very night the detective came to ask about it.

64

The 'Cuda Club was not listed in the phone book and searching the internet wasn't much more productive. Shaun was able to find a number for a Mark Bellos, the apparent founder of the group. But when he dialed the number it was answered by a laundromat. A search for the name Mark Bellos turned up a Marcos Bellos in a northern suburb.

Shaun called the number listed and on the third ring a woman answered, out of breath.

"Hello," she said. "Sorry. No one ever calls the landline anymore."

Shaun introduced himself and explained why he was calling. The woman confirmed that her husband was indeed the founder of the club, but that he had just left for work and would be there until the evening. At Shaun's request the woman gave him the address of Mark's employer.

Mark Bellos, the sports car enthusiast, was a furniture salesman at a department store in the mall. Shaun arrived shortly after the mall opened and made his way to the furniture where customers were already searching for bargains. He stopped at the edge of the department and looked for someone that met the description of the man he needed to talk to.

"That's a good choice," a man behind him said.

"Pardon me?" Shaun turned to him.

"That sofa is a nice choice," the man said. "One of our best. And at that price, it's quite a bargain."

Shaun considered the sofa for a second. If it was one of their best he wasn't sure he would want to see more. He said, "I'm looking for a Mark Bellos."

The smile faded from his face. "Oh. Okay then. I'll send him out."

Shaun sat on the sofa the salesman claimed to be among the best in the store and could not get comfortable. He finally settled for sitting on the edge with his arms resting on his knees. That is how he was sitting when another salesman walked up to him.

"Great sofa," the man smiled broadly.

"Save it," Shaun raised his palm to the man. "It's not a great sofa and no matter how many times you guys say it is, it does not make it so. Besides, I'm not here to buy a sofa. I'm here to see you."

"Do I know you?" The man held his smile.

"Is your name Mark Bellos?"

"Yes."

"Is there somewhere we could talk?" Shaun asked. "It won't take long."

"Do I know you?" the man repeated.

"No," Shaun pulled his badge out and flipped it open. "I'm Officer Shaun Travis. I need to ask you some questions."

"What's this about?" The color left Mark's face.

"Are you the founder of the car organization called The 'Cuda Club?"

"Yes," Mark was tentative. "Why?"

"I need to get some information about your members," Shaun said.

"That's all?"

"For a start," Shaun nodded.

"What do you need to know?"

"I need a list of their names, addresses, phone numbers and such," Shaun said.

"That's easy," Mark said. "I can give you the same list I gave the other guy."

"Other guy?"

"Another guy asked me for the same thing a couple days ago," Mark said.

"Was the other guy a cop?"

"Didn't say he was," Mark shook his head. "Just asked for a list. Wanted to mail a magazine or something."

"Was he an older man?" Shaun asked. "About so tall?"

"Sounds right," Mark agreed. "You know him?"

"I might," Shaun said. "Could I get that list?"

"It's on my computer at the house," Mark said. "I can get it for you after work."

"Can your wife access it?" Shaun asked. "It's important that I get it as soon as possible."

"I'll call her and tell her to get it for you then," Mark said. "What's all this about anyway?"

"I really can't say," Shaun said.

"Figures," Mark said. "Must be important though."

"You could say that," Shaun was patient. "Could you make that call now?"

"Okay," Mark pulled out his phone. "I'll call right now."

Mark told his wife where to find the membership list for the club and explained that Shaun would be back by to get it. He assured her he was not in any trouble and it was perfectly safe to give out the list. When he finally hung up he shrugged. Shaun grinned and left the store. He headed back to Mark Bellos' place of residence.

65

"They found what?" Charles' voice cracked at the end of his question.

"Possibly the weapon used to kill your daughter," Jack answered.

"In my house?"

"Front hall closet," Jack specified.

"How did it get there?" Charles sat in the large leather chair behind his desk. Jack had come to his office to talk to him. "I mean, how is it possible?"

"The killer must have put it there," Jack said, vaguely.

"Who?"

"Detective Peterson says it was you," Jack said.

"It wasn't," Charles' shoulders fell in defeat.

"I know," Jack said.

Charles considered the detective. "I appreciate that. What do I do now?"

"You do what you should have done yesterday," Jack advised. "Go find a motel, pay cash and hide."

"I can't hide knowing the police are looking for me," Charles said.

"There's no warrant yet," Jack said. "Go to the motel and don't watch the news."

"I'm an attorney, detective," Charles reminded him. "No judge is going to believe that. And if it goes to trial, how is it going to look if I run?"

"Charles," Jack said. "Listen to me. Detective Peterson doesn't have the clout to get judges to issue search warrants with as little as they had on you. Someone else is pulling the strings on this. I think whoever that person is had something to do with your daughter's murder, or knows who did. It's probable they planted the weapon in your house, got the warrant issued and told Peterson to search. If that's the case, there is no telling what other evidence has been planted to point at you. Holing up in a motel for a few days may be the least damaging thing a jury might hear."

"But why?" Charles' normal controlled demeanor crumbled. "Why did they kill Lisa? Why are they framing me? Who are they? What did I do to them?"

"I don't know, Charles," Jack said. "But I am going to find out."

"You have an idea though." There was little hope in Charles' eyes. "You think you know."

"I have some leads to follow," Jack assured him. "I do have some ideas. Nothing substantial. Not yet anyway."

"Who?" Charles demanded.

"I can't tell you that," Jack said.

"I need to know," Charles said. "I need to know who so I can try to understand what I may have done to provoke them. What would make them kill Lisa and destroy me?"

"I can't tell you, Charles," Jack repeated. "If I told you, you might do something we would both regret. You could be hurt. I might be wrong."

"I won't do anything," Charles said. "I just need to understand what is happening."

"No," Jack shook his head. "Not now."

"Please, detective," Charles pleaded.

"You go get to a motel," Jack ordered. "Call my cell and let me know where you are. When I know something more, I'll give you a call."

Charles' head dropped lower than Jack thought should be possible. He let it hang a moment before looking back up at Jack. "I need to know if I am somehow responsible for her death."

"I know," Jack said softly. "But you're not."

"I couldn't live with myself if I'm responsible," the lawyer confessed. "You know what I mean?"

"I know," Jack said again. "But no matter what the reason behind her murder, even if it was someone seeking revenge against you, you are not responsible."

"I didn't kill her," Charles said. "I know that. But I didn't protect her either."

"What would you have done?"

"I don't know," Charles admitted. "If I knew she was in danger ..."

"You didn't," Jack interrupted. "There's nothing you could have done. There's nothing you can blame yourself for."

"It doesn't work that way, detective," Charles sighed heavily. "If she were killed out of revenge for something I did, as long as I can breathe knowing she no longer does, I will hate myself."

"Check into a motel, Charles," Jack insisted. "Get some rest. Let me find her killer, then we'll worry about everything else."

"You'll keep me informed?"

"As much as I can."

"Okay," Charles stood and started putting things into his briefcase. "I'll go to a motel. I'm tired. And the prospect of going to a big empty house really isn't that appealing to me right now anyway."

"Good," Jack said. "Do you need a ride?"

"No," Charles lifted the case from his desk. "When I bought my last car I gave my old one to Lisa. It's parked out front."

"Don't forget to let me know where you are," Jack patted Charles on the back as the lawyer moved around the office toward the door. "Meanwhile, I'm going to find a way to prove you didn't kill Lisa."

"How are you going to do that?" Charles asked.

The man's face had a sunken quality to it. His eyes were deep in the center of dark rings. The wrinkles around his lips and brow were pronounced. He looked like a man with little to live for. Jack reached out and patted his shoulder again. "By finding out who did."

66

Terrance woke up and was not sure where he was. It was not his room. The familiar ceiling fan was not spinning above him. He rolled his head from side to side until he found the clock on the bedside table. He was in a motel room and the clock showed eight-oh-five.

He sat up so quickly his head swam. He was always in the office by eight. How could he be late? He glanced around the room and saw two cardboard boxes with various items jutting out the tops. One lay open with clothing folded over the edge. The night before came back to him in a rush and threatened to send his head reeling again. As he remembered he reached for his phone, scrolling through contacts until he found what he needed.

"Chief Singleton's office," Kelly said.

"Kelly this is Terrance," he said. "I'm going to be a bit late. I have some business to take care of before I come in."

"Is everything okay?" she asked. She had been his secretary for nearly ten years and had never known the man to be late.

"Fine," he responded. "There are some things I need to take care of. I'll be in around lunch."

"Lunch?" She wanted to be sure she heard him right.

"Earlier if I can," he said. "Take messages and let people know I'll be available this afternoon.

"Okay, I will."

He set the phone down and turned the television to a news channel. Listening to the newscaster read the talking points of the day, he stepped into the bathroom and turned the shower on to start the hot water. A quick shower cleared his senses and he dressed in his usual suit. Because his department-issued car was at the house he called for a cab and watched the news until they arrived. When the cab's horn blared he did not remember a single news item.

He stood, smoothed out his slacks and left the motel room. The cab was parked behind the Barracuda and Terrance waved at him to let him know he was coming. He tested the motel door to be sure it was locked. When he turned back again his gaze fell on a BMW that had just parked a few spaces away. The man behind the wheel was familiar. Terrance made his way to the taxi keeping an eye on the driver of the BMW. As he climbed into the taxi the man exited the car and stood straight. Terrance recognized him immediately. It was Charles Reagan.

67

Heather had trouble falling asleep and when she finally did she slept much later than she meant to. She tried to call her brothers when she woke but neither answered. She chose not to leave messages, believing what she needed to say should be said in person, or at least not in a recording. Showering quickly, she dressed and left the house in a rush. She needed to talk to them before they learned Terrance had moved out. It would be hard enough explaining what happened. If they found out on their own, it would be impossible.

She wasn't sure what she was planning for the future. Nothing was ever going to change if she and Terrance stayed together. And she wasn't ready to spend the rest of her life with the status quo. One night with Jack had shown her that. Not that she had any illusions that she and Jack had a future. She wouldn't even consider it if he were interested. He was too close to Terrance and she wanted to get as far away from her husband as she could.

She was sure he would not want the house, so they would have to sell it and split the money. She could also sell most of the furnishings and the years of accumulation might be worth something. Once she was done and had cash in hand, she could pack her things into her car and vanish.

Disappearing would upset her brothers and they would probably be suspicious of Terrance. They would suspect foul play. It would be wise for her to leave them a letter. But that was something she would worry about when the time came. For now she needed to let them know what was going on.

She turned onto a busy street and regretted it. Traffic was moving too slowly for her and she took the first opportunity to turn again. She drove two blocks trying to go around the bulk of rush hour when she found herself at a standstill. This time the traffic wasn't just heavy, it was jammed. She slapped the steering wheel and let out an almost primal yell. She needed to get to the courthouse before Paul started the day's docket or she would never get to him before B.J. got to him. And finding B.J. before he learned something would be almost impossible.

Even as little kids B.J., not the smartest kid around, had a special talent for finding things out. He overheard things, walked in at the opportune moment, or hurt someone until they told him what he wanted to know. Usually it was the last, yet he still had that knack for the other two. Heather knew that before the day was done he would know that Terrance was no longer living at the house. And if that happened before she had a chance to talk to her brothers, things would surely turn bad.

She was determined to get to Paul before anything happened. B.J. would not act without Paul. He was the leader. His IQ was high and they all knew it. For B.J. that meant he would believe anything Paul told him. He trusted his older brother to a fault.

Sitting in traffic she remembered the day her brothers attacked the man who raped her. Paul had made the plan, had explained exactly what they would do and coaxed B.J. into doing it. Paul was smart enough to know that he was no match for a grown man. But B.J. was big for his age. The youngest of the three of them, even then he was close to six feet tall and weighed over two hundred.

Later in his life B.J. would struggle with the weight, working out nearly every day to keep the muscle on and the fat off. But when they were young, he was in top shape without even trying. Paul urged him on and they jumped the man while he slept. Paul was calculating in the assault, a born leader with his army of one. But B.J., once started, was hard to stop. The man was nearly dead before Paul could pull his brother back. At the time, Heather was proud of her brave brothers. But when she thinks back on what they did that day, she sometimes gets a chill down her spine.

She glanced to her right for a second then back to traffic. An image registered in her mind and she looked back thinking she had seen Terrance standing in a row of cars. A cab was pulling away and there was a man there. Not Terrance, but a man she had not seen in many years, not since his picture had graced the pages of newspapers in connection to his wife's death. It was Charles Reagan. The man was unlocking the door to a motel room. She stared at his profile for a moment. She felt a sense of sorrow for him. Losing his wife then and his daughter now. How lonely he must be.

A horn blared behind her and her eyes snapped forward. Traffic was moving. She followed, glancing back again at the motel. Charles was gone, but parked among the cars she saw something she hadn't before; Terrance's Barracuda.

68

Jack was ten minutes late and the governor's assistant was clearly impatient. Jack grinned at her back as she speed-walked down the hallway toward the study. Jack was inclined to walk slowly. It was petty but at the same time he got a kind of thrill knowing he was ruffling the woman's feathers. She glanced back and he quickly replaced his grin with a stoic stare.

"Detective," the woman sounded alarmed. "We don't have all day."

"I won't need all day ma'am," he nodded. He did not walk any faster and he was amused by her narrowing eyes as she frowned before she turned away.

The study door stood open and the woman stopped in front of it, her hands on her hips. He thanked her politely as he stepped past her and into the room. She nodded to him, though her eyes burned into his. He grinned as she pulled the door closed behind him.

In the study, the governor and his wife sat side by side on a leather sofa. The governor stood as Jack entered and the detective waved him back down. Jack crossed the room and took the politician's hand in a firm shake then offered the hand to his wife. Betty Mitchell looked at Jack's hand then to his eyes. She made no attempt to take the hand.

Jack withdrew and sat in a chair opposite them. He pulled out a notebook and flipped through the pages until he came to a clean one. He folded the used pages back and took a pen from his pocket. The couple watched without a word.

"I apologize for being late," Jack said when he was ready. "Police work doesn't always follow a schedule."

"I understand," the governor said. "Let's get on with this, shall we."

"It would be best if I spoke with Mrs. Mitchell alone," Jack anticipated the governor's response.

"I do not agree," the governor responded predictably. "I believe anything my wife might have to say about our daughter, she can say in front of me. I want to be here to assure you don't upset her unduly."

"Very well," Jack turned to the governor's wife. "May I call you Betty?"

"Mrs. Mitchell," she said softly.

"Okay," Jack looked at his blank notebook and up again. "Can you tell me about the last time you saw Elizabeth alive?"

"Why did they let him go?" Betty asked.

"Pardon me?"

"That boy?" Her voice was low and Jack had to strain to hear her. "He killed my baby and they let him go. I want to know why."

"Mrs. Mitchell, there is a chance Timothy Waters did not kill Elizabeth," Jack explained. "That's why I'm here. I need to research the facts to find the real killer."

"He killed her," she snapped. "Terrance proved that twenty years ago. That low-class trash of a boy killed my girl and you let him go."

Jack stared at the woman a second, then at the governor who sat quietly next to her. He did not touch his wife. He offered gentle words to keep her relaxed. Her eyes locked on Jack's and she acted as if her husband wasn't there.

"Why did you let him go?" she demanded.

"I need to conduct my investigation, Mrs. Mitchell," Jack said. "If you believe Waters killed your daughter, that is fine. I do not have the luxury of letting emotions direct my search. I need facts. And if you want your voice to be heard, to be a part of the findings, I need you to answer some questions."

She stared at him with contempt, then to her husband who nodded his agreement, a gesture that surprised Jack. He had been against this interview from the start. But the woman turned back to Jack and let her hands, which had been tightly clasped in front of her, separate and open.

"What do you want to know?"

"Elizabeth's last day," Jack repeated. "Was there anything different that you remember? Anything that did not raise an alarm at the time, but maybe did after she was killed?"

"I did not see my daughter that last day, detective," Betty looked down at her shoes. "I saw her the day before that. And I am ashamed to say we fought."

"Can you remember what you fought about?"

"The last conversation we had together?" she smirked. "I remember it like it was yesterday. I have played it over and over in my mind for twenty years."

"And?"

"We fought about that boy, about Timothy," she said.

"What?" the governor turned to her. "You never told me that."

"Why would I, Steve?" she said to her husband. "She was dead. Why would I tell you that the last time I saw my daughter alive, I forbade her to see the boy she claimed to love? Why would I tell you that? Tell me why?"

"Because she was our daughter, not just yours," he yelled. "I had the right to know. I can't believe you kept that from me for all these years."

"You went on your crusade to change law enforcement," she said. "You didn't have time for me. Do you even know how old your other children are?"

"Excuse me," Jack interrupted. "I really need to get on with this."

"Detective, do you have children?" Betty lashed at him.

"No, I don't."

"Then you can't understand what it's like to have a part of you taken away," she said. "Elizabeth and I were not close. Not as close as we should have been. I always blamed it on her age, figured when she got older we could make up for the teen years. But she never got older. We never made up. She died angry with me."

"Mrs. Mitchell," Jack tried to steer the conversation. "Why did you forbid her to see Timothy?"

"Because he wasn't good enough for her," she said. "He was nothing. He had few choices to become anything except the nothing he was. I wanted more for my daughter than that."

"When you fought, did she tell you that she was planning to meet with him?"

"No."

"Did she tell you she was thinking about running away with him?"

"No," she gasped. "She wouldn't possibly . . ."

"Did she tell you she was pregnant?"

The governor and his wife sat with their mouths gaping, mirrored reactions to unexpected news. Jack had expected this from Mrs. Mitchell. He was sure she wouldn't know the whole truth about her daughter. But watching the governor, he remembered how Simon Penske told him that the then-mayor had made him keep the pregnancy out of the coroner's reports. Jack was confused, thinking Terrance's demand for suppression of that detail had been at the order of Mitchell. It was possible that his wife finding out the truth had him upset, but Jack saw more in the man's eyes than concern for an uncovered secret.

"What did you say?" the governor asked.

"She was pregnant," Jack repeated.

"That's impossible," Steve said.

"I would have known," Betty echoed his sentiment.

"It was possible," Jack countered. "Your daughter's autopsy revealed a pregnancy. It was covered up."

"Why?" Betty asked.

"According to the coroner," Jack turned to the governor, "you ordered him to leave it out of the findings to protect Elizabeth's image."

"How could you?" Betty lashed out at her husband.

"I did no such thing," he defended. "This is the first I've heard of it. I thought this boy was away at college."

"He was," Jack confirmed.

"Then how?"

"The baby wasn't his," Jack said.

"Then whose was it?" Betty asked.

"That's what I'm trying to find out," Jack answered. Then to the governor, "You're saying you didn't order the autopsy records changed?"

"Of course not," Steve said.

"And you didn't know Elizabeth was pregnant?"

"No."

"Then there was only one person who did know," Jack thought aloud.

"Who?" Steve insisted.

"Terrance Singleton."

69

The chief of police rode back to his house in the back of the cab he had called for that morning. He thought it ironic that Charles Reagan was checking into the same motel where he was staying. Did the lawyer see him and recognize him as the detective who tried to have him locked up for killing his own wife? Surely the man would have responded to seeing him if that were the case.

He should probably find another place to stay. It would not do to have a confrontation with the man and he really didn't want to run into the lawyer, even if Charles didn't recognize him. There would be plenty of time to find another motel later.

The cab pulled into the driveway and Terrance paid the driver. He stepped out of the yellow car and stood looking up at his house, the house he would never live in again. Heather's car was gone, and he considered going in to get some more of his things but there was nothing else he wanted. He opened the door to his unmarked car and started the engine. Letting it idle he looked at the house again.

He remembered when they bought it shortly after they were married. The two of them had been happy then and he longed for that time. The house was to be a new beginning to go along with their new lives as a couple. That beginning turned out to be the beginning of the end. Soon after moving in they started spending a fortune keeping the house up to date. Then came the problems having children, followed by the fights. She felt alienated. He felt ignored. When she discovered his affairs, it was all over. Yet here they were, twenty some odd years later, just now getting around to really finishing it.

Had they ended things right away everything would have been different. Not just for him. Her life would have been better too. He was sure of that and he thought she must know it as well. It was probably that bit of knowledge that finally convinced her it was time to move on. No more guilt. No more hate. Just start fresh and hope for something better.

He drove away from the house for the last time watching the structure shrink in his rearview mirror. There was no sorrow or remorse. He was energized. Things were finally going to change. Things were finally going to improve. All he had to do was get through the mess he was in and that would be it.

He drove toward the department and caught himself whistling. He couldn't remember the last time he had whistled. He smiled at the thought of something so simple being so exciting to him. He was starting to whistle again when his phone rang. He reached into his jacket pocket and pulled the phone out, checking the caller ID to see who it was. He knew of the warrant issued for Charles Reagan's house, so he was not surprised Bret's name appeared on the small screen. He moved his thumb to the talk button, hesitated, then slid it to the power button. He pressed this button and held it until the phone powered off. He tossed the phone in the passenger seat. He wasn't quite ready for the world just yet.

70

Mrs. Bellos was standing on the front porch of her home holding the list of club members in her hand when Shaun pulled up. He took the list and flipped hurriedly through the five typed pages of names, addresses and phone numbers. It surprised him that there were so many.

"They aren't all still members," the woman seemed to read his thoughts. "Mark never got around to updating the list."

"I see," Shaun folder the pages. "And this is the same list you gave Larry?"

"Who?"

"The older cop who asked for the list," Shaun clarified.

"Oh, yes," she agreed. "This is what Mark gave him. Such a nice man. Mark said he was murdered."

"Yes ma'am," Shaun said.

"And you think the killer may be one of our members?"

"We don't know," Shaun admitted. "But we're going to take a look."

"I hope you find him," she called to Shaun's back as he returned to his car. "The killer, that is."

"So do I," Shaun put the list in his pocket and slid into his car. As he drove away he pulled the list out again and looked it over. No names jumped out at him. He tried to turn the pages and keep his eye on the road but lay the list in his lap as his phone began ringing.

"Officer Travis," he answered.

"Shaun, this is Jack."

"What's up, Jack?"

"You have any idea where to get a picture of a nineteen-seventy-two Barracuda?"

"As a matter of fact I might," Shaun turned into the driveway of a large ranch style house. Two children playing in the yard looked up with interest. Shaun waved at them then backed out again to complete his turn around.

"Good," Jack said. "I need you to get one and meet me at Tina Shelton's place."

Jack gave Shaun the address and the line went dead. Shaun parked his car in the Bellos' driveway and sat for a moment while he wrote down what Jack had told him. When he raised his head, Mrs. Bellos was standing in the doorway of the house looking at him.

"Is there a problem?" she asked the approaching officer.

"No," Shaun smiled. "No problem. I was needing another favor."

"A favor?"

"Yes," Shaun said. "I was wondering since your husband is such a big fan of the car if you might have a photo of a 1972 model?"

"I'm sure he does," she sounded like a woman who was less enthused with the car than her spouse.

"I need to borrow one if I could," he explained. "I'll be sure you get it back."

"Hold on," she stepped back into the house. "I'll see what I can find."

She was gone only a few minutes before reappearing. She stepped back into the sunlight saying, "Will this do?"

In her hand was a calendar featuring the Barracuda. It was open to the month of May. The picture gracing the page was of a 1972 'Cuda painted red with black racing stripes. Shaun took the calendar and admired the photo.

"This will work fine," he concluded, returning to his car once more. "Thank you."

"You can keep it," she said. "He has several of them."

Shaun waved to her and drove away a second time. He looked at the image of the car. It was the kind of car his father may have driven as a teen. There weren't many on the road today. If Tina Shelton identified the car, it wouldn't take much to track down owners of the vehicle. But he had a feeling that Jack already knew one of them. He turned east toward the address the detective had given him.

71

The phone rolled over to voice mail after four rings. Bret hung up and called again. The second time it went to voice mail immediately. Frustrated he put the phone away, scowling. He had enjoyed the look on Jack's face when the bloodstained bat was found. But all that was gone now. He needed an arrest warrant issued for Reagan and he couldn't find anyone.

Bret took hold of the bloody bat sealed in a large clear plastic bag, the kind reserved for weapons like rifles and such. He gripped it as if he were going to swing at a fastpitch and tapped it against the table where the evidence they collected was piled. A technician was working on the ground, organizing the bags and boxing them. Bret hated when things did not move along as they were supposed to.

Resting the bat on his shoulder he dialed another number. He waited for the ring, waited for the answer that never came. Angry, he swung the bat down and struck the table. The technician jumped and dropped a handful of evidence bags. Bret frowned, disgusted.

"Get this stuff packed up and to the lab," he barked.

The technician gave him a look that said, 'That's what I'm doing' then started gathering what he had dropped. He mumbled, "Yes, sir."

Bret did not notice the man's sarcastic response. He dropped the bat and walked away toward the street. The neighborhood was upper class and there weren't many curious spectators. The officers assigned to crowd control didn't have much to do. Two of the men were standing next to their patrol car talking when Bret approached. As soon as they saw him they stood up straight.

"You two are with me," he pointed at them. "Get in your cruiser and follow."

The officers glanced at one another then complied. A few minutes later Bret was driving south with the patrol car right behind him. He tried both numbers again with no success. He slapped the dashboard and checked the rearview mirror to be sure his backup was still following. By the time he drove into heavy traffic he was furious.

He was forced to stop, waiting for traffic to move again. He drummed on the steering wheel to let some of his tension out. When the cars started to move, a car in the next lane did not. Even as he looked, his eyes were drawn to another car parked in the motel parking lot across the street. It was Terrance's '72 'Cuda. He knew it was his from the personalized tag. He noted the name of the motel before continuing on his way.

His tires screeched as he turned into the attorney's parking lot. The patrol car followed close behind and both stopped in front of the office building. Bret was already halfway to the entrance when the officers came to a stop. Inside, the three of them formed a half-circle around the surprised receptionist's desk.

"We're here for Charles Reagan," Bret looked past her to the door beyond.

"He isn't here right now," she responded.

"Tell him Detective Peterson is here," Bret said. "He'll see me."

"He isn't here," she repeated.

Bret's anger flared and he walked around her to the closed office door. He did not slow as he pushed the door open hard enough to knock a framed diploma from the wall. He scanned the office but as the receptionist had said, there was no Charles Reagan.

"Where is he?" Bret demanded.

"He told me he was leaving for the day," the woman informed him. "Asked me to cancel his afternoon appointments and everything for tomorrow."

"Where did he go?" Bret loomed over her.

"I don't know."

"Sure you do. He would have let you know how to reach him in a hurry. So tell me."

"I text him his messages," she shrank away from him. "I don't know where he is."

Bret stood over her, breathing heavy and letting his mind race with possibilities. He was sure she knew something and right then he was ready to make her talk. He raised a hand toward her as if he might grab her throat.

"Uh, Detective," one of the officers said. Bret turned to the two of them, not knowing which had spoken. "She doesn't know. Let's go."

Bret's chest heaved and his fists clenched. He said, "We have his car. Did he call a cab?"

"No, sir," she whimpered.

"Then how did he leave?" he demanded. "Did he take your car?"

She shook her head.

"How did he leave?"

"He took his daughter's car," she finally said. "It's been parked out front since she . . . well, you know."

"He took her car?"

"Yes." Barely a whisper.

"What kind of car is it?" he asked.

"A BMW," she said. "White with four doors."

Bret began to relax a bit and he started to leave. "I'm going to check into this and you can believe me when I say we will find him. If I find out you lied to me about knowing where he is, I'll be back and I will put you away."

The officers led the way out. They were already through the doorway when the receptionist spoke in her soft, weak voice.

"The other detective might know where he is," she offered. "You might ask him."

Bret stopped mid-step, his large frame taking up most of the entrance. He squared his shoulders and twisted his thick neck to look at her. His voice was low and menacing. "What other detective?"

72

Jack was sitting in his car in front of Tina Shelton's house when Shaun pulled up behind him. The two men stepped out of their vehicles and climbed the sidewalk to the modest home. The young grandmother smiled when she opened the door.

"Hello, Detective," she said. "What can I do for you?"

"I have that picture I wanted you to identify," Jack said taking the calendar from Shaun. "It's very important you take your time and study the picture before you jump to your answer."

"I understand." Her gaze was on the object in his hand.

Jack held up the calendar so she could see the picture of the car. She studied it a moment trying to do as Jack requested and take her time before making her decision. Jack waited a moment before asking his question.

"Is this the car you saw Elizabeth get into twenty years ago?"

"It's hard to say," she admitted. "This one is painted different, sportier. But it definitely looks similar."

"But you're not sure?" Jack's frustration was obvious to the woman and to Shaun.

"I'm sorry," Tina said. "I wish I could be of more help."

"What about this car looks like the one you remember?" Jack was not ready to give up.

"Well," she leaned a little closer. "I mean the body looks right. It's hard to say with that paint. It's so different."

"What about the mirrors?" Jack asked. "Or the front grill?"

She twisted her face a little. "It was kind of far away."

"You told me you would recognize the car if you saw a picture," he accused.

"I know and I'm very sorry," she lowered her head. "I thought I would be able to."

"It's all right," Jack said. "You didn't think of anything else did you?"

"No," she shook her head. "I really don't remember much."

"Okay," Jack said, "Well, we've taken enough of your time. Thanks for trying."

He looked at the picture of the car again trying to decide where to go next. The old man at Lisa's apartment building came to mind, but if he couldn't make a positive ID it would cause more problems for Jack than it would fix. He closed the calendar and handed it back to Shaun who was tucking it under his arm when Tina came to life with excitement.

"That's it," she cried out, pointing at the back of the calendar.

Shaun turned the calendar in his hand to expose the back where a small copy of each month's photo was represented. He turned it to the woman who pointed at the eleventh photo in the set. Shaun flipped to November in the calendar and folded it over on its spine. He turned the larger photo to Tina.

"That is it," she squealed. "That is the car I saw Beth get into."

Shaun turned the calendar to Jack. It was another 1972 Barracuda. Rather than the bright red paint with a thick black stripe running from the front to the back, this car was a dark brown with no special markings at all. It was the same model, but with the more subdued paint job it looked like an entirely different car.

"You're sure," Jack knew she was but needed to hear her say it.

"Positive." She was adamant.

"Thank you," Jack smiled. "You've been very helpful."

"I'm glad," she said, and she meant it.

Jack looked at the calendar again. "Let's go show that to one other person, just as a formality."

"Then what?" Shaun walked beside Jack.

"Then, we go talk to a judge," Jack said. "I think we have him."

73

Terrance pulled into his parking space at almost one o'clock. When he stopped the car he sat staring up at the building. He had spent a couple of hours driving around the city where he had grown up.

He drove by his schools, one of which was no longer a center for education. After that he passed through the old neighborhood and the house his parents had occupied for fifty years before his father's heart attack. His mother refused to return to her home after the funeral and spent the last two years of her life in a home for the elderly. The place was depressing to Terrance so he had not visited her very often. It was something he regretted now. She passed away less than a year before he married Heather.

He finished his tour of the past across the street from the home of his high school sweetheart. Not the house she lived in when they were kids, but the one she lived in now with her husband and three kids. He had run into her at a convenience store a couple of years ago. After all that time, he recognized her immediately but she had not recognized him. He followed her home and had all the information about her he wanted to know within an hour.

She was married to a construction foreman. Her children, ages 15, 12, and 9, attended the same school Terrance's kids would attend if he had any. He had watched them grow and change over the last two years. Had things been different would this have been his life? They had been too young to get married. He had been too immature to know what a great woman she really was. They had been so close then. It was hard to imagine she didn't recognize him. Or maybe she only pretended not to know him. He couldn't blame her if that were true.

Today he only saw her once as she walked out to her car and returned carrying a small box. He blushed when he saw her. He had loved her, that fresh love of youth. It was a feeling like no other.

A feeling he had spent a large part of his adulthood trying to revive. It was too late now. He stayed longer than he should have before going to work.

Entering through the side entrance reserved for officers and detectives raised an eyebrow or two. A few of the men he passed nodded in greeting but most avoided making eye contact with their superior. It wasn't difficult. With his head bowed slightly, Terrance didn't see half of them as he walked down the hall to the stairwell. Purposely avoiding the busier corridors where someone might stop him for a question or something, he didn't come across anyone during his climb to the fourth floor. No one from the stairwell to his office acknowledged him.

"Chief," Kelly said when he entered, "I've been trying to reach you."

"Kelly?" Terrance said with a start. "I thought you would be at lunch."

"Not yet," Kelly said. "Detectives Peterson and Mallory have been trying to reach you."

"They have?" Terrance tilted his head. "I can't imagine Mallory working with Peterson."

"Not together," Kelly corrected. "They both called saying you haven't been answering your phone."

"Yeah, I had my phone off," Terrance shrugged. "Did they say what they wanted?"

"No," She picked up the messages she had taken. "Jack insisted on knowing where you were, which I couldn't tell him. And Detective Peterson kept yelling at me, saying I was screening your calls."

"He sounded upset then?" Terrance frowned.

"Oh, yeah," she stifled a nervous laugh. "Said something about you not being where you're supposed to be."

"Did he say anything about where I was supposed to be?"

"I assume he meant here," she offered.

He nodded. "Why don't you go to lunch? Take the afternoon off."

"Really?" she smiled broadly.

"Sure," he started for his office. "Just don't be late tomorrow."

"Thank you," she started gathering her things. As he opened his door she stopped. "Chief? Are you okay?"

"Yeah," he furrowed his brow. "Why do you ask?"

"Well, you've never been late before," her eyes dropped to her hands, "and you're not usually . . ."

"Nice?"

"That's not what I meant," she blushed.

"I know what you meant," he said. "I'm fine, go to lunch."

She left without another word, glancing back before disappearing from sight. When she was gone Terrance went into his office and closed the door. He let out a heavy sigh as he turned the phone on his desk around to face him. He dialed and waited.

"You were looking for me?" he said.

"It's about time," Bret said through his teeth. "I wanted an arrest warrant for Reagan. Now, he's given us the slip."

"The slip?"

"It means we can't find him," Bret said.

"I know what it means," Terrance snapped. "It just surprises me."

"Why is that?"

"Because I know where he is."

74

"You sure that's what you want?"

"I don't know what I want," Heather admitted. "But I know I don't want things to go on as they have."

Her brother, Judge Paul Watson, sat across from her in the small diner. She came into his chambers, which was unusual. Something told him she needed his full attention. His morning docket had been light and he chose to shuffle them all to later in the day or later in the week so he could take some time with Heather. She wrung her hands and glanced around nervously.

"What's wrong then?" Paul asked her.

"That's just it," she put her hands in her lap. Paul was the oldest of the siblings and the only one to have their mother's last name. His father had been a one-night stand and according to their mother, she didn't even know the man's name. She told them once that he had been an athlete, but another time she said he had been a businessman. Heather's skin was pale next to Paul's dark features. "There shouldn't be anything wrong. I should be happy to be getting on with my life, but I feel like I'm losing something."

"The two of you have been together a long time," Paul theorized.

"We've hated each other for the last twenty years."

"Once you've been apart for a while you'll be fine with it," Paul agreed. "But for now, you are experiencing a huge change. The comfort of knowing what you're coming home to is gone. You're resisting change is all, not mourning the loss of a two-timing husband."

"We actually had a nice conversation last night," Heather sipped from her coffee, not sure what to add.

"Heather," Paul spoke in the fatherly tone he always used to convince others he knew what he was talking about. "A civil conversation does not make up for him cheating on you and making your life miserable."

"You know what bothered me most?"

Paul hesitated. He could tell they were getting to the point and he was unsure he wanted to go there. "What?"

"When we finally agreed to end everything," she said, "when we told each other it was time to move on, he wasted no time. He packed last night and left."

"What did you expect him to do?"

"I don't know. I thought he'd take a few days to find a place to live," she started wringing her hands again. "I didn't think he'd be in such a hurry."

"Heather," Paul's voice softened. "It's been a long time coming. The two of you have been locked in a loveless marriage so long you think it's normal. In Terrance's mind, he left a long time ago. Packing his bags and leaving is just a formality."

"But why couldn't he at least wait until morning?" she asked. "Why did he have to sneak out in the middle of the night?"

"It doesn't matter," Paul insisted. "I told you twenty years ago to get away from him. You told me you wanted to make him suffer. And he has suffered. There is no excuse for the things he did. But you have made him pay for his sins. He was ready to go. You need to let it all go."

"I don't know if I'm ready," she confessed. "Last night I was, but now I'm not so sure."

"You have to."

"I saw his car this morning," she said.

"You did?"

"Yeah, that damned car he drives when he's out prowling," she sniffed. "I was stopped in traffic and I looked over and there it was parked in front of a seedy motel. And you know what my first thought was?"

"What?"

"The first thing to come to my mind was jealousy," she laughed. "I thought that son-of-a-bitch was cheating on me again. Can you believe that?"

"It doesn't mean anything," Paul assured her. "Things are changing. It's natural for your emotions to go a little haywire."

"They definitely have," Heather rubbed at her eyes.

"I'll tell you what," Paul said. "My afternoon docket is pretty light today. As soon as I'm done here the three of us can go to dinner and celebrate. You, me and B.J., just like old times. Your new life is about to set sail and we're going to christen the ship."

"I'd like that." The edges of her lips rose slightly, but her eyes were still heavy.

"It's settled then," Paul patted her hand.

"What about B.J.?"

"I'll make sure he comes," Paul said. "He'll want to."

"No," Heather shook her head. "I mean what about him and Terrance? They've never liked each other. I'm afraid B.J. will do something stupid."

"I'll talk to him," Paul wasn't sure what to say to his kid brother. He was more affected by their mother's lifestyle than any of them. He always made it clear to Heather that he would not accept his sister living the way their mother had. One man, one marriage. It was one of the reasons Heather had stayed with Terrance for so long. It was the only thing Paul and B.J. had ever fought about. Well, not the only thing, but the most passionate. "He'll have to understand."

"I should talk to him," she suggested.

"No," Paul was adamant. "I'll talk to him. He loves you Heather, but you also remind him of mom. Until he gets used to the idea of you and Terrance divorcing, we don't want him thinking about her any more than necessary."

"You're right," she sighed. "I just don't want him finding out before you talk to him. He might get the wrong idea."

"Well, you know Terrance isn't going to tell him. So how would he find out?"

"I don't know," she grinned. "Okay, I'll wait for you to tell him."

"Good," Paul let a smile spread across his large black features for the first time since they entered the diner. "Now walk me back to my chambers."

They walked down the sidewalk talking about the years they lived together in their mother's house. They talked about the different paths they had taken and the similarities between them as well. It was good to talk, something Heather hadn't done in years. Between last night with Terrance, and now, she enjoyed two real conversations. She hoped it was a sign of what she might expect in her future.

As they entered the offices, a secretary handed Paul a stack of messages, which he thumbed through rapidly. He stopped, continued, stopped again.

"What's wrong?" Heather saw the concern in his eyes.

"He's been trying to call," Paul said.

"Who?"

"B.J." Paul held out the messages. "He's called a half dozen times."

"Do you think?"

"Come into my chambers," Paul was already through the door. "I'll call."

A moment later they were in the chambers with the door closed. Paul was sitting in his oversized leather chair with the phone pressed to his ear. His eyes were locked on Heather as he waited.

"Yes, B.J.," he said cheerfully. "You've been calling? Yeah, Heather and I had coffee together this morning. We were thinking you might join us for dinner."

Paul was silent for a time, listening intently.

"Where?"

Silent again.

"Okay. I'll handle that. You'll be there for dinner though, right?"

He hung up the phone and smiled at his sister.

"He'll be there tonight," Paul said. "I told you he would."

"Why was he calling?"

"He's on his way to the Kensington Inn on Third. Has some business to take care of."

Heather's eyes widened and the color left her face.

"Heather?"

"That's where I saw Terrance's car."

75

"Where are you?" Jack asked after identifying his caller as Charles.

"The Kensington," Charles answered.

"Listen," Jack said. "I think I know who killed your daughter."

"You have him?"

"No," Jack said. "Not yet. I'm not sure where he is. But until I find him I don't want you to leave your room."

"But, Jack," Charles started.

"Don't leave your room," Jack repeated. "I'll bring you something to eat. I need to ask you some more questions, too, about your wife."

"My wife?"

"I'll explain when we get there."

"We?"

"I'm bringing Officer Travis with me," Jack explained. "We need to be sure before we start pointing fingers. No room for error on this. We have to be absolutely sure. Do you understand?"

"Not really," Charles admitted. "I'll take your word for it."

"Okay," Jack said. "We're on our way. What do you want for lunch?"

A few minutes later a knock on the door surprised Charles. He was not expecting anyone so soon and had placed the 'Do Not Disturb' card on the door to assure housekeeping would not bother him. He thought about ignoring the knock altogether but it might be Jack. The detective may have been nearby when he called.

He slid off the bed where he had been sitting, working on his laptop trying to get some overdue letters written. He stretched not realizing how long he was in that one position. His legs cramped. Reaching for the doorknob he thought better of it and sidestepped to the window. Slowly pulling the curtain away he looked outside at who was knocking. Unfortunately the man was standing with his back to the window. It was easy enough to conclude it was not Detective Peterson though. This man was not nearly that large. Charles returned to the door and opened it.

"May I...?" Charles began, letting his voice fade as he looked into the face of his visitor. "You?"

76

"Tell us what room he's in," Heather pleaded.

"I've already told you I can't do that," the desk clerk used a practiced calm tone. "I rang his room and there was no answer. That's all I can do unless you want to leave him a message."

"Sir," Paul stepped up to the desk. "I am a judge and it is very important that we find this man."

"I don't care who you are," the clerk smiled. "Unless the guest has given permission to give out his room number, you will need a warrant to get it."

"We don't have that kind of time," Paul said.

"Forget it, Paul," Heather was pulling the door open. "B.J. might already be here. We can look for his car and for Terrance's. We can find them without this jerk's help."

Paul glanced at the clerk then followed Heather out the door. The clerk watched them through the window until they were out of sight. He debated calling the police but there was no crime being committed so he went back to the book he had been reading before the two came in.

Paul and Heather walked across the parking lot to where Terrance's Barracuda was parked. Three cars down was Terrance's car from work. He had to be here and if he wasn't answering his phone something must be wrong. Paul noticed another unmarked police car parked all the way at the end of the row.

They stood staring at the line of windows on this side of the building both upstairs and down. They narrowed their search by location and windows that shown a light in the window. They skipped those that did not have the curtains drawn and were left with three possible rooms. Paul walked up to the first door and knocked. There was no answer. Heather was in front of the second staring without moving.

"What is it?" Paul called to her.

She raised a finger to her lips but did not take her eye off the door. He walked up to her and stood behind her. The door to the room she was looking at was ajar. They had no visual of the inside, but they could hear the muffled voices of the men inside. The brother and sister exchanged glances. They could not make out the words, but there was a definite strain between them.

"What do we do?" Heather asked. The problem was everyone in that room could be armed and they were not.

"We intervene," Paul responded moving toward the door. Heather reached out to slow him but he kept moving. She hesitated then moved in behind him trying to look over his shoulder as they neared the room. They closed the distance and the voices inside the room grew louder, more distinct, more angry.

Paul pushed the door open and stepped into the room and became the immediate focus of two armed men. Standing by the window Bret held his pistol at arm's length, pointed at Paul. On the far side of the room Terrance was in a similar stance. When the men identified the newcomer they both swung their weapons on each other as they had been when Paul entered. It took a moment for Paul to see a third man sitting on the floor between the two beds. He knew the man from seven years ago. It was Charles Reagan.

Heather's gaze moved from one gunman to the other and back again, finally falling to the frightened image of a man on the floor. She did not know Charles, did not understand why he might be in Terrance's room. Nor did she care. The guns in the hands of the two men were all she could focus on, though she was not sure how to react.

Paul stepped toward the center of the room, arms outstretched and palms up as if to stop both lanes of oncoming traffic. He turned his head slowly from Terrance to Bret and back again. "Let's put the guns down. We can talk this over."

"Get Heather out of here, Paul," Terrance said.

"I wish I could, Terrance," Paul said. "You know she doesn't listen to me. If she did, she would have never married you."

"Just get her out of here," Terrance repeated his request. "Bret and I are going to settle this."

"Damn it, Terrance," Paul snapped. "You know I can't do that."

"The hell you can't," Bret broke his silence. "Get her out of here."

The door, which had quietly swung closed behind them, resting against the jam unlatched, erupted as two more men burst into the small room.   Again guns swung wildly and everyone took a defensive stance.   Heather was knocked to the ground and Paul found yet another weapon pointed at his face.

"Police!" Jack shouted.   He was on one knee, sweeping the room with his gun.   The irony did not evade him that everyone in the room that was armed carried a badge.   Shaun stood behind him, his weapon panning from Terrance to Bret and back.

Eyes and weapons shifted from one to another until each of them settled on whom they considered the biggest threat.   Terrance held his gun on Bret.   The other three all trained their sights on Terrance.   Charles shrank back closer to the wall and Heather slowly stood again.

"Put the gun down, Terrance," Jack suggested.

"Yeah, Terrance," Bret mimicked.   "Put the gun down."

"No," Charles whispered.

Jack glanced at the lawyer then returned his concentration to Terrance.

"Are you out of your mind, Jack?" Terrance asked.   "Why are you telling me to put my gun down?"

"You know if you don't put your gun down this can only end badly," Jack reasoned.

"I'll put my gun down if he puts his down," Terrance indicated Bret.

"What do you say, Bret?" Jack remained focused on the chief. "Put your gun down so we can resolve this peacefully."

"Forget you, Jack," Bret said.   "I'm not putting my gun down."

"B.J.," Heather pleaded.   "Please."

Jack's eyes shifted to Heather then to Bret.   "Bret's your other brother? What's going on here? Judge?"

"Paul, get her out of here," Bret ordered.

"B.J., you can't do this," Paul said.   "Let's talk it through."

"Why are you here, judge?" Jack demanded.

"It's a family matter, detective," Paul said.   "And you being here isn't helping."

"Charles Reagan is not a member of your family," Jack pointed out.   "Now let's try again.   What's going on here?"

"I don't know about anyone else," Bret said.   "But I'm here to arrest a murder suspect."

"Terrance, it's your turn," Jack said.   "Why are you here?"

"Cut the crap, Jack," Terrance sneered.   "You know Charles didn't kill Lisa."

"Yes, I know," Jack agreed.   "But how do you know?"

"This isn't the time, detective," Paul said.

"When is the time?" Terrance asked.

"Terrance?" Heather looked at her husband.

"Put the gun down and we can talk," Jack offered.

"You want to talk, Jack?" Terrance asked. "Let's talk."

"Terrance!" Bret stepped forward, his weapon raised menacingly.

"Peterson!" Shaun spun and targeted the detective. "Stand down!"

"You stand down, officer," Bret turned on Shaun.

"B.J.," Paul said, holding his hands out non-threateningly. "Let's all stand down."

"Let's get Charles and Heather out of here," Jack suggested. "We don't need them here."

"Nobody leaves," Bret said waving his gun from target to target.

"B.J.," Paul appealed to him, "do you want Heather to get hurt?"

"No," Bret relaxed a little.

"Then let her leave," Paul said.

"Okay, she can go," Bret agreed. "But not the lawyer."

"That's not going to work, Bret," Jack said. "They both go."

"He's not going anywhere," Bret responded. "He's my suspect and I'm taking him in."

"He didn't kill his daughter," Jack argued. "You heard Terrance. You have nothing to charge him with."

"I'll charge him," Bret said.

"That's the way it works isn't it?" Terrance said. "Lock up the most convenient person."

"Like Timothy Waters?" Jack asked. "He wasn't guilty was he?"

"No," Terrance admitted. "I still blame him sometimes, but he didn't kill her."

"What happened, Terrance?" Jack continued. "I know you were having a relationship with Elizabeth. What happened the night she died?"

"Don't say anything, Terrance," Bret said.

"I loved her," Terrance was barely audible. "She invited me to that house that night. Wanted to talk about the future."

"So you went there to talk," Jack prodded him. "What happened then?"

"Nothing happened," Terrance said. "I went there to discuss our future and all she said was she couldn't see me anymore. She was going to go away and live with Timothy."

"Is that why you killed her?" Jack asked.

"Killed her?" Terrance turned to Jack. "I didn't kill her. I loved her."

"Terrance," Bret warned. "You want to end up in jail?"

"I thought things were going to change for me," Terrance said. "Heather and I weren't doing so well. So, I thought I'd move on. Then she dumped me."

"Terrance," Paul spoke in a low even tone. "Where are you going with this? I think it would be best if you thought about what you're saying."

"I drove around all night that night," Terrance ignored him. "Never went home. Was just sitting there trying to decide what to do next. When the call came over the radio, I recognized the address."

"If you want me to believe you didn't kill her you're going to have to give me more than that," Jack said. "Being alone in your car all night isn't much of an alibi."

"When I got there," Terrance continued, "I had to go inside to see. I was hoping it wasn't her, that some other girl had gone there after Beth left. Of course, that wasn't what happened. She was there lying on her side like she was sleeping, but she wasn't. I thought Timothy had come back and killed her. But then I saw Heather's purse."

"Terrance!" Bret took another step forward, firing a shot into the chief's chest.

77

Jack spent half the night interrogating everyone to determine who played what role in the events of the evening. Terrance took the hit square in the chest but his vest protected him. The wind was knocked out of him and he fell to the floor. The chief's gun-hand tensed when the bullet struck him and he accidentally shot Paul in the shoulder. The judge was recovering from surgery.

Bret refused to stand down, even after shooting his brother-in-law and Jack was forced to shoot him. The first shot into his vest only stunned him a moment before he opened fire again. Jack and Shaun both returned fire, killing the detective. Heather was witness to her brother's death and the wounding of both her husband and other brother in one night. Charles was unharmed and grateful.

Jack was sitting at a table in the hospital's cafeteria transposing his notes so they would be easier to read. He was able to talk to Paul before he was sedated and got most everything else out of Heather before he arrested her. He sent Shaun home a couple hours ago, congratulating him on a job well done.

Jack grew aware of someone nearby and looked up from his papers to where Charles was standing next to his table. His suit was disheveled and his eyes were so dark and sunken Jack wondered how long it had been since the man had slept. When he was settled in the seat across from Jack, the detective said, "Thought you went home."

"Wasn't ready to go," Charles set his own coffee on the table. "Needed answers."

"I have some for you," Jack set his pen down.

"Is Singleton dead?"

"Vest," Jack shook his head. "Knocked him out but the vest saved his life."

"Can you help me make sense of what happened last night?" Charles asked. "I think it would help me to know."

270

Jack explained, "When Heather Singleton found a diamond necklace in her husband's sock drawer, she didn't say anything, just waited for him to give it to her. He never did. The next time she saw the necklace it was around the neck of the mayor's seventeen-year-old daughter.

"She was furious and decided to follow Terrance that night," Jack said. "Unfortunately, that was the night they met at the empty house. When Terrance left, Heather broke into the house by breaking out a small window by the back door. She confronted Elizabeth who broke down and admitted she was pregnant. At the time, Heather thought Terrance was going to divorce her and buy the house for him and Lisa. She snapped and strangled Elizabeth."

"Terrance arrived at the scene, saw Heather's purse, and realized what must have happened," Jack continued. "He arrested Timothy Waters and created enough evidence to send him to prison, with the help of Heather's brothers. Paul was the presiding judge at the trial. And Bret, who was a rookie at the time, used his uniform to pull over and get rid of the only witness who might be able to help Timothy. The problem was guilt ate at Terrance, so he destroyed the evidence he planted so that Timothy would be able to get out when he appealed. That took twenty years."

"How does this tie in to my family?" Charles asked.

"Tracy was killed because one night when Bret was on patrol," Jack said, "he saw her come out of an all-night diner with Terrance. They embraced before going to their cars. Bret was furious that Terrance would be having another affair and followed your wife home and killed her."

"My wife was having an affair?" Charles was beside himself. "With Singleton? And he tried to frame me for her murder just like he did with that Timothy Waters?"

"Not exactly," Jack put his hand on Charles' shoulder. "He did have an affair with Tracy, but it wasn't seven years ago. It was twenty-two years ago before he got involved with Elizabeth Mitchell. But Tracy disappeared. Her family would not tell where she went and Terrance never found her. He ran into her in a small grocery store and he bought her coffee and they discussed the old days."

"And she was killed for that?"

"In a manner of speaking," Jack nodded.

"And my daughter?" Charles asked. "Why did they murder Lisa?"

"Lisa was very much the same as your wife," Jack said. "When Terrance heard Timothy Waters was going to be released he had an urge to make things right, at least to a point. And that included your daughter."

"Lisa?"

"When we were investigating Tracy's death, Terrance suddenly understood why she had disappeared all those years ago," Jack said. "She was pregnant like Elizabeth had been. Tracy was having his baby. Lisa was his daughter."

"No," Charles slapped the table. Everyone in the room looked their way. "She was my daughter."

"I know, Charles, no one can take that from you," Jack said. "But Terrance was her biological father. And Terrance wanted Lisa to know. Wanted to help her out financially and everything. But in spite of his precautions, Bret found out and thought he was having another affair."

"He killed Lisa to get back at Terrance?"

"For cheating on his sister," Jack agreed. "Only that was too much for Terrance. He knew he couldn't leave me on Lisa's case because Heather's brothers would be watching and if I got too close to the truth they might try to come after me. Timothy being released reopened that case and Terrance hoped that by putting me on the case, I would find out what happened."

"Which you did," Charles sighed.

"Completely by accident," Jack admitted. "And not before Bret killed one of the men helping on the case. Larry found out that Terrance and Bret both belonged to the same car club, and that Bret, at the time, drove a similar model car."

"Thank you, detective," Charles said. "It helps to know."

"I'm glad it's over," Jack sighed.

"It will never be over, detective," the lawyer stood and collected himself. "One thing that is for certain is that it will never be over."

THE END

Thank you for reading!

Dear Reader,

I hope you enjoyed reading **Murder Revisited** as much as I enjoyed writing it. At this time, I would like to request, if you're so inclined, please consider leaving a review of **Murder Revisited**. I would love to hear your feedback.

Amazon: https://www.amazon.com/dp/B084DGQDS6

Goodreads:
https://www.goodreads.com/author/show/18986676.William_Coleman

Website: https://www.williamcoleman.net

Facebook: https://www.facebook.com/williamcolemanauthor/

Many Thanks,

William Coleman

Other novels by William Coleman:

THE WIDOW'S HUSBAND

PAYBACK

NICK OF TIME

Printed in Great Britain
by Amazon

87421953R00161